killing grounds

DANA STABENOW

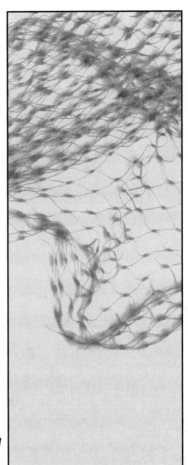

a kate shugak mystery

killing
grounds

G. P. Putnam's Sons / New York

G. P. Putnam's Sons
Publishers Since 1838
a member of
Penguin Putnam Inc.
200 Madison Avenue
New York, NY 10016

Library of Congress Cataloging-in-Publication Data

Stabenow, Dana.
    Killing grounds / Dana Stabenow.
        p.   cm.—(A Kate Shugak mystery)
    ISBN 0-399-14356-4 (alk. paper)
    I. Title.   II. Series: Stabenow, Dana. Kate Shugak mystery.
PS3569.T1249K55   1998   97-23900 CIP
813'.54—dc21

Printed in the United States of America

10   9   8   7   6   5   4   3   2   1

This book is printed on acid-free paper. ∞

Book design by Ellen Cipriano

AUTHOR'S NOTE

For those who persist in looking up
Kate's home ground on a map,
I would remind them that
there is a reason we call it fiction.

However,
if it will make you feel better,
for the purposes of this book
the coastline of Alaska has been altered
to include Alaganik Bay,
two hours (or so) by bowpicker southeast of Cordova.

Cordova is a real place and it does exist.
Shitting Seagull isn't a real person and doesn't.
Real Cordovans are much more fun than he is.

killing
grounds

It was a cloudless summer day. Salmon leapt free of the blue surface of the water, only to fall back with flat smacks that echoed across the bay. The fishing period had opened at twelve noon exactly and the tender wouldn't be taking delivery from fishermen for hours yet, although cork lines were already bobbing with the kind of frenzied energy that promised a busy and productive period.

Fishermen were making ready to launch skiffs, but on board the tender *Freya* there was time to open deck chairs in the bow, time to prop feet on the gunnel, time to eat roast beef sandwiches on homemade bread, heavy on the horseradish, time to make lazy comments on the skill or lack thereof shown by the skippers of the forty-odd boats setting drift nets as close as they could get to the markers of the creeks without setting off the fish hawk.

The fish hawk in question, a twenty-eight-year-old man named Lamar Rousch, hovered around the perimeter of the action, his little rubber Zodiac looking flimsy and vulnerable and outnumbered next to the battle-scarred hulls of the fishing fleet. Clad in the brown uniform of the Fish and Wildlife protection branch of the Alaska Department of Public Safety, Lamar stood rigidly erect at the controls of the Zodiac, as if by doing so his height might be mistaken for five-foot-one, instead of a mere five feet. Kate could relate. She saw him wave Joe Anahonak and the *Darlene* back from the markers on Amartuq Creek, the buzz of the outboard on the back of the Zodiac sounding like an irritated wasp.

Joe flashed an impudent grin, a jaunty wave, and moved maybe ten feet south of the mouth, the stubborn set of his shoulders clearly indicating his determination not to be corked. It happened, if you got careless or unlucky, a moment's distraction and another fisherman more on the ball would drop his net into the water between you and the creek markers, and you lost the advantage of being closest to the narrow funnel through which coursed hundreds of thousands of gleaming red salmon. Sleek and fat from five years of feeding off the nourishing depths of the north Pacific Ocean, the salmon were frantic now to regain that section of stream bed upon which they had been spawned, there to lay their own eggs and die, coming at last to rest and rot upon their ancestral gravel.

Not for the first time, Kate reflected on how improvident nature was. She couldn't remember the exact numbers, but it went something like this: Of the four thousand salmon eggs hatched by a single salmon each year, only two thousand made it downstream to salt water. Of those two thousand, only one thousand made it out into the deep ocean. Of those one thousand, eight returned to Prince William Sound. Of those eight, two made it upstream to spawn. Two survivors from a clutch of four thousand. As always, looking out across a bay filled with a great school of leaping, gleaming salmon, all of whom had returned home against unimaginable odds, she was awed by a natural design engineered with this many built-in backups, and respectful of its continued success.

The local guarantor of that continued success ran his Zodiac in between the mouth of the creek and Yuri Andreev's *Terra Jean*. Without expression, Yuri removed his drifter from the area of contention. Joe Anahonak tossed out a cheery greeting, which Yuri ignored with dignity, narrowly avoiding the outer buoy of a setnetter. The setnetter yelled at him from the beach, and he ignored that, too.

The setnetters were out in force, launching their nets from shore instead of from a boat, trusting to the tides and currents and the salmon themselves to scoop up their share of the mighty schools swarming into the bay. From the *Freya* the setnetters' gear looked like one long uninterrupted line of white corks interspersed with orange anchor buoys, a carefully graded string of beads against the deep blue throat of the bay.

The day before, there had been no sun and that throat had been a dull, drab green. Kate washed down the last bite of roast beef with a long swallow of tepid water and, catlike, stretched her five feet to about five and a half, trying to expose as much of herself to the sun as was physically possible. Her brown skin had already taken on a darker hue, and in this idle moment she wondered if perhaps she ought to crop the bottom of her T-shirt after all. The sleeves were already gone, as was the collar, as well as most of the legs of her oldest pair of jeans. Too much effort on a full stomach, she decided, and closed her eyes against the glare.

She was content. Kate loved the fishing industry and everything to do with it, from the first gleam of silver scales beneath clear ripples of creek water in the spring, to catering to the separate idiosyncrasies of setnetter, drifter and seiner, to the hundred physical differences of the fleet itself, wooden and fiberglass hulls, Marco-made or rebuilt PT, dory to bow-picker to purse seiner. The hard work had yet to start for her, but when it did she would love that, too. It was deeply satisfying to play a part in what was essentially a rite that went back to the first time man went wading into the primordial soup whence he came, for the bounty left behind that, unlike him, had never known the incentive to grow legs and walk on dry land. Her family had been fishing in the Gulf of Alaska for a thousand years. It was a tradition she cherished, and honored in the practice thereof.

Next to her the old man grinned. "Ain't this the life?"

"Ain't it though." She yawned hugely. The sun poured down over everything like warm gold. Wavelets lapped at the hull, an ephemeral zephyr dusted her cheek. A small swell raised the hull and for a moment the *Freya* strained against the force of the incoming tide. Kate opened one eye, but the bow and stern anchors held and she closed it again. She heard a deep sigh, and let her hand slide down from the arm of the chair. With an almost voluptuous groan, Mutt rolled over on her side, legs in the air. Scratch my belly, please. Kate smiled, her eyes still closed, and complied.

There was a faint shout somewhere off to starboard.

Nobody moved.

There was another shout, louder this time, followed by others, growing in volume and alarm.

Mutt huffed out an annoyed breath and raised her head to look at Kate. Kate sighed heavily, opened her eyes and looked across at Old Sam, one deck chair over. Old Sam swore creatively and rose to walk to the railing, shading his face with one hand. Off the port bow he saw a bowpicker—the *Tanya*, he thought, narrowing his eyes—with two sweating, straining, swearing men in the bow. Most of the net was in the water and the men seemed to be playing tug-of-war with it. They pulled back on the net, the net pulled them and the boat forward, they pulled back, the net pulled them forward. Old Sam watched, amazed, as the bowpicker left a wake of tiny whirlpools, moving drunkenly but steadily southward, toward the mouth of the bay and Prince William Sound beyond.

"Goddam," Old Sam said respectfully.

Kate's chair creaked and footsteps sounded on the deck behind him. "What?"

The crow's-feet at the corners of the old man's bright brown eyes deepened. "Well, either Captain Nemo needs a shore launch, or Doug's got himself a halibut tangled in his lead line."

Kate squinted in the light. "It's pulling them against the tide." They watched, fascinated, as even the cork line was dragged below the surface. The net jerked suddenly and the bowpicker lurched left to scrape its port side along the starboard side of the *Angelique*. Rhonda Pettingill, looking up from untangling a fifty-pound king from her gear, was too astonished at the sight to do anything but stare. When the *Tanya* cut the cork line of the *Marie Josephine*, Terry and Jerry Nicolo were more forthcoming.

"Well, shit," Old Sam said, and scratched behind one ear. "Why don't they just cut 'er loose?"

"Um," Kate said.

He looked over at her. "What?"

She shoved her hands in her back pockets, one hip cocked, as she admired the tan of one splayed knee. "The *Tanya* just lost a set of gear last week, didn't they? Got hung up on a deadhead off Strawberry Reef?" She let him think about it for a minute. "And you know how anal Doug gets about losing to a fish anyway."

"Well, shit," Old Sam said again, and sighed, his brown, seamed face settling into mournful lines. "And here I was just settling into a gentleman's life of leisure. Pull the goddam hooks, Shugak, while I yank her chain."

"Yes, boss," Kate said, grinning, and went to do as she was told.

The deck of the *Freya* shuddered as the last link of dripping chain rattled up. Moments later they were under way, threading a slow, careful, no-wake path through boats and cork lines and skiffs and frantically picking fishermen. Beneath the surface of the water enormous schools of salmon, their silver sides darkened to slate by the water, arrowed back and forth in ardent attempts to gain the mouth of the river.

The *Tanya* had reached the mouth of the bay by the time the *Freya* caught up with her. In the bow, Doug, a dark-haired man, all muscle and bone, worked in furious silence next to a short, rotund blond whose usually beaming face was set into equally determined lines.

A window rattled down and from the bridge Old Sam shouted, "I'll put us alongside, Kate, you swing the boom over!"

The mast rose up from the deck just aft of the focsle. Kate lowered the boom and freed the hook attached to the shackle. Both swung over the side. "Ahoy the *Tanya!*" she shouted, her husk of a voice carrying clearly across the water. "Doug! Jim!"

Doug looked up just in time to catch the hook as it swept by. Water boiled up from the stern as Old Sam put the *Freya*'s engine into reverse and brought the tender to a sliding stop. Doug and Jim loaded the hook with as much cork line and net as it would hold. Kate gave the opposite end of the line a few turns around the drum and started the winch. It whined in protest at the heavy load, and the *Freya* listed some when the net cleared the water.

She listed some more, nearly enough to ship water over the starboard gunnel, when the mammoth halibut cleared the surface. The fish was flat, brown on top and white on the bottom, and had both eyes on the brown side. It flashed dark and light as it fought to be free of the net, succeeding only in tearing more holes in it. Kate was ready with the .22, but before she could raise it to her shoulder Doug had vaulted up onto the *Freya*'s deck and snatched the rifle out of her hand. At the expression on his face she sensibly took a step back. It was an automatic rifle and the five shots came so rapidly they sounded almost like one, followed by a long, repeating echo.

Doug held the rifle against his shoulder, finger on the trigger, as seconds ticked down. The halibut gave a last convulsive heave, ripped out another six feet of mesh and subsided. Kate said nothing. As much satisfaction as Doug had taken in finishing off the monster that had finished off his gear and probably a week's worth of fishing, it was as much necessity as revenge. They didn't dare bring the halibut on board before it was dead. It was big enough to kick the *Freya* to pieces.

Laid out on the deck, the halibut's snout poked into the door of the focsle and its tail bent up against the front of the galley. The ventral fins almost but not quite overlapped either side.

They crouched over it in wonder. "Sweet Jesus H. Christ on a crutch," Old Sam said prayerfully. "How big do you think, Doug?"

Doug was still mad. "I think it's just too damn bad I can't kill it twice."

"It's a downright dirty shame we don't have a scale big enough to handle the sucker," Jim said wistfully. "Betcha ten bucks she weighs five hundred pounds."

"Six, maybe," Kate said.

"Seven," Old Sam said, and spat over the side for emphasis.

"This mother's eight hundred if she's an ounce," Doug snapped. Everyone else maintained a prudent silence, broken by the scrape of a boat against the portside hull. Kate looked around in surprise, and rose at once to her feet, her face lit with pleasure. "Auntie Joy!"

"*Alaqah*," Auntie Joy said, her round face peering over the gunnel, "that is some fish you got there, Samuel."

"It sure as hell is, Joy-girl." The old man stood to offer her a hand. "Get your ass on up here and grab a knife, we can use the help."

The old woman laughed, and Kate couldn't help the grin that spread across her face. It was matched by identical grins on the faces of the three other women still seated in the New England dory warped alongside the *Freya*'s starboard hull. "Hi, Auntie Vi. Hi, Auntie Edna. Auntie Balasha, I didn't know you were in the Park."

Auntie Joy took Old Sam's hand and with an agility that

belied both age and rotundity climbed over the gunnel to the deck. The other three women followed. Kate made the introductions. "Doug, Jim, this is Joyce Shugak, Viola Moonin, Edna Aguilar and Balasha Shugak. My aunties." She said it proudly, if inaccurately. Only one of them was really an auntie, the other three were great-aunts and cousins, but the relationships were so convoluted, involving Kate's grandmother's sister's husband who had divorced his first wife and married again and moved to Ouzinkie, that it would have taken half an hour to unravel. Balasha was the youngest of the four of them, a mere child of seventy-six. The rest of them were in their early eighties, although Auntie Vi never got very specific about it. They were as brown as berries, as wizened as walnuts and as round and merry as Santa Claus. It raised the spirits just to breathe the same air they did.

"You on your way to fish camp, Joy-girl?" Old Sam said.

Kate remembered then, the family fish camp a mile or so up Amartuq Creek, the very creek across the mouth of which Yuri Andreev had tried to cork Joe Anahonak not half an hour before.

"Yes," Auntie Joy said, "we fly George in from Niniltna, and come from town on the morning tide." She beamed. "Fish running good, huh?"

"Real good," Old Sam said.

As if to corroborate his judgment, they heard a whoop off to port. Pete Petersen on the *Monica* had just hauled in what looked like a seventy-five-pound king, which was selling delivered to the cannery for three dollars a pound.

Kate looked at Old Sam. "We're going to need this deck pretty soon."

Old Sam nodded. "Get the knives."

Kate went to the focsle. A storage area formed where the bow came to a point, the focsle served as food locker, parts store, tool crib and junk drawer. It was black as pitch inside, and Kate held the door open with one hand while she fumbled with the other for the flashlight hanging from a nail on the bulkhead to the right. The focsle was so crammed that the flashlight didn't help much; she scraped her shin on a crate of eggs, caught her toe on a small cardboard box full of dusty brass doorknobs and snagged her braid on a bundle of halibut hooks before she found the sliming knives.

They were broad, sharp blades with white plastic handles, and when she brought them out on deck they got down to the almost mutually exclusive jobs of butchering out the halibut and salvaging Doug and Jim's gear. The four old women pitched in next to them, each producing her own personal knife in a gesture that reminded Kate irresistibly of the rumble between the Sharks and the Jets. The aunties' knives had long, slender, wickedly sharp blades with handles carved variously of wood, bone and antler, with which they outbutchered even Old Sam, who had only been doing this for a living for sixty years.

To everyone's surprise and to Jim's ebullient relief, the gear was in better shape than it had looked with the halibut caught in it. Doug said nothing as his brown, callused hands measured the gaping holes that would have to be mended before they could fish again. It wasn't like there was a net loft up on the nearest beach, either. Kate remembered that his wife, Loralee, had had a baby six months before, a Christmas baby named Eddie, a chuckling, fair-haired child with enormous blue eyes like his mother's and a jaw squared with a lick of his father's stubborn.

Doug must have felt the weight of her gaze and looked up, eyes narrowing on her face. Kate, who had a lively sense of self-preservation, refrained from offering sympathy. Doug would have taken it for pity and as a matter of pride refused any offer of further help, and if Kate knew her aunties, an offer of help was forthcoming.

Next to her Auntie Vi spoke. "You got needles and twine?"

Doug's gaze moved from the young woman to the older one. "What?"

Patiently, Auntie Vi repeated, "You got needles? You got twine?" He said nothing and even more patiently she said, "To mend your gear?" She gestured at the other women. "My sisters and me, you got needles and twine, we help mend." She waited.

He looked from her face to the faces of the other three. They were impassive. He looked back at her. "Well, sure," he said slowly. "I've got needles, and twine, too."

"I've got a spare case in the focsle," Old Sam put in, and looked at Kate. Kate, nursing her scraped shin, sighed heavily and went back to the focsle.

Auntie Vi gave a decisive nod. "Good. We fix."

"I don't know," Doug began, and Auntie Vi said, patience gone, "*Freya* not going nowhere. We hang the cork line from the bow, one end from *Tanya,* other end our dory, use Samuel's skiff to mend from, work toward middle." Doug opened his mouth and she beat him to it. "We reef the net to cork line as we mend."

Doug still looked doubtful, but Jim slapped him on the back. "Sure, it'll work. There's no chop or swell, and with all of us working we'll get it done in no time. Maybe even before the period's over." He knew, and Doug knew it, too, that this was an offer they couldn't refuse. The four old women between them had more net-mending experience than the rest of the fleet combined.

Doug was a proud man, with an innate disinclination for accepting handouts and an even stronger dislike for being beholden to anyone. Kate, watching him, saw him bite back that pride and bow his head to necessity and, perhaps, to the generosity of age and experience as well. With their years on the river, the four aunties had probably torn up their share of gear. They knew what it was like to watch impotently as the year's catch passed them by, and they knew, too, what a hungry winter was like. "Thanks, Viola. I—Thanks."

She shrugged. "We helping each others. You help us sometime."

And that was that. In less time than it took to tell it, they had the gear draped over the bow of the *Freya*, Auntie Edna and Auntie Balasha mending toward the center from the dory, Doug and Jim mending toward the center from the *Tanya*, and Auntie Vi and Auntie Joy darting back and forth in the *Freya*, plastic needles flashing in the sun, talking and laughing nonstop.

It isn't easy, mending a wet net, but they did it. The task was made easier by the fact that the gear was fifteen mesh, or fifteen feet deep from cork line to lead line, for fishing the shallower waters near shore. Still, it was fifty feet long, and mending a net on water was a tricky business at best, swell or no swell, and it was two hours before the eight of them manhandled the mended net back to the *Tanya*'s deck and Doug and Joe rewound it on the reel in the bow.

"Hold it," Jim said as Doug prepared to cast off, and

vaulted the gunnel to the *Freya*'s deck. He slipped and almost fell in the gurry and blood left from the halibut that Kate and Old Sam had been butchering out as the others mended the *Tanya*'s gear. Before she could nip out of the way he had scooped Auntie Vi up in his arms, bent her over backwards and thoroughly kissed her. He pulled back and grinned down at her. "Thanks, Viola. I'd propose but I'm already married. Want to shack up instead?"

Auntie Vi flushed deep red and scolded him in Aleut, with a couple of extra words Kate recognized as being Athabascan and profanity thrown in for good measure. The other three aunties were rocking with laughter, and Jim, grinning widely, jumped down to his own boat.

Even Doug was smiling. "Thanks, aunties," he called as they pulled away. "I owe you one. Hell, I owe you ten!"

"We'll save you some steaks!" Kate called, and the two men waved once before getting back to the serious business of fishing salmon for a living.

They watched the *Tanya* find a spot to set their gear and turned their own attention to the halibut. It had white flesh but its blood was as red as any salmon's, and a considerable amount of it was spread across the *Freya*'s deck, mixed in with seawater that had kept it fluid.

Kate had always been interested in the stomachs of everything her family shot and ate. The stomach contents of game were stories in themselves. She remembered a Sitka doe once that had had a belly full of seaweed dotted with blueberries and a couple of pop-tops. Halibut were especially fun to excavate since they spent their lives vacuuming up the floor of the ocean. This monster's most recent meal had consisted of a Dungeness crab, two pollock, about a hundred tiger shrimp, a can of cat food with holes punched in it, a small piece of coral and one dark brown rubber hip boot, a little the worse for wear.

"Tell me there's not a foot inside that boot," Old Sam commanded. Unenthusiastically Kate investigated. The boot was empty. Everyone relaxed. They all knew halibut were bottom feeders, and they all knew what sank to the bottom of the ocean when it fell overboard, and they all knew that halibut liked their food ripe. It didn't stop them from eating halibut, or crab either, for that matter, but a foot in the hip boot might have given them indigestion afterwards.

They pitched the guts over the side and began carving the carcass into cookable chunks. The halibut cheeks alone would be enough for an evening meal for the six of them. When they finally got the spine out the resulting fillets were immense.

So was the heart. "Jesus," Old Sam said. "Look at that, will ya."

He handed it to Kate. She needed both hands to hold it.

The dark red lump of grainy flesh pumped once against her palms. In one leap she was at the railing, where she dumped the still-beating heart down on the gunnel and backed away. Old Sam cackled with laughter, and the four old women giggled. A tinge of color darkened Kate's face. She should have tossed the damn thing over the side and be damned to it.

Mutt came to her rescue. She stood two feet from the rail, neck stretched to its farthest limit, the stiff hairs on her ruff raised, lips curled back from her teeth, nostrils flaring. She looked at Kate, eyes wide, and didn't find any help there. She turned back to the halibut heart, extended her neck another inch and sniffed once at the jerking flesh. Her lip curled even farther and she backed up a step, uttering a low "woof" deep in her throat. That sound had been known to stop a brown bear in its tracks; unintimidated, the halibut heart kept on beating without pause. A rumbling growl and Mutt backed away on stiff legs, yellow eyes never leaving the palpitating lump of red flesh, and retreated to the bow, where she stayed until they got back to Cordova the next morning.

Kate felt like joining her. Cut out from its chest, separated from its body which even now was being boned and sliced into steaks behind her, the organ beat on relentlessly, heaving up and down on the black-painted surface of the gunnel. "How long's it keep doing that?" she said.

Old Sam shrugged. "I seen 'em beat for hours after getting cut out of a body. Just ain't ready to give up, I guess." He grinned at her. "Bothering you, girl?"

Kate drew herself erect and lied like a trooper. "Of course not."

Old Sam laughed, and the damn halibut heart kept beating while she hauled buckets of water up over the side to wash down the deck. It kept beating as she wrapped and stowed the halibut fillets in the walk-in freezer next to the engine room below aft, and it was still beating when Old Sam moved them back to their original anchorage just in time to meet the first laden bowpicker as she waddled up, hold spilling a mound of fish from gunnel to gunnel.

"Okay, girl, get them hatch covers off," Sam bawled from the bridge. "Time to hunt and gather."

They were lucky in that the fish were running so well, encouraging the fishermen to off-load full holds into the *Freya* and go back for more. If the fishing had been slow, the holds of the smaller boats would not have been filled by the end of the period, and they would have hauled their own fish back to the canneries in Cordova, where they would have earned a penny extra a pound, a penny Old Sam regarded as by rights belonging to him. Since Kate was earning a deck boss share, she felt kind of proprietary about it herself.

The hatch covers, long boards twelve feet in length, came off to reveal the square mouth of the *Freya*'s hold. With a revulsion Kate didn't understand herself she moved the still-beating halibut heart to the stern, out of the way and, truth be told, out of her sight.

She would have thrown it overboard if Old Sam hadn't been watching her every move with a gleeful eye. Old Sam would have thrown it overboard if he hadn't taken a perverse delight in how much it bothered her. Between the two of them, the halibut heart was destined to thump up and down on the gunnel until the end of the season.

She laughed at herself, at the both of them, until a hail from an approaching boat reminded her to get to work before Old Sam had even more cause to flex his testosterone, and she trotted forward again to catch the line tossed her by Tim Sarakovikoff. He skippered a trim little bowpicker called the *Esther*, named for his mother, who would be proud when she heard her namesake had been first in the period to come alongside.

Maybe an inch taller than Kate, with broad shoulders and arms roped with muscle, Tim was flushed with pleasure and triumph and had fish scales caught in his eyebrows. "Am I first up?"

"I don't see any other fish in our hold," Kate said.

He peered down the open hatch. "No shit?"

Kate grinned. "No shit."

An answering grin split his face, clear-skinned and topped with straight brown hair that flopped into his eyes. For just a moment Kate allowed herself to fall in love with his clean-limbed youth, his obvious ability, his sturdy self-sufficiency and his joy in his work. "Come on," she said, slapping his shoulder. "Let's pitch us some fish."

The boom swung over the side, and Kate let out enough line to lower the brailer, a wide tube of netting suspended from a circle of steel, to the deck of the *Esther*. Tim donned rubber gloves and stooped to pitch fish into the brailer until it was full, when Kate swung the boom back over the gunnel and centered the brailer over the *Freya*'s open hold. She recorded the weight of the fish from the scale attached to the boom (an innovation for the old girl; thanks to her antediluvian skipper, the *Freya* was moving into the twentieth century just as the century itself was moving out), tugged on another line, and the bottom of the brailer opened up and salmon cascaded into the *Freya*'s hold in a silver stream, redeemable on shore for groceries and school clothes and rent and boat payments.

There was a shout to port when Tim, dizzy with delight at the final count, went into the galley to get Sam to write up his fish ticket. Kate looked around to see Yuri Andreev and the *Terra Jean* warp alongside. Yuri had evidently managed to catch a few fish in spite of not being able to cork Joe Anahonak.

It was late for kings, but the *Esther* had brought in three and the *Terra Jean* five, so Kate limbered up the small scale and weighed each individually, reporting the results to Old Sam, ensconced in bleak formality at one end of the galley table. Tim was seated a respectful distance down the bench, the four aunties between, sitting like little brown birds in a row, steaming coffee mugs in their hands, eyes bright and inquiring.

Old Sam never joked with the fishermen as they came aboard to deliver; he'd spent seventy-five summers fishing and tendering on the waters of Prince William Sound and he took the business seriously, as seriously as he took his reputation for fair dealing. If Old Sam wrote a fish ticket that reported Tim Sarakovikoff had delivered five thousand pounds of reds to his, Sam's, hold, then by God there were five thousand pounds of reds with Tim's brand on them to be delivered to Kamaishi Seafoods in Cordova, the same five thousand pounds for which Tim would be paid hard cash money at the going rate per pound at time of delivery when he got back to town, or at the end of the season, whichever he preferred.

Whenever Kate got a moment in the frenzied hours that followed, she looked up to find the fleet drifting, nets out, their crews moving up and down cork lines in skiffs, hauling the net up wherever they saw a cork bob and picking the salmon caught in the mesh of the net below the surface of the water. It was hard, backbreaking work, but Alaskan fishermen were the last of the independent businessmen, stubborn, self-reliant, always cantankerous, frequently adulterous and, in Kate's admittedly biased opinion, wholly admirable. The state had done its best to regulate where they fished, but the fishermen still delivered to whoever they damn well pleased, which was probably whoever paid them the most per pound, but could also be whoever had pissed them off the least, and the opportunities for pissing off an Alaskan fisherman were legion. They were sovereign unto themselves and fiercely beholden to none, so long as the Mother of Storms saw fit to let them be, and so long as they got their boat payments to the bank on time.

The *Dawn*, the *Rose*, the *Darlene*, the *Deliah*, the *Tiana*, the *Danica*, the *Priscilla*, all came, delivered fish and went. An hour before the period ended, the *Tanya* pulled up to port, Jim beaming and Doug nearly giddy with relief. They delivered three thousand pounds and took their ticket away rejoicing, Jim this time outright proposing to Auntie Vi and taking his rejection in good spirit. A skiff came alongside so loaded down it was shipping water, a redheaded woman in yellow rain gear at the kicker, a setnetter delivering from the beach. She was followed by Mary Balashoff, another setnetter from the opposite end of the beach. Kate thought she saw a third and equally loaded skiff put off from the beach and tie up to a drifter, but she was too busy to pay much attention.

The *Freya*'s trim line was a lot lower in the water than it had been that morning when the *Esther* returned for a second time, her young skipper's triumph having given way to weariness, but it was a happy fatigue, and when Kate told him he was high boat for the period his broad brown cheeks flushed like a boy's. "Am I really, Kate?"

She smiled, almost as tired as he was. "You really are."

He stood there, dazed and delighted, savoring it. He was nineteen years old, and it was only his second summer of fishing on his own. "Wait till I tell Dad." He grinned suddenly. "Wait till I tell Mom!"

Kate laughed. "Should keep her happy for a while."

"You don't know my mom. She'll say any boat with her name on it ought to be high boat every period."

"And she's right," Auntie Joy said sternly from behind them. They turned and saw the twinkle in her eye.

Tim tried to frown and failed. "Ah, you women all stick together."

"Make her come out and pick her own fish," Kate suggested.

He brightened. "I like that plan."

Thinking of Esther, a dignified elder with a passion for bingo, Kate quite agreed, and Auntie Joy laughed her joyous laugh.

There was a vicious thump and scrape against the portside gunnel. "Hey!" Kate said, turning.

Water roiled up from the screw of the white-hulled drifter with the flying bridge and the reel in the stern. She was riding low in the water, silver salmon slipping across the deck as her skipper manhandled her into place. A chunky, sullen young man of perhaps fifteen stood in the bow and hurled the bow line at Kate, who just missed catching the lashing line with her face. "Hey!" she said again, and stooped swiftly to gather the line up and hurl it back at the boy with interest.

He dodged out of the way as it whistled past, missed his footing and went over the side. There was a loud curse from the flying bridge, and Kate looked up to see a scowling man slam the throttle into neutral and slide down the ladder to the deck. He snatched up the stern line and tossed it to Kate. It looped neatly into her hands this time, so she made it fast and came forward to catch the bow line when he retrieved it to do the same. By the time they were done, the boy had hauled himself on board by way of one of the white Styrofoam bumpers hanging over the far side of the drifter, and the man went to stand over him. When he stood on the deck, dripping and shaky, the man backhanded him once, a blow that was deceptively effortless in execution and immensely effective in result, knocking the boy back into the water.

"Hey!" Kate said a third time.

Next to her Tim shook his head. "No, Kate," he said in a low voice.

Auntie Joy stood stony and immobile, all trace of laughter wiped from her face.

The boy's head broke the surface of the water.

"That's for fucking up the docking," the man's dispassionate voice said. He waited until the boy hauled himself back on board, knees visibly trembling this time, before backhanding him a second time, same hand to the same side of the face, same parabola over the side into the water.

Tim grabbed Kate's elbow and held on. "No."

It took longer for the boy to surface this time. Just about the time Kate was deciding to go in after him, he did. The man said, still without inflection, "And that's for putting the fucking bumpers on the wrong side of the fucking boat."

"Hey," Kate said, her torn voice coming out in a broken growl. "There's no call for that."

The man turned his head to regard her out of cold eyes. "Mind your own fucking business," he said without inflection.

Kate clenched her hands. Tim grabbed her elbow again. "No, Kate," he repeated.

This time the boy had barely enough energy to pull for the side of the boat and wrap both arms around the bumper. He hung there, head burrowed into his arms. He was trembling so badly that boy and bumper virtually vibrated against the hull of the drifter. The man spat into the water next to him and reached down one long arm to grasp the boy's collar and haul him aboard. The boy collapsed on the deck in a wet, coughing heap.

The wake of a boat passing by caught their hulls. The rocking motion rubbed together the sides of the *Freya* and the white-hulled drifter, which had no name, only an f/v number issued by the Alaska Department of Fish and Game stenciled on the bow. The man went down the side of his vessel, unfastening the white rubber cylindrical bumpers from the free side of his vessel and transferring them to the side scraping against the *Freya*. The boy was still hiccuping noisily in his puddle of salt water and salmon scales, and in passing the man hauled back his foot and kicked him almost casually in the side. "Get your gloves and start pitching fish."

Kate pulled against Tim's grip, and he said again, more

urgently this time, "Don't, Kate. Really. Don't. I know this guy. You'll just make it ten times worse on the kid."

As they watched, the boy managed to fight his way to his feet, move to a locker and pull out a pair of rough-surfaced, reddish-brown rubber gloves—monkey gloves they were called, Kate didn't know why. He looked across at the two of them, eyes narrowed and hostile, his right cheek swollen and beginning to bruise. "What are you looking at?"

Tim said nothing. Neither did Kate said, and the boy said, "You ready or what?"

His voice was as flat and brusque as the man's. Behind them the door to the galley opened and Old Sam's stern voice called out, "Tim, get your butt in here, boy, you want your ticket."

Kate drew a deep breath, and matched her tone of voice to the boy's. "Yeah," she said, and bent to the controls. "We're ready."

Tim faded from her side. Man and boy bent to their task, filling a brailer so that Kate could transfer their catch to the *Freya*'s hold. She had to admit the two of them worked well together, bending, snagging fish by their gills, pitching them up and over the rim of the brailer. Of course, from what Kate had seen it was in the boy's best interests to work well. She cursed herself for not catching the damn rope the first time the boy had thrown it, and dodged back just in time to get out of the way of a fifty-pound king that sailed across the gunnel to hit the deck with a loud thud.

Her eyes lingered on the figure of the skipper. His movements were nimble, his feet stepped light as a cat's, his hands were deft and sure in the bulky monkey gloves, as they had been at the controls of the drifter.

He looked up and saw Kate looking at him, and straightened up slowly to return like for like. He took his time about it, his dark eyes moving slowly over the polished black helmet of her hair, the clear hazel eyes beneath lids folded to give her face an exotic Asian cast, the high, flat cheekbones, the smooth brown skin interrupted by the ropy scar that bisected her throat, the taut muscles and smooth curves of her body displayed to advantage in cut-off jeans and a cut-down T-shirt.

At first astonished and then repulsed, she gave him look for look, insolent and derisive, letting her face show her revulsion. He was short and thickset, with long arms and a heavy jaw. His face looked as if it had been chipped out with a pickax, blunt-featured and brutal. His skin was clear, his eyes gleamed, and his hair, as dark as his eyes, was as thick and shining as a bear's pelt.

Her scrutiny didn't bother him; he even smiled a little, a slight lifting of the corners of his mouth. Involuntarily she looked toward the bow. Mutt was there. Lying down, true, but watching, her chin on her paws, yellow eyes unblinkingly fixed on the stocky figure of the drift fisherman.

He followed Kate's gaze. The little smile widened. Even at this distance Kate could see the hair raise ever so slightly on the back of Mutt's neck, and she was glad when the boy's exhausted voice echoed up from the hold of the drifter, "That's it, we're empty," and she was able to turn to the boom controls and bring the brailer back over the *Freya*'s hold.

She caught a glimpse of Auntie Joy, who had either remained standing at the door to the galley during the drifter's delivery or come out again. The old woman's face was still, and there was something in her eyes that brought Kate to a standstill. "Auntie?" she whispered, without knowing why she was whispering. "Auntie, what's wrong?"

A bumper caught between two hulls squeaked in protest and Kate turned to see the drifter captain vault the *Freya's* gunnel in one smooth, easy motion. It wasn't anything she hadn't seen skippers and deckhands do fifty times already that day, but he made it look natural, even graceful, like Mutt taking a fallen tree in one easy stride on a run through the Park. He made no move to come closer, but somehow he seemed to fill up the deck with his presence. Again Kate looked toward the bow. Mutt was sitting up now, looking at her, waiting for a signal.

The man nodded. "Joyce."

Auntie Joy, her face stiff, nodded. "Mr. Neamy."

He grinned. His mouth was wide and overfilled with large white teeth. "Meany. But I told you to call me Cal." His voice was a deep, soft purr of sound.

He stripped the gloves from his hands and tossed them back to his boat. The boy made catching them into an act of personal survival, which it probably was. Cal Meany watched without expression as the boy snatched the gloves from the air with one hand, lost his balance and went down hard on one knee to avoid going into the water. "Wash the hold and the deck down," his skipper said, and turned back to Kate, allowing his eyes to drop to her breasts. "Who are you?"

"The deck boss," she said shortly. "Sam!"

A grizzled head poked out the door. "Yeah?"

"Got another ticket to write."

"Call 'em off."

She called off the numbers and he took them down. "Well, come on in then, Mr.—"

"Meany," the man said. "Calvin Meany."

"And don't forget your goddam permit card like the last

three assholes pretending to be fishermen who came on board," Old Sam growled.

Meany walked aft to the galley door, reaching in his back pocket for his wallet. Auntie Joy was standing in front of the door. He paused, looking down at her. "Have you given any more thought to my proposition, Joyce? We could make a lot of money together, you and me."

Auntie Joy stepped to one side without answering. He shrugged. "Think it over. It's the right thing to do, for both of us." He opened the door and stepped inside.

Kate looked from the closed door to her aunt. "What was all that about?"

Auntie Joy looked at her and through her. "Nothing."

"Nothing? What do you mean, nothing? What's that guy talking about, the two of you making money together? How did you meet him? What does he want?"

"Nothing," Auntie Joy said again, her voice as stony as her face. She turned as if to go back in the galley, hesitated and then walked around Kate to climb up into the bow. Mutt watched her go by, and then padded after her, sitting down to lean her shoulder against Auntie Joy's knee. A worn, gnarled hand came down to rest on the dog's head.

Kate looked from them to the drifter. The boy was hauling buckets of water up over the side and splashing them over the deck of the drifter. He raised his head to find Kate watching him. His mouth set in a thin line. "What are you looking at?"

The *Joanna C.* pulled up to the *Freya*'s starboard side and Kate was spared the necessity of a reply.

The fishing period was over at six sharp that evening. They took their last delivery at seven-thirty, the rest of the boats hauling their last loads into Cordova themselves. The *Freya*'s galley menu offered up deep-fried beer-batter halibut cheeks at ten o'clock that night. The heart of the great fish was still beating on the railing, a dull red, humping lump of flesh in the slanting rays of the sun, single-minded, single-purposed, inexorable, as the four old women clambered down into their dory and set off for the mouth of Amartuq Creek.

They weighed anchor and were in Cordova by one a.m. Kate and Sam donned boots and rain gear to climb into the hold with three members of the cannery's beach gang, there to fill the brailer lowered by boom from the cannery dock. One brailer at a time, they emptied the hold, and when the last fish had gone and the hold had been hosed down and the hatch covers replaced and the *Freya* had been refueled and moved to her slip in the small boat harbor, the heart beat on beneath the rays of the rising sun. Fishermen and beach gang and fuelers alike were awed by it, by the sheer force of nature it personified. They moved around it, careful not to touch it, speaking in whispers.

Kate carried the sight of it with her to the chart room bunk, which probably accounted for the jangled state of her dreams.

Although even that was better than lying awake worrying about the boy on Meany's boat, or the expression on Auntie Joy's face as she looked at Meany, to which Kate could still put no name.

She woke next morning to sunshine and the smell of coffee. Old Sam was gone, but he'd left the pot on the stove. Mutt was stretched out on the focsle, basking in the morning sun, the remains of what looked like the knee joint of a humpback whale lying next to her. With some trepidation, Kate sidled up to the starboard galley door and eased it open a crack to peek around the jamb. No halibut heart, and the gunnel was scoured clean. Old Sam must have taken it uptown with him for show-and-tell over the bar. Immensely relieved, Kate closed the galley door firmly behind her.

It was a long, narrow room the width of the beam of the ship, less the deck space between bulkhead and gunnel on both sides. A bench ran along the forward bulkhead, with a table bolted to the deck in front of it. The opposite bulkhead was lined with sink, cupboards, stove and refrigerator, this last a modern-day concession to the finicky habits of Old Sam's sissy deckhands (this said with a choleric eye rolled in Kate's direction). He still grumped about missing the cooler that had hung next to the starboard-side door, the one he had used for thirty years, and the cupboard and counter space usurped by the refrigerator. Rectangular windows lined the forward bulkhead sill to sill, letting in a lot of light and satisfying Old Sam's inquisitive eye with a 180-degree view of his surroundings.

The immaculate room was trimmed with wood varnished to a deep chestnut glow. An old oil stove, polished to a dull black shine, put out a steady wave of heat and caused the kettle sitting on top to give a low, comforting whistle. Kate poured herself a cup of coffee and sat down with her feet up on the seat to take advantage of Old Sam's view.

The harbor was still and quiet in the early-morning hours, the fishermen sleeping off the last period. Boats were rafted two and three together, leaving barely a skiff's width of water between the slips. Transient parking was, as usual, empty of so much as a kayak, nine hundred feet of vacant slip space. This while the rest of the harbor was jammed to the breakwater and the fishing fleet jostled for moorage.

Kate detected the fell hand of Shitting Seagull.

She looked up. The harbormaster's office, a small, neat house sitting on the edge of the fill just before the dock and ramp that led down to the harbor, seemed deserted.

But then maybe Gull was only luring potential offenders into a self-incriminating complacency.

Behind the small boat harbor was the town of Cordova. Perched at about one o'clock on the curve where Prince William Sound met the Alaska coastline, it was a stair-step settlement built of wooden clapboard houses, many of them on pilings pounded into the sheer side of the steep coastline. Cordova had once been the southern terminus of the Kanuyaq River & Northwestern Railroad, a hundred-mile track that carried copper ore from the fabulous Strike It Rich lode in the Teglliq Foothills from 1911 until 1936, and many of the buildings looked like they dated from that time.

The town's tiers culminated in the twenty-two-hundred-foot peak of Mount Eyak, a sharp point that contrasted with the rounded peak of Mount Eccles, a whole hundred feet higher. Between them the peaks guarded a narrow strip of land linking Orca Inlet, Cordova's access to Prince William Sound, and Eyak Lake, a glacier-fed body of water whose opaque, gray-blue tint changed only when it froze a hard, unforgiving white. East of Eyak Lake began the thirty-mile-wide Kanuyaq River delta, a vast expanse of rushing, silty water interrupted by migrant sandbars the size of Manhattan. Between the rapid current and the glacial silt, a bowpicker averaged one impeller per summer. Kate wondered sometimes if it was worth it. She would have bet most fishermen did, too.

It was a big town, as far as Alaskan towns went, supporting a population of three thousand. Access was by boat or plane; the only road out had been under construction when the 1964 Alaskan earthquake hit. The project was abandoned, although a recent governor had made a stab at restarting it from the other end, only to have his Cats halted in their tracks by the Environmental Protection Agency—but not before the Cats had gleefully bulldozed the spawning grounds of entire schools of red salmon.

The town was half-asleep in winter and wide awake in summer when Outsiders from Anacortes and Bellingham and Seattle flooded Cordova in drifters and seiners. A few married locally and took their brides south for the winter. Fewer still stayed the winter to fish for king crab, to build homes and raise families and become sourdoughs instead of lowly chee-chakos, a distinction they took smug pride in pointing out to their fair-weather colleagues. The competition to be high boat was fierce and enthusiastic, and pitched battles were fought at sea and refought on shore, fights over corking and short counts by tenders—something the fishermen were always accusing the tendermen of doing and the tendermen were always denying in duels of honor at local bars.

North of Cordova many glaciers funneled around the peaks of the Chugach Mountains; from the south the Mother of Storms took her best shots. In spite of both, the area had a temperate climate, which meant it rained a lot.

But not today.

An insistent growl made itself evident low down in Kate's belly. She drained the last of her coffee, roused Mutt and went out in search of breakfast.

The Coho Cafe was a shoebox-shaped room with booths down one side, kitchen and counter down the other, and half a dozen tables jammed between. A grimy bank of windows stretched across the far wall, overlooking the harbor, from this angle nothing but a forest of masts. Other than a signed, matted and framed picture of Susan Butcher and Granite on the wall behind the cash register, the decor was utilitarian, Early American Greasy Spoon—bleached-out tan Formica on the counter and tabletops, faded blue linoleum underfoot, the latest coat of white enamel paint on walls and ceiling already yellowing beneath an accumulating layer of yellow grease. There wasn't a matching set of chairs at any table, and the counter stools were flaking chrome from their legs. Coffee the color and consistency of diesel fuel was served in thick white porcelain mugs, food on thick white porcelain plates, and the silverware was plain stainless steel worn so thin you could cut your tongue if you were unwise enough to lick your spoon.

The cafe was packed, people rafted at tables the way boats were rafted to slips in the harbor. The swinging doors between kitchen and counter were constantly in motion and the jeans-and-T-shirt-clad waitresses rattled around the room like pinballs, lighting up one table of raucous, raunchy men after another. "Order up!" blared through the pass-through every thirty seconds.

A heaping plate of eggs scrambled soft with ham and home fries whisked beneath Kate's nose, followed by what had to be the world's largest cinnamon roll, and her stomach growled again. There wasn't an empty chair in the place, and she was debating whether to wait for a stool at the counter or to move on down the street to try her chances at The Empty Mug, when she heard her name called. Looking around, she saw an arm waving at her from a corner booth next to the windows. "Kate! Kate! Over here!"

She didn't recognize the voice, and she couldn't make out who it was against the light from the window, but her stomach made up her mind for her and she threaded her way through the tables and chairs and wildly gesticulating hands.

Arriving at the booth, she discovered Lamar Rousch. He was occupying his entire booth in isolated splendor, probably because he wore the brown uniform of the fish hawk, by any other name smelling as sweet as a state trooper.

"How are you, Kate?" Lamar said, pumping her hand. "I just ordered. Sit down, take a load off."

"Sure." Kate slid in opposite him. Terry Nicolo scowled at her for consorting with the enemy.

Kate returned a bland smile, which widened into something more genuine when the waitress arrived. A cheerful, gum-popping teenage heartthrob with long blond hair tied back in a ponytail, she looked maybe one day out of her cheerleader's uniform. She plunked down a plate of eggs over easy, link sausage, home fries, two slices of wholewheat toast and a side order of French toast.

"Hey, Kate." The heartthrob wrestled an order pad from a rear pocket that was extremely reluctant to give it up. All activity in the restaurant paused until the extraction was complete. The pad slid free and up went a collective sigh at the resulting wiggle as the jeans slipped back into place. "What can I get you for?"

"Everything," Kate said comprehensively.

The heartthrob cocked her head. "Three scrambled soft, bacon crisp, home fries, biscuit with honey?"

"And coffee," Kate said, bowing her head in the presence of greatness. "You know me so well, Ruthie."

Ruthie flashed a grin and stuck her order pad back into her hip pocket, sliding it home with another tiny wiggle. The fisherman sitting directly behind her choked and coughed coffee all over his bacon waffle. "Just you remember to tell Dandy Mike I turned eighteen last month."

"You bet," Kate lied, and Ruthie swished off, if it was possible to swish in jeans. Judging by the whiplash her wake caused, it was. "So, Lamar," Kate said. "When's the next period, Wednesday or Friday?"

Lamar had cornflower-blue eyes and fair, straight, silky blond hair that he kept in a brush cut in the secret hope that it would make him look like an ex-Marine. It only succeeded in drawing attention to the plump pink curves of his babycakes cheeks, giving him all the authority of a cherub. He spread whipped butter over his French toast in a painfully even layer. "Give me a break, Shugak. I haven't even got the escapement numbers yet, let alone the cannery pack."

"Yeah, but I saw you coming down Calhoun Creek late yesterday afternoon. You must have some idea how many fish got up the river."

Loud voices sounded from the counter, followed by a crash of crockery. "It's Craig off the *Rose*," Lamar said, rising up to peer over the back of the booth. "And Les off the *Deliah*."

"I thought Les broke it off with Craig," Kate said, leaning to look around him, just in time to see Joe Anahonak grab both men by the scruffs of their necks, shake them like dogs and assist them ungently out the door, to the accompaniment of general applause.

"He did," Lamar said, settling back in his seat. "Looks like he started up again."

"Or not," Kate said, leaning back to look out the window. Craig and Les picked themselves up and marched off in opposite directions, one with a rapidly swelling eye and the other checking to see that he still had all his teeth. "I saw Les cork Craig's line yesterday about two minutes after the official opening."

"Ah." Lamar nodded his appreciation of the difference.

Ruthie arrived with Kate's breakfast. The eggs were perfect, the bacon crisp, the spuds done and the biscuit hot. Conversation, at their table at least, suffered a momentary lapse.

It went on nonstop around them. One table over, a burly

man in a checked wool shirt and a gimme cap with a Gulf logo on it said, "I didn't do squat in herring this spring. Those goddam Japs are getting pickier about what they'll take every year."

"You're lucky you caught anything to show them," the man next to him said. His eyes were bright blue in a tanned face, lines fanning out from the corners, the result of squinting at the same horizon for thirty-five years. He was the only one at the table without a hat, which probably meant he was the only one at the table with any hair left. It was pure white and thick and combed carefully back from a broad brow. "We had five boats and a spotter plane and we barely caught enough to pay for fuel."

There was a grunt of agreement from the table next door. "There hasn't been a decent run of herring since the spill."

"It's not just the herring," someone else said. "It's the salmon. If it weren't for the hatcheries, we'd be up the creek our own selfs."

"Yeah, but because of the hatcheries we've got humpies coming out our ears and no place to sell them."

"Why don't sport fishermen have to apply for limited-entry permits?" someone else demanded. "Tell me sport guides aren't commercial fishermen, and I'll call you a liar."

"They ought to have to fill out fish tickets, same as us," someone else agreed.

"And pay the raw fish tax."

"Not to mention the enhancement tax," the first man added, "to restore the creek habitat they tear up every year with those friggin' speedboats."

"It all goes back to the spill," the first man insisted stubbornly, and there wasn't a lot of disagreement.

Watching their faces, Kate saw anger and a consistent, pervasive bitterness that would never go away. The ten-million-gallon, eight-hundred-mile-long spill of Prudhoe Bay crude was nine years old, but it might as well have been yesterday. These men had been fishing Prince William Sound since they were old enough to walk the decks of their fathers' boats. They fed their families and paid their mortgages and put their kids through school with what they wrested from the jealous grasp of the Mother of Storms.

When the TransAlaska Pipeline project had first been proposed, shortly after the discovery of nine and a half billion barrels of oil and twenty-five trillion cubic feet of natural gas seven thousand feet below the surface of Prudhoe Bay, these same fishermen, who individually had more hands-on experience of Prince William Sound than any twenty tanker captains, drunk or sober, had lobbied long and hard for an overland, transCanada route, as opposed to the all-Alaska route that would culminate in Valdez and require shipping by tanker.

Supported in their efforts by economists and environmentalists alike, they were roundly defeated by a coalition of local and state businessmen frankly drooling at the prospect of opening up to development an eight-hundred-mile corridor of Alaskan wilderness. The fishermen freely prophesied disaster, and the grounding of the *RPetCo Anchorage* on Bligh Reef sixteen years later was a Pyrrhic victory for their viewpoint.

There is no worse triumph, Kate thought, than the one that results only in saying, "I told you so."

She leaned forward, fork momentarily suspended, the better to look at the faded T-shirt worn by a fisherman a few tables down. *Don't Shoot,* it read, *I'm Not Denton Harvey!*

She sat back in her seat. "Who's Denton Harvey?"

"Huh?" She pointed, and Lamar leaned out to look, only to turn back to her with a wide grin. "The superintendent of Whitfield Seafoods."

"Oh?" Whitfield was one of the major fish buyers and processors in Prince William Sound, but until now she hadn't known the name of its superintendent, and she would do her best to forget it at the first opportunity. She made it a point of honor to tune out fishing politics, which seemed to be dictated from Seattle and Tokyo and acquiesced to by a weak-kneed state legislature in Juneau. So long as the check for her deckhand share cleared the bank, she went home happy. "What's with the T-shirt?"

"He put the price of reds in the toilet the first week of July last year—something like fifty cents a pound, I think it was—and of course all the rest of the processors followed his lead."

"Ah."

"Yes. I sent him a thank-you card."

Kate was amused. "What'd it say?"

Lamar's grin widened around a mouthful of toast. He swallowed and quoted, " 'Thanks to you, Denton, I didn't have to duck once this summer. Keep up the good work!' "

Kate laughed. "Denton Harvey superintendent at Whit-field again this year?"

Lamar beamed. "He sure is. Gotta love the guy."

Kate didn't, but she sympathized. The fish hawk was not the most welcome sight to rise up over a fisherman's horizon, and over the years more than one fisherman had been moved to express his displeasure, sometimes at the business end of a .30-06. "Listen, Lamar, you ever hear of a guy name of Calvin Meany?"

"Cal Meany?" Lamar's coffee cup halted, suspended in midair. "What do you want with that asshole?"

"Just curious. He delivered to the *Freya* yesterday. I've never met him before."

"Lucky you," Lamar said, and paused when their cheerleader came around with the coffeepot. He stirred four packets of creamer into his coffee with more vigor than was necessary.

Kate used six. "So you know him," she said, sipping cautiously at the still-dark brew. She didn't gag at the resulting taste, but only because she was a strong woman.

"Yeah, I know him." Lamar fortified himself with a long swallow. "He lives in Anchorage. He's got the setnet site east of the beach from Amartuq Creek, right next to the Flanagans'."

"What?" Kate was confused. "No, he's not a setnetter, he's a drifter, he delivered off the—ah, that's right, a no-namer, all he's got is an AK number on the bow."

"No, he owns the setnet site, too, and God only knows what else."

"Wait a minute. I thought you couldn't own two permits, I thought it was against the law."

Lamar set down his mug, and leaned forward, eager and earnest. Lamar loved his job, almost as much as he did explaining its labyrinthine ramifications to the unenlightened, maybe even more than he did catching a perpetrator and soon-to-be felon in the act. "You can't own more than one drift permit, Kate. But you can own a drift permit and a setnet permit and a seine permit and fish them at different times of the year. Of course," he added, "that's just here, in Prince William. You can't own a drift permit in Prince William Sound, another in Cook Inlet and a third in Bristol Bay. Or you can," he amended, "but you can't fish them all the same year, Prince

William in June, Bristol Bay in July, Cook Inlet in August, you can't do that."

"You can't follow the fish," Kate said, nodding.

"Exactly."

"So who's fishing Meany's setnet site while he's drifting?"

"His brother. And," Lamar added, "before you ask, they've got a formal lease agreement. I checked."

"So, they're within the letter of the law." If not its spirit, she thought, and thought again of the boy, and of the boy's sullen fury, and of the expression on Auntie Joy's face. In the normal course of events Auntie Joy and Calvin Meany would have had nothing to do with each other, personally or professionally. Auntie Joy lived in the Park, Meany lived in Anchorage. Auntie Joy fished a mile up the creek, Meany drifted. Auntie Joy fished subsistence, Meany commercially. They were forty years apart in age, a world apart in culture. How had Meany managed to come into contact with Auntie Joy and offend her to the point of speechlessness?

As if he'd been reading her thoughts, Lamar said, "Are Joyce and Viola up at fish camp this year, Kate?"

Evidently he had been too busy to see the four aunties the day before. With perfect truth Kate said, "I haven't been up the creek yet this year, Lamar."

He raised a skeptical eyebrow. "There's still an injunction against subsistence fishing there."

Tim Sarakovikoff burst through the door and rescued Kate from dancing any further around the truth. He grabbed the first fisherman he saw and babbled out the news. The second man, at first disbelieving, asked him a question. Tim gave a violent nod. The fisherman turned to the man next to him and repeated the news. Tim spotted Kate and hustled over. "Kate! Have you heard?"

"No, what?"

Tim saw Lamar and paused, but only infinitesimally. "Denton Harvey, that prick, is sticking it to us again! He's dropping the price on reds to fifty cents a pound!"

Kate set her mug down. Across the table Lamar beamed. "Gotta love that guy."

Fortunately for his continued survival, his comment went unnoticed. "We're not even a week into fishing," Jerry Nicolo said hotly. "It's not like the market is saturated."

"Fucking farmed salmon are gonna put us all outta business," a loud voice said from across the room. "Norwegians, Scots, even the fucking Canucks are getting into it."

"No way."

"It's a fact. They got fish farms in B.C. now. I hear pretty soon the Japanese are gonna be starting some up."

"It's that fucking spill," Dewey Dineen said morosely. "Nobody wants to buy Alaskan salmon anymore."

"It's that goddam Harvey again. This time I say we shoot the bastard and use him for halibut bait!"

"Don't blame Harvey," another man said, "blame the goddam Japs. Hiroshi Limited's the major stockholder in Whitfield."

"So you want to fly to Tokyo, Dick?" someone else said. "Maybe take the matter up with Hiroshi-san personally?"

A stocky man sitting at the counter turned on his stool and surveyed the room, mug in hand. His jeans and plaid shirt weren't any different from what anyone else was wearing, but they were too clean, and the jeans might even have been ironed. "I'll beat Harvey's price a penny a pound."

His words were not greeted with loud hosannas; the drop in price had been too substantial for a penny a pound to make too much difference.

"Delivered to the dock in Cordova," he added, drained his mug and walked out.

"Who was that?" Kate said.

"Joe Durrell," Lamar said. "Independent fish buyer from Anchorage. Middleman for restaurants from Anchorage all the way down to San Diego. First buyer in when the first king hits the Kanuyaq, first buyer out when the last red goes up. He's not interested in anything else."

"Looks like he's going into wholesale," Kate said.

"He does that sometimes. Never by much, just by a cent or two, and there's always a couple of fishermen pissed off enough to sell to him instead."

"What's he do with the salmon?"

Lamar shrugged. "He's a middleman for the gourmet fish processing industry. Probably a lot of folks with more money than sense willing to pay top dollar for the first king up the Kanuyaq."

"But they won't be," Kate said, adding, at his look, "the fish he buys after today. They won't be the first fish up."

Lamar smiled kindly at her. "That's why they call it marketing, Kate."

Kate sat back in the booth. "Right. My mistake."

The shock of Tim's news was giving way to indignation. Four out of five of the men in the room had boat and insurance payments due in September. Three out of five of them would lose their impellers at least once during the summer, two of the five would snag a drifting log, known colloquially as a deadhead, in their gear—or a monster halibut, Kate thought—and rip it beyond repair, and at least one of the five would have trusted his rebuilt engine one season too many, break down and miss out on the remainder of the fishing season altogether. They all went head to head with the IRS every year of their working lives, which bureaucracy failed repeatedly to understand why fishermen had difficulty in making quarterly tax payments on arbitrarily set dates that had nothing whatever to do with when fish were or were not in the Sound.

And now, with the prospect of the first good run in five years, the price per pound was dropping almost before they'd had a chance to get their nets wet. It wasn't five minutes after Tim had burst into the room that the word "Strike!" was hanging in the air.

A brunette shorter than Kate whose brown uniform was belted around her petite body with as much style as a burlap sack came in the door and spotted Lamar. She waded through the incipient mob to their table. Strong men gave way at her approach, probably due to the sour smell of vomit that emanated from her in a miasmic cloud. It reached the booth well in advance of the trooper herself.

Lamar looked her over, taking in the stained front of her uniform shirt, and said with more severity than Kate had thought him capable of, "Becky, I told you, you go up to count fish, not watch the trees. Leave the flying to the pilot and you'll be fine."

An expression of nausea crossed Becky's face, and she swallowed hard.

"So what's the story?" Lamar said.

She fished a slip of paper out of her pocket. "We're over," she said, handing it to him.

Some of the stain had soaked through the pocket. Lamar

touched only corners of the paper with the tips of his fingers, and held it as far away as he could and still read it. He nodded. "Way over. Okay then, put out the word. We're open Wednesday, six to six."

He handed the paper back, and Becky folded it and stowed it carefully in the same pocket as before. Kate wondered if it would become part of the official record of this fishing period. She also wondered how many official records were marked with the puke of fledgling fish hawks, trying to reconcile their stomachs with a profession that kept them in the air in a small plane for half of their working lives. It was one way to weed out the faint of heart.

Lamar's words were overheard, and on any other day it would have been enough to move the subject off Denton Harvey, the price drop and the incipient strike. Not today.

Lamar was aware of it. "For what it's worth," he said, and adjusted the flat brim of his round-crowned hat just so over his eyes in a gesture worthy of Chopper Jim. "Be seeing you, Kate."

She watched him thread his way through the crowd, babycakes face stiffened into as much of an expression of authority as he was capable of with those cheeks, his diminutive sidekick trailing along behind like a limp, smelly tail.

Kate rescued a patient Mutt from the sidewalk outside and walked back down to the boat harbor. The only other person she saw was one lone fisherman squatting on his hatch cover, needle and twine in hand, mending his gear.

The harbor, on the other hand, was as full of boats as Kate had ever seen it, possibly because there was a whole float of pleasure craft, sloops, Liberty Bayliners and Boston whalers, all with improbable names like *Windrover* and *My Retirement* and *Happy Hour,* crowding out honest working boats with honest names, names of mothers and wives and sweethearts and daughters and recently even a few sons. The pleasure craft ran slip rentals through the roof, and their owners usually came down only once a year to fish in the Kanuyaq River Silver Salmon Derby. Kate curled her lip at them and moved on.

The next row was a distinct improvement,

where twenty-five- and thirty-foot bowpickers and drifters lined up gunnel to gunnel. Seiners with flying bridges and crow's nests and masts with booms cocked just so nosed into the next row of slips in a lordly line. They seemed a little bit longer, their paint jobs just a little bit whiter, than the drifters. If seiners had noses, they would have been just a little bit elevated, all the better to look down upon their less elegant—and less profitable—counterparts.

At the floats closest to the entrance of the harbor she found the crabbers, massive craft a hundred feet in length and more, deep-draft vessels with cold storage for the shellfish and hot showers for the crew, the closest a fishing fleet got to a luxury liner.

Kate reached the end of the slip. Dwarfed between Derek Limmer's *Largane* and Max Jones's *Asgard* was a boat with a wooden hull eighty feet in length, similar in design to Old Sam's *Freya*, with a high bow, a round stern and a cabin set aft of amidships. Unlike Old Sam's meticulously cared-for craft, this old bucket's sides were peeling black paint, the metal bulwark topping the gunnel in the bow was rusted through, and to add insult to injury, fireweed was growing from her trim line. Her name, once bold white letters a foot high, was a faded, ghostly presence, pride broken, spirit gone.

Unconsciously, Kate pulled her hands free of her pockets, squared her shoulders and raised her chin, coming more or less to attention. Mutt, padding ahead of her, halted and turned to cock an inquiring eyebrow.

The *Marisol* had been sailing the waters of Prince William Sound since before Kate was born. Her father had deckhanded for Eli Tiedeman during many very successful crab seasons, but it wasn't crab fishing Kate remembered in connection with the *Marisol*, it was a week when she and her mother had flown out from Niniltna to board the *Marisol* to go deer hunting on Montague Island.

It had been late fall, she remembered, a cold, clear, crisp November day. The limit had been four that year, four deer per hunter, and the party had split up in hopes of catching everyone's limit. Zoya had gone with Eli, Eli's wife Luba with their son, Ed.

Kate had gone with her father. She was six years old and armed to the teeth with a .22 rifle that was as tall as she was. It might have slowed down a very small deer at point-blank range, but Stephan had insisted from the time Kate could walk that she become accustomed to always going armed on a hunt.

There was only a thin crust of hard snow on the ground, and it crunched underfoot as they hiked Montague to the north. Eli had anchored the *Marisol* inside the lee of Jeannie Point, and there was a nice long beach where the deer often came down to eat seaweed and lick salt off the rocks. Zoya and Eli had headed up Torturous Creek, Luba and Ed up Jeannie Creek, and Stephan had made for the swamp that drained into Nellie Martin River. It was four miles as the crow flies, and slow going on foot through heavy brush and the occasional stream and an unending series of deserted marshes. Kate had found some blueberries still hanging on the bushes. They were as big as the top joint of her thumb and frozen solid. She held them in her mouth, the cold, smooth sphere melting into a half-sweet, half-tart mush. Stephan had laughed at her blue tongue.

They'd found their deer, a fat doe, on a little rise overlooking the Nellie Martin, probably on her way to the beach. Stephan brought her down with a single shot, just above and behind her right shoulder. Together, he and Kate had fashioned a yoke with the rope he'd brought and they'd begun the hike back.

As they were coming into a small clearing at the bottom of a hill, Stephan had paused for a breather. He looked up, to see three grizzlies watching them from the top of the hill, a female and two males. The males were smaller than she was, but a grizzly, big enough to start with, looks twice its size outlined against snow, and the three of them together looked like all four horsemen of the Apocalypse. Even the first week of November, the last thing Stephan had been thinking about was bears, because any decent, upright, law-abiding bear was in hibernation by then. He was carrying a bolt-action .30-06 with five rounds, one of which he'd used on the deer and the other four of which were in the pocket of his mackinaw.

He dropped the rope and reached for the ammunition. At the same time, the female caught the scent of the dead deer and exploded into a run. Her sons were right behind her.

As long as Kate lived, she would never forget watching those bears tear down that hill in their direction, looming larger and larger against the snow. She unshouldered her .22.

"No," Stephan said. "Run, Kate. Run!"

She ran a few steps and stopped, out of his eyesight, and watched, the .22 held in both hands across her chest. Her world narrowed down to her father and the bears, and suddenly everyone seemed to be moving in slow motion, slow enough for her to notice things and think about them, slow enough for her to feel the smooth metal of the .22's barrel and the slick wood of its stock against the palms of her hands, slow enough for her to feel the bite of below-freezing air on the skin of her cheek, to smell the scent of pine, to taste fear bitter on her tongue, slow enough to notice the sun traveling the sky just above the horizon, two sun dogs guarding it like scimitars to the right and to the left.

The three bears came at a gallop that covered the earth, claws tearing at the crust of snow and kicking it up in little puffs. One of the males caught his paw on a bush and tumbled forward into a somersault, his velocity carrying him as fast as his brother was running.

Her father's hand was shaking so badly he dropped the first round. It seemed to take forever to hit the ground, brass casing glinting in the slanting rays of the sunset. She had time to notice that her father didn't even swear. By sheer effort of will he steadied his hands and fed the remaining three bullets into the magazine and slid the bolt home.

The bears were less than fifty yards away when he brought the rifle up to his shoulder and sighted down the barrel. The first shot echoed in her ears, *bang, bang, bang, bang,* the rhythm sounding like a fading heartbeat. Slowly, ever so slowly, Kate's eyes followed the line of the barrel. The female was still coming, so were the males, and she thought Stephan had missed.

Then the female stumbled and went down, sliding forward another ten feet on her belly, her immense frame so agile in action, so incongruously awkward in death. The two males barely checked. Again, her father fired, again the echo, *bang, bang, bang, bang,* and the male on the right squealed and stumbled. He got back up, still squealing, and made for the edge of the trees, limping badly on his right foreleg. His brother skidded to a halt and howled a protest. The other bear answered him in kind, and he wheeled about to hurl defiance at Stephan. Stephan kept his eye to the sight but held his fire. The third bear gave off the grizzly's signature sound, a cross between a donkey's bray and a pig's squeal, and retreated to the top of the hill.

Kate, meanwhile, returned to real time. First she heard the sound of her own heart, beating rapidly high up in her throat, then her breath, then her father's voice. She looked up to find him staring down at her, slanted hazel eyes so like her own, thoughtful and considering.

"You didn't run," Stephan said.

Kate swallowed hard. "No," she admitted.

"I told you to run."

"I couldn't, Dad," Kate said. "I couldn't leave you."

She'd been six years old and armed with a single-shot .22, and she had refused to back down or run away. Her father's slight smile betrayed his pride, and she straightened her shoulders. "All right," he said. "Let's get back to the boat."

"What about him?" Her chin indicated the sounds of the wounded male.

Stephan glanced at the sky. "It's almost four o'clock. It'll be dark in an hour. I'm not chasing around after any wounded grizzlies in the dark." He stooped to pick up the rope handle tied to the deer.

"We're taking the deer with us?"

"We worked too hard for her," he said. "I'll be damned if I leave her for them." He looked at her. "You can shoulder your rifle now, honey," he said, his voice gentle.

She looked down in surprise. Sure enough, she had the rifle up, the butt pulled firmly into her shoulder. Her cheek hurt, she realized, from where it had pressed against the stock. Her muscles stiff and sore, she reset the safety. She didn't re-shoulder it; she carried it in both hands across her body, ready.

Stephan gave it a long, thoughtful glance, her face another, and said nothing.

When they got back to the beach, the others were there before them, Zoya and Eli with a stringy old buck and Luba and Ed with a couple of fat two-year-olds. They had been going to butcher out on the beach, but when they heard Stephan and Kate's story they loaded the four carcasses in the dory and headed for the *Marisol*.

Stephan strung their doe up by her hind legs from the boom. She was so fat, and her brown pelt so smooth and soft. Her eyes were open, big and brown, staring at the deck. Kate couldn't look away from them. Stephan noticed, and came around to see what she was looking at. He reached over Kate's shoulder and put a hand over the doe's face.

Almost thirty years later, Kate could still remember the gentleness of her father's hand that day. It had worked; with the doe's eyes closed Kate could help with the butchering out and even take an academic interest in the contents of the stomach—seaweed and an incautious hermit crab that hadn't let go of the seaweed when the deer nibbled it up. The crab was still alive, and Kate tossed it in the water and hoped it made it back to its own tidal pool.

The next morning, Kate had been left on the boat while the grown-ups (including Ed, who was only five years older than Kate, a fact she pointed out to her father) went ashore and tracked down the wounded bear. He'd died overnight, and they returned to the *Marisol* that evening with two bearskins and three more deer. Stephan had grinned at her as he swung a leg over the gunnel, and her determined pout had dissolved like mist beneath a rising sun.

It had all been a very long time ago, but it was a memory

Kate treasured, a memory inextricably entwined with the sorry shadow warped into the slip before her. Once the *Marisol* had been catered to, fussed over, no copper paint too good for her hull, no deckhand too young or too small to help scrub down her decks after a fall hunt. She leaned forward to rest her forehead against the flaking bow. "That's okay," she whispered. "You were high boat for a long time, and back when it counted, too."

The blistered wood felt warm to the touch.

"Damn shame, isn't it," a voice said behind her, and Kate jumped a foot in the air. Mutt cocked a quizzical eye, and Kate felt her cheeks getting hot.

"Hold still a minute, you got some paint on your face," he said, and raised a hand to swipe at her cheek.

She suffered the attention because her back was to the *Marisol,* but as soon as she could she stepped out of reach. He inspected his fingers and raised his hand. There were flecks of black paint on them.

"Thanks, Gull," she said gruffly. "How are you?"

"Fine, Kate, just fine," he said. He waved a proprietary hand at the boat harbor, rather in the manner of a medieval baron presenting his domain while retaining all rights and authority thereto, including scutage and droit du seigneur.

Kate understood. She could look, but she couldn't touch.

Shitting Seagull had been born Ernest Lee Weustenfeld in Nooseneck, Rhode Island, fifty years before. So far as she knew, she was the only person in Alaska who knew this. But was it her fault that while she was paying Old Sam's slip rent one morning Shitting Seagull had seen a forty-foot pleasure cruiser trying to sneak into transient parking and had hot-footed it down the ramp to chase them off, leaving her alone in his office with nothing to read but the detritus on his desk, which just happened to include a letter from his sister in East Matunuck? A sister who called him Ernie LEE (the emphasis seemed natural to Kate) and, signing herself "Your sis, Sissy LU," wanted to know when he was abandoning the Alaskan wilderness and returning to the bosom of his family, and oh, by the way, that useless bastard Kenny JOE had left her again, this time for that bleached bitch Leona ANN (it seemed that everyone in rural Rhode Island had two first names, a custom Kate thought had been rightfully restricted to south of the Mason-Dixon Line) and she was short for the rent, could Ernie LEE oblige? Just while she got on her feet, of course, and little Ernie LEE and little Martha RAYE sent oodles of love and wanted to know when their Uncle Ernie LEE was coming to visit? And not to forget the Eskimo yo-yos he'd promised them.

Ernie LEE didn't go by his given name in Cordova, however. Upon further investigation, Kate concluded that it was probably all Hawkeye's fault. On a shelf in the harbormaster's office sat the collected works of James Fenimore Cooper, as well as everything ever written by M. Scott Momaday, Dee Brown, James Welch, Louise Erdrich, David Seals, Thomas King, Tony Hillerman and Barbara Kingsolver. There was a two-foot-high stack of back issues of Indian Country Today piled in one corner. A folder of photocopied microfiche articles on the Alaska Native Claims Settlement Act spilled off the filing cabinet.

Kate, a trained detective as well as a natural snoop, feared the worst, and time proved her right. Ernie LEE was a wannabe Indian. He had migrated first west and then north, rejecting White America and all that it stood for (in his mind, broken treaties, Custer and Wounded Knee) and wholeheartedly embracing the Native American ethic and everything it represented (in his mind, sovereignty, Black Elk and Wounded Knee). He was a card-carrying member of AIM, tithed regularly to the Free Leonard Peltier Committee and was eager to explain the legal differences between being a Native American and an Alaska Native—even to Alaska Natives, who suffered in silence, because after all, Shitting Seagull did control access to the small boat harbor.

He got the harbormaster job because he was seven feet two inches tall, weighed 350 pounds and had hands like the shovel on a front-end loader. The mayor took one look at Ernie LEE and saw an immediate end to any unnecessary roughhousing or drunken boat driving down on the docks, which until then had contributed heavily to the repairs and maintenance of slips and pilings.

On his side, Ernie LEE took one look at Cordova and knew his odyssey was over. He settled in, not bothering to look for a place to live other than the room behind the harbormaster's office, where he slept on a cot beneath army blankets, cooked on a hot plate and read sitting on a Blazo box, his back to the wall and his feet on the windowsill. He had one pinup: Wilma Mankiller.

As far as the name went, after some tactful inquiry Kate gathered that Ernie LEE had read something somewhere about Native Americans naming their children after the first thing they saw after the child's birth. Since his mother (probably Carolina MOON or Georgia PEACH) had not had the foresight to do so, after much thought he had decided to rectify his lack. He fasted three days and three nights in a lotus position (it didn't matter that yoga wasn't a necessarily Native

American practice, it was indigenous to somewhere and it was spiritual in nature and that was enough). On the fourth morning, just before sunrise, eyes firmly closed, he uncranked himself—painfully—into an upright position, hobbled to the door and felt his way outside. He'd been unable to keep from speculating what he would first see, and was guiltily aware of choosing names in advance of the culmination of the ceremony. Morning Star? Rising Sun? Tall Tree? White Cloud? Flying Eagle?

Breathless with anticipation, he opened his eyes. At that moment, a twenty-three-inch immature female specimen of *Larus glaucescens,* startled awake from her roost on the harbormaster's roof by the vibration of the opening door, launched herself from the ridgepole and unloaded right in Ernie LEE's face.

In other words, a seagull shit on him.

Now another, lesser man might have rejected Native American traditions at this point and moved on to a less stressful spiritual discipline, such as the Jesuit priesthood, but it must be said that Ernie LEE had the courage of his convictions. If a seagull shitting on him was the first thing he saw on the morning of his spiritual birth, then Shitting Seagull was the name by which he would be known from that time forward. It was a decision that gave the fishing community no little enjoyment, and the city clerk heartburn every month when she had to print out his paycheck. A prim throwback to a more Victorian era, she wouldn't say "shit" if she had a mouthful.

"So, Gull," Kate said. "How's business?"

Gull considered. "Busy," he pronounced. "Lots of in-and-out, like usual this time of year."

They were walking down the slip, back toward the ramp,

when movement caught the corner of Kate's eye. Gull walked on a few paces before he realized he was alone, and stopped to look around. "Kate?"

She held a finger to her lips, and he, surprisingly light-footed for one of his bulk, came back to stand next to her. "What?"

She pointed with her chin. He looked, and his face darkened. "Ah."

It was Cal Meany, boarding his drifter, and he wasn't alone. She had a mass of dark hair that rioted around her face in artificial curls and a figure lush enough to give the Pope whiplash. Her plaid shirt was unbuttoned and her jeans were falling down and her back was against the bulkhead of the cabin on Meany's boat. As they watched, one of his hands fumbled with his zipper. A second later the woman let out a shriek that echoed around the boat harbor. Meany clapped a hand over her mouth, wrenched the door of his cabin open and stumbled inside, her legs wrapped around his waist. The door slammed shut behind them.

Gull had turned a delicate shade of red, and he looked everywhere but at Kate. Kate herself was unmoved. The encounter had had all the tenderness and respect of a couple of Doberman pinschers in heat. She looked around the harbor, wondering how many other witnesses there had been. Meany had conducted his amour on the side of the boat facing away from town, but that didn't mean much between periods in the middle of the fishing season.

"Bastard," Gull mumbled, still red.

"You know Meany, Gull?" Kate said, starting to walk again.

"Damn straight I do, that prick is the biggest poacher in

town. I mean to tell you, Kate, it's hot and cold running babes the year round. And he's *married*," he added, outraged, like no one in Alaska had ever committed adultery before. He added accusingly, "And so is she."

"Who is she?"

"Myra," he said. "Myra Sarakovikoff."

"Not Tim's wife?" she exclaimed. She hadn't made the wedding, and so had not yet met the bride.

Gull gave a gloomy nod. "Meany likes his married, because he is, too," he said. "Makes it easier to avoid scenes when they'll both be in trouble if they get caught." They came abreast of the last slip before the ramp, the timbers lining the edges painted yellow, and black letters spelling out "Transient Parking Only." The big man's face darkened. "And Meany's always sneaking into transient parking when I've got my back turned. Last time I ran him off with a shotgun. I'll use it, by God, the next time he tries to pull that crap."

Kate regarded the empty spaces, enough for a dozen bowpickers or two dozen pleasure craft or four or five crabbers, her tongue firmly between her teeth. "Umm."

"Damn fishermen, anyway," Gull grumbled. "They're always whining and complaining about how long it takes to get a permanent slip, like that's some excuse to take the transient spaces instead. I mean, if you think it takes forever to get a permanent slip in this harbor, you ought to hear what the parking situation is like around Enif Prime, especially since those pushy Nekkarians insisted on a whole friggin' degree of arc for their ambassadorial entourage."

"Crowded, is it?" Kate said sympathetically.

The harbormaster gave an indignant, emphatic nod. "Like salmon up a creek on a morning in July!"

"That *is* crowded," Kate agreed. She regarded him from one corner of her eye. He had a broad, smooth face (he plucked his whiskers out by the roots) dominated by high, wide cheekbones, widely spaced brown eyes, eyebrows that looked as if they could use a good raking and a mop of thick, naturally curly hair the color of wet sand that would not stay in braids, but Gull didn't let that stop him.

In his authority as harbormaster, Shitting Seagull retained the right to reserve transient parking for ships belonging to such extraterrestrial visitors as wandered out this far on the galactic rim. He had been doing so for twenty years, ever since he first took on the job. The mayor would have fired him for this partiality except that each month, rent for transient parking accumulated in the city account at the National Bank of Alaska, twenty cents per foot per day, for nine hundred feet of dock. It was deposited directly into the account, in the exact amount required per foot of slip space. When rents had gone up two years before, the amount had obligingly adjusted itself accordingly.

The mayor decided what he didn't know wouldn't hurt him, although it made sport fishermen in for the day a little irritable, because no one could see the visiting spaceships except Gull. The same size and mass that allowed Gull to keep the peace in the harbor had kept anyone, thus far, from arguing the point. It was infinitely easier to raft their boats together two and three at a time.

Besides, Alaskan fishermen, a race who embraced eccentricity as a way of life, were rather proud to call Gull one of their own, especially when they got a couple of beers down him and he began to hold forth on the price per pound of bantha tongue on Tatooine.

So Kate walked the floats with Shitting Seagull, Mutt padding patiently behind, listening as Gull rebroadcast the latest headlines from abroad, a tale involving the secretary-general of the Council of Planets, centrally located on Deneb Prime; the son and heir of the warlord of Dubhe; the nubile daughter of the prime minister of the United System of Sidus Ludovicianum; a rare element called merakium found only on, you guessed it, Merak; the Free Traders; and pirates from Spica Four.

Kate was enthralled (this was better than a Heinlein novel—hell, it was better than *Star Wars* on Bobby's VCR, with or without popcorn), and was just about to request a definition of "nubile" on Sidus Prime when a shout came from the head of the gangway at the end of the dock.

She looked up and saw a tall man with dark hair and blue eyes in an almost ugly face, a boy who was obviously his son, waving madly, and Old Sam with his nasty grin dwarfed between them.

Gull, thrown off his rhythm, frowned up at the end of the dock. After a moment his brow cleared. "Hey, isn't that Jack Morgan? Who's that kid with him? Kate?"

But when he looked around she was already running for the gangway.

5

They left that evening at ten o'clock, and dropped anchor in Alaganik Bay a little after eleven. With the sudden facility of prepubescence, Johnny crashed in the spare stateroom across from Old Sam's, who was already bunked down and out if the snores rattling the door in its frame were any indication. Kate and Jack rendezvoused in the bow, beneath a clear sky with a rim of light around the horizon, no clouds and no stars, either, because it was too light to see them. It would be too light until September.

"Goddam, woman, I have missed the hell out of you," Jack said, and without bothering to wait for a reciprocal declaration grabbed her up into a comprehensive embrace that escalated rapidly.

"Hold it," Kate managed to say after a moment.

"Funny," he said, "I was just about to ask you the same thing."

She smothered a laugh. "Jack, no—"

"Not the 'n' word, not now." He lifted her to sit on the gunnel and moved purposefully between her legs.

"Jack!"

"What!" he bellowed.

"Knock it off!" somebody yelled from another boat, and somebody else cursed and added, "Can't a person get some goddam sleep around here?" The comment was followed by a long, loud wolf whistle, and at least three heads popped out of cabin doors.

Kate stiff-armed the extremely aroused and extremely frustrated male away from her. "That's what."

She was not unaffected by having her legs wrapped around Jack Morgan for the first time in three months. Johnny had spent spring break with his grandmother in Arizona, and Jack had spent his in the loft of Kate's cabin. It had been an extremely active ten days, followed by a long and very fallow three months interrupted only by Kate's too brief spring shopping trip to Anchorage. Considering Jack lived in Anchorage and Kate lived on her homestead in the Park, they took what they could get when they could get it. But not here, and not now, with half the boats in the bay moored side by next to the *Freya*'s gunnels.

She cleared her throat and pulled herself together. Her voice, already husky from the scar tissue that would never fade from her throat, rasped with an unconscious frustration it did Jack's heart good to hear. "In case you hadn't noticed, we've got boats sitting at anchor all around us, not to mention we've got four rafted to starboard and three to port." She was reminding herself as much as she was explaining to him.

His teeth, which had returned to nuzzling her neck, let

go of her earlobe reluctantly, and she shivered. He raised his head and looked around, for the first time registering the seven boats rafted to the gunnels and the others anchored a dozen deep on both sides. "Shit," he said, with feeling. "Where's your bunk?"

"No, Jack," she said.

The bellow was back. "What do you mean, no!"

There was another comment from one of the boats rafted to port. Kate said, "I am not going to make love with you in the chart room bunk."

"Why not!"

"For one thing, Johnny and Old Sam are sleeping in the staterooms below, for another the bunk is too narrow, and for a third sound carries over water." She couldn't help grinning at his woebegone countenance, and raised a hand to his cheek. "Be patient, we'll find a time and a place."

"Patient," he grumbled, and caught one of her fingers between his teeth. She gave some thought to the less than comfortable but undeniably private possibilities of the focsle. Reminding herself to be strong, she tried to pull free, thinking only to move Jack out of the reach of temptation.

He wasn't having any; he sat down on the gunnel and hauled her into his lap. "Just so you know what you're missing," he said, and his grin flashed in the half-light.

They sat there for an hour, talking in low voices of Jack's custody battle over Johnny with ex-wife Jane, now apparently over and the enemy routed, of the murder case pending against Myra Randall Wisdon Hunt Banner King, of E. P. Dischner's uncanny ability to thus far escape indictment, of Jack's caseload. In turn Kate told him of the size of Dinah's belly ("Bernie says odds are even it's twins"), of Dandy Mike's latest ménage à quatre, of his father's behind-the-scenes maneuvering of the Niniltna Native Association board, of Harvey Meganack's attempts to open up new areas of Iqaluk to clear-cutting, of the Bingleys' slow and shaky attempts toward recovery. He listened in silence, and when she was through said briefly, "You miss her more than you thought you would."

"Emaa?" Kate thought about that for a moment. "I don't," she said at last. "They do."

"Who is they?"

She waved a hand. "All of them, everyone in the Park, the tribe, Park rats, Park rangers—Dan O'Brian came to see me this spring, did I tell you? He wanted me to talk to the elders about the Taiga caribou herd, he says it's so big that the fish hawks are thinking about going for a same-day fly-and-shoot hunt in January."

"In January? I thought caribou season started in September."

"It does, but they figure the trophy hunters will all be gone by January, so it'll be locals taking game for meat. But to get back to my point, Dan came to me to talk over something he could just as easily have bounced off Billy Mike or even Auntie Vi."

"You're standing in for her."

"For Emaa?" The image of her grandmother rose up before her, solemn, stern, commanding. "They think I am."

"The tribe elected you to the council yet?"

"No," Kate said, "and they won't, either."

Jack detected the note of truculence in her voice and as a matter of self-preservation decided to change the subject. "Speaking of Auntie Joy—"

"What about her?"

"Didn't you tell me once she's got a fish camp up Amartuq Creek?"

"Not according to the federal government."

"She still suing them?"

"Uh-huh."

Jack grinned. "What is it with the women in your family, you take a vow with Rabble Rousers, Inc., before you're allowed into puberty or something?"

"Emaa trained us well." Kate had meant the words to be a joke, but they were too true to be laughed off. "Amartuq where you and Johnny want to go fishing?"

He nodded. "Do you think it'll be a problem?"

Her answer was oblique. "The period opens at six a.m. The fishermen won't be delivering until ten or so. I'll give you a ride up the creek in the skiff." She raised her head to look at him, a suggestion of a smile on her face. "Be warned. She might let you fish."

He eyed her expression. "Just not with poles and lures?"

She grinned. "I've always liked that about you, Morgan, you're very quick."

"Not when it counts," he said with a cocky grin.

A smile spread across her face. "No."

He couldn't resist kissing her under that kind of provocation, and he had a good try at talking his way into her bunk, but she held out for dry land and privacy, and in the end he unrolled his sleeping pad and bag on the hatch cover and she ascended to her lonely bunk in the chart room.

It hadn't been a lonely bunk until she climbed into it with the knowledge that Jack Morgan was lying thirty feet away and one deck down.

"What the hell," Old Sam said the next morning. He was standing in the wheelhouse, coffee cup in hand, staring hard out the windows. Kate, zipping her jeans, padded forward in bare feet to look over his shoulder at the gray day outside.

It was six-thirty and the seven boats rafted with the *Freya* had yet to cast off. The other dozen or more boats had yet to up anchor. She reached around Old Sam and picked up the binoculars. There was a setnet out; through the glasses she could see white corks bobbing against dull green ripples close to shore. She moved around Old Sam and craned her neck. And there was one drifter, after all, a white drifter with no name lettered on the bow.

It wasn't that everyone had overslept; there were men and women on the deck of every boat within eyesight. They all seemed to be staring at the lone drifter, and from the collective set of jaw on the bay, not liking what they were seeing. Not at all.

Kate nipped the mug out of Old Sam's hand and took a deep swallow of coffee. "Strike?"

"Looks like it, goddammit," Old Sam said. "Look at that."

Kate's gaze followed his long arm. There was a convulsive ripple over the surface of the water, and several flashing bodies leapt into the air at once, smacking back into the water with loud splashes. The corks on the only two nets out were bobbing energetically, and Kate could see a figure from the no-name drifter preparing to climb down into his skiff, a figure even at this distance identifiable by the width of his shoulders and the thickness of his chest. "Cal Meany's still fishing," she observed.

"That setnetter, too," Old Sam said, snatching his coffee back.

"What do you want to bet it's Meany's site?"

"No bet." Old Sam drained his cup. "Goddammit," he said again. "And we were just inches away from a decent season."

"It's not over yet," Kate said.

They looked at each other, thinking the same thing. When fishermen got this pissed off, it might as well be.

Hard on the heels of that unsettling thought came a loud crack! over the water. They both instinctively ducked down.

Old Sam swore. "What the hell was that?"

"I don't know," Kate said, beginning to rise to peer up over the console, and ducked back again when there was another loud crack! followed by a rapid rat-a-tat-tat-tat-tat! and a long, loud whistle, followed by a distant explosion. There was a flare of color through a window. "What the hell?" She stood up, in time to see a shower of lavender stars fall from the sky, fading rapidly into oblivion. It had already been light out for five hours.

"I'll be goddammed," Old Sam said, rising to stand next to her. "I totally forgot." Kate looked at him, and he whacked her across the shoulders. "It's the Fourth of July, Kate! Independence Day, by God! Fireworks and hot dogs and beer and boring speeches by pissant politicians and freedom and justice for all!"

Kate counted backwards in her mind. The opener had been two days before, and it had been July 2. Yes, indubitably, today was the Fourth of July.

"So what do we do now?"

Her question was punctuated by another pyromaniac getting an early start on the celebrations with a cherry bomb. A fountain of water rose up from a space between two boats and smacked down again, liberally dousing both decks and the fishermen thereon. Old Sam waited until the cursing stopped before answering Kate's question. "Have breakfast. I'm hungry."

Jack made the toast while Kate scrambled eggs with cheese and onions and potatoes. "So do we get to go fishing, Dad?" Johnny said, buttering his toast with a lavish hand and loading on a half a jar of strawberry preserves.

Jack raised an eyebrow at Kate, who shrugged. "No reason why not. The commercial fishermen are on strike, but to my knowledge that's never stopped a sport fisherman."

"Or a subsistence fisherman," Old Sam said.

"Solidarity, anyone?" Jack said brightly. Nobody laughed, nobody even smiled, and he reflected on the foolhardiness of joking in Alaska about something as serious as salmon.

"Doesn't look like anybody'll be delivering fish anytime soon," Kate said, "so I'll take the two of you up Amartuq in the skiff after breakfast." After an acid remark on the unreliability of wimmen and how a sure-enough boat jockey had only his fool self to blame if he hired one for a deckhand, Old Sam waved his assent.

"Is he mad?" Johnny said in a low voice as they cast off.

"Nah," Kate said as she started the kicker and the skiff pulled away from the *Freya*. "He's ecstatic. I'm living proof that all his worst suspicions about women in the workplace are true. The next time he gets together with Pete Petersen they can damn my whole sex without fear or favor."

"If he feels that way," Jack said, "how come he even lets you on board?"

She grinned. "If I didn't work summers on the *Freya,* I'd have to find another tender. Old Sam isn't about to turn me loose on the unsuspecting fishing population."

Probably, Jack thought, Old Sam wasn't about to allow the population to turn itself loose on an unsuspecting Kate. Probably Kate knew that, because nearly every summer Kate could be found weighing fish on the deck of the seventy-five-foot fish tender, at the beck and call of the crustiest, crankiest Alaskan old fart ever to wet a toe in the Gulf of Alaska. "I thought he liked women. You're always telling me stories about Old Sam's girlfriends. That nurse in Anchorage, for instance."

"He loves women," Kate said. "Just not on the deck of a boat, and in particular not on the deck of the *Freya.*"

"How does he like them?" Jack said, pretty sure he already knew the answer but unable to resist.

"Naked and stretched out on a bed. It's our proper place in the cosmic scheme of things."

"I heard that."

So had Johnny, whose eyes were the size of dinner plates, but neither adult was paying any attention to him.

Jack looked at Kate, at the tilted hazel eyes bright with humor, the breeze generated by their passage pulling a strand of her hair loose from its braid and bringing a glow to her cheeks, and knew a mighty temptation to tackle her right there in the stern of the skiff.

Unfortunately, the presence of his son and heir was something of a hindrance, not to mention fifty fishermen who seemed to have gone collectively insane.

All around them salmon jumped and splashed, the school a dark swath beneath the water that cut back and forth between the boats riding at anchor. Cases of beer had appeared on every deck, and aluminum lawn chairs upholstered in plastic green plaid unfolded themselves in bows and on the tops of cabins. A skiff whizzed by, towing Tim Sarakovikoff water-skiing on his hatch covers. His face was split wide in a grin, and he swerved toward them. Kate ducked in time, but Jack was sprayed and Johnny was drenched.

The boy whooped. "Hey, come back here, let me try that!"

"No way," Jack said.

"But Dad—"

"No," Jack said, and with firm hand sat Johnny down hard on the bow thwart. Johnny pouted.

They passed Cal Meany's drifter, his net paid out over the stern, white corks bobbing like popcorn popping as the fish hit it. He and his son were moving up and down the cork line, picking fish so fast their hands blurred in action. The skiff was already two-thirds full. Not a few fishermen were eyeing them with less than favorable expressions on their faces, and several comments were made in raised voices, "scab" being the nicest epithet hurled.

"Is that going to be trouble?" Jack said as they left the no-namer behind.

Kate nodded. "Probably."

"Should we do something?"

"Like what? Tell Meany to stop fishing? He'd tell you to

fuck off. Tell the fishermen to leave Meany alone? They'd just beat the shit out of you first."

Johnny leaned around his father to see if she was kidding. Her face was calm and unsmiling. He sat back, sober and a little regretful. He was going on adolescence, and this might be the closest he'd ever come to a shooting war. He was kind of sorry to be missing it.

They passed the markers and entered the mouth of the creek, a broad stretch of water gray-blue with glacial silt, sandbanks on either side and a few sprouting midstream. Kate reduced speed and threaded a careful path upstream. No matter how many times you'd been up the Amartuq and no matter how well you thought you knew him, he was a noisy, contrary, temperamental beast who delighted in surprise ambushes that usually resulted in the loss of a kicker, if not a hull. Sandbars changed sides, deadheads lurked around every bend, boulders shifted location beneath the force of the spring runoff, until you thought you could hear a deep, mocking laugh in the rush of the water beneath the bow. Kate took her time. If they hit something, at least they'd hit it slow.

Alders and cottonwoods and the occasional scrub spruce crowded the banks. "Look!" Johnny said, pointing. A grizzly lumbered out of the brush and waded out belly-deep into the water. As they watched, he caught a gleaming salmon in his claws and sat down in midstream to eat it. His matted pelt shone golden brown in the morning sun just breaking through the overcast. He didn't bother to look around at the noise of the outboard, concentrating on brunch instead.

Around the next bend a wolverine snarled at them from beneath a clump of diamond willow. On the other side of the creek a family of otters played tag. Jack grabbed his son by the shoulders and turned him to look at a lynx crouched on the branch of a cottonwood, tufted ears cocked forward over glowing cat eyes. Two trumpeter swans paddled in a calm backwater, while high above an eagle beat his enormous wings steadily homeward.

Jack shook his head. "You've sure got the wildlife out here well trained, Shugak, I'll say that for you."

Johnny was bug-eyed and speechless. Kate was unable to repress a grin, well aware of the absurdity of taking any responsibility for the perfection of the day or the proliferation of the wildlife, but proud that Calm Water's Daughter was putting her best foot forward nonetheless. What The Woman Who Keeps the Tides was up to in Prince William Sound she preferred not to think about.

Fifteen minutes later the left side of the creek spread out into a wide, flat area of sand and tall grass. A log cabin with a roof sprouting green moss sat on the bank behind. A smaller creek ran next to the cabin and into the bigger creek, and where the two met sat what looked like a miniature version of what pushed riverboats up the Mississippi a hundred years before.

"What's that, Kate?" Johnny demanded.

"A fish wheel."

"Cool," he breathed. "What's a fish wheel?"

"You'll find out," she promised him.

Of the two of them, Jack had more experience with that sweetly promising tone of voice. He looked apprehensive. She saw the look and smiled at him. He did not feel reassured.

A woman came to the door of the cabin, saw them and called out, "Vi, Edna, Balasha, come see! Katya is here!"

Kate cut the outboard engine and the bow of the skiff nosed up onto the gravel. Johnny jumped out and tugged them in the rest of the way, Jack following more slowly. Mutt took the bow in one leap and galloped madly up the bank as Auntie Joy and Auntie Vi and Auntie Edna and Auntie Balasha came out of the cabin, laughing and chattering excitedly, taking turns patting Mutt, who ducked her head at each in turn, very much in the manner of royalty granting an audience. When etiquette was satisfied, she led the way down the bank with her tail at a lordly angle, escorting the four old women as if it were their first trip down to the water's edge.

Kate climbed ashore last, and looped the bow line around a low-hanging branch of diamond willow.

Auntie Vi said with a twinkle, "The old man fire you, or you quit?"

"Auntie!" Kate shook her head in mock reproof. "Old Sam can't fire me, I'm too good to lose. And I can't quit," she added, "because without me nobody would deliver to him." Everyone laughed. "You know Jack Morgan, don't you, aunties? And this is his son, Johnny."

Jack inclined his head in a gesture that was half nod, half bow and all respect. Jack had always been good with Kate's elders, possibly because he knew he would never have gotten anywhere with her if he hadn't. Johnny followed his example, the gravity of good manners resting easily upon his youthful shoulders.

"Jack and Johnny are on a fishing trip. We just stopped in to say hi."

Auntie Joy inspected father and son with bright eyes, head cocked to one side, looking like a plump, inquisitive bird. "You go up creek to fish?"

Jack nodded. "Yes, Joyce. We do."

"What for you go up creek? You stay here. Plenty fish for everybody. Okay, girls?"

Auntie Vi agreed heartily. Edna and Balasha, who didn't live in Niniltna and therefore didn't know Jack as well as the other aunts did, were shier but just as hospitable, which had as much to do with the expectation of the free labor such guests would provide as it did with innate hospitality. When Calm Water's Daughter sent such a gift up the creek, one was wise to accept it without complaint.

"It's settled then," Auntie Joy said. She beckoned with an imperious finger, and Jack bowed to the inevitable and meekly shouldered pack and pole and sleeping bag and empty coolers up the bank and into the cabin. Johnny, who by rights could have expressed serious annoyance at this hijacking of his male-bonding fishing trip with his dad, looked at Kate for inspiration. She grinned at him. He was a good kid. He sighed, shouldered his own gear and followed his father.

And the gates of mercy closed behind them, Kate thought, and followed both her men up the bank, still grinning.

Auntie Joy bustled around and produced spiced tea in chipped mugs. She had to call Balasha and Johnny up from the creek, where Balasha was instructing Johnny in the mysteries of the fish wheel. "You should see how it works, Dad," Johnny said around a mouthful of Oreo. "It's so cool, it's like this paddle wheel, only the blades scoop up salmon in them. And Balasha let me eat some eggs right out of the fish!" He demonstrated, holding his hands over his head with an imaginary salmon stretched between them. "You squeeze, and the eggs just shoot out into your mouth!"

"Mostly," Jack said, reaching out a hand to pick a cluster of pink eggs that had adhered to his son's cheek.

Johnny grinned at him, unrepentant.

"What did they taste like?"

"Cold and salty." Johnny smacked his lips together. "Better than popcorn. Yum!"

Balasha said something in Aleut to Auntie Vi, who replied briskly. Kate caught the word *qaryaq*, which meant salmon roe, and *"Siksik!"* which meant, sort of, "No way!" and all four women looked on the boy with approval. Johnny, apparently, was in. Unaware, he crammed another Oreo down after the *qaryaq*.

"So, Auntie Joy," Kate said. "Has Lamar Rousch been around yet this year?"

Auntie Joy curled a lip. "That boy don't come back since I run him off last year."

Johnny looked curious, but he knew enough to shut up and listen.

"Lamar's the fish hawk for this area, and this fish camp is on federal land," Kate explained.

"Why's a guy working for the state enforcing federal law?" Jack asked.

Kate shrugged. "Probably because of the federal cutbacks in the Parks department. Dan O'Brian's crew is stretched pretty thin. He probably asked Lamar to keep his eye out."

"Humph," Auntie Joy said.

"Of course, this is federal land only according to the federal government," Kate added. "It wasn't federal land until statehood, and our tribe has subsistence fished here since, hell, I don't know, since forever."

"As long as the water runs and the grass is green, we been here," Edna said. She blushed when everyone looked at her in surprise, and ducked her head.

She had invoked the traditional words included in every treaty the federal government had entered into with the Native American peoples, "so long as the water runs and the grass is green"—a phrase that was supposed to imply forever regarding the terms of the treaty, but in reality had meant only until something of value was discovered on the lands the treaty referred to, something like gold or water rights or grazing lands or town sites or uranium, anything Manifest Destiny could be applied to and that therefore could be overrun by wannabe miners and ranchers and settlers and railroad builders.

And national park managers, Kate thought, who wanted to annex every square foot of land they saw and keep it pristine and inviolate, unsullied by human hand. They failed to recall that the indigenous peoples who came across the Bering land bridge during the last Ice Age had had their hands all over anything that had the remotest possibility of nutritional value and were every bit as much a part of the landscape and the wheel of life as the fish and the birds and the mammals. It wasn't until salmon started being taken commercially, in fish traps owned by Outside consortiums based in Seattle—fish traps that spanned the entire mouths of creeks and trapped whole schools of fish in their comprehensive maws—that the fish runs began to suffer their drastic declines.

She waited in case Edna wanted to say more, but the old woman had lapsed into her customary silence. "Like I was saying, Johnny, we've always fished subsistence here, but then the feds selected this creek at statehood, and they closed the fish camp down. Five years ago, Auntie Joy and Auntie Vi petitioned for it to be reverted back to subsistence use. The feds turned them down."

"And?"

"And, they sued."

"It still in court?" Jack asked with the cynicism born of long experience with the legal system.

Kate nodded. "They lost at the state level, big surprise. They're appealing to the supremes."

In sudden realization Jack sat up straight on his log. "You mean we're busting a federal law, fishing on this creek?"

Kate's smile was sardonic. "Oh no, *you* can sport fish here all you want, so long as you've got a state fishing license and the fish hawks declare the stream open." She nodded at the circle of women. "It's the aunties who aren't supposed to." She hooked a thumb over her shoulder in the direction of the creek. "That fish wheel's illegal as all hell. Lamar comes upstream every year and tells Auntie Joy so, doesn't he, auntie?"

"Humph," Auntie Joy said again.

"Lamar's not that bad, auntie," Kate said gently. "He's nowhere near as bad as some of the other fish hawks have been over the years."

The old woman's face relaxed, and she sighed. "I know, Katya. But his rules are not our rules."

Auntie Vi was not so generous. "Who is he, this park ranger, tell us what to do like he own everything? He don't own the creek. He don't own the fish. Nobody own them, so everybody own them." She sat back on her stump, dismissing the matter.

"Vi is right," Auntie Joy said, and added reasonably, "And besides, how our children and grandchildren living, if we don't teach them the old ways?" She waved a hand at the shack full of drying racks standing behind the cabin, a quarter of them hung with the limp red carcasses of red salmon. Split, boned, soaked in brine, they would be left hanging until the oil ran, when the dried alder would be lit and the shack filled with smoke to dry, flavor and texture the meat. "Who knows how to smoke fish when we're gone, if we don't come to the river and teach the children?"

"We always looking for children to come to fish camp." Auntie Balasha sighed. "But children don't come much no more."

A memory of the deer hunt with her father flashed through Kate's mind. As small as she had been, as young as she had been, as unskilled as she had been, still Stephan had been determined that his child would learn the traditional ways, at the very least be able to feed and clothe and house herself without being dependent on anyone else. He had died the following year, but by then the pattern of self-reliance was set, forming the fabric of her life.

She looked around the circle at the four old women, and saw her father staring back at her from every face.

Edna surprised them again. "No, the children don't come, but the white men do. They come with their planes and their powerboats and their four-wheelers, all the time making noise, leaving garbage all over." She leaned forward. "You know what I hear about those ones? They don't even eat the fish! They put them on the wall of their house, to look at! Why? Why is that?" she demanded. "Fish is food, for hungry in winter, not pretty for wall of house." She sat back and stared accusingly at the two white men in their midst.

Jack looked undeniably guilty.

"Gee, Dad," Johnny said, "maybe we should—"

"We eat everything we catch," Jack said hastily. "Don't we?" he appealed to Kate.

"I don't know," Kate drawled. "What about all those trophies you've got lining the walls of your den back in Anchorage?"

There were gasps of horror from all four old women.

"Den?" Johnny said. "We got a den?"

"Kate," Jack said ominously.

"Let me see, now, there's a moose, and a Dall sheep, and a goat, and two bearskins, and three king salmon, and I think there's even a wolverine." Kate added, "And he flies and shoots caribou the same day, too, and not for meat, for the racks, can you imagine?"

"No," Auntie Joy said, aghast.

"*Ayapu*," Auntie Vi said, appalled.

"*Alaqah!*" Auntie Edna said, deeply offended.

"Kate," Jack said.

She went for broke. "Not to mention all those Outside hunters he flies out to Round Island to take walrus illegally for their tusks."

Auntie Balasha went so far as to put a hand to her breast and nearly swoon from shock.

"Kate!"

She couldn't hold it back any longer and burst out laughing. The four women joined in, rollicking back and forth on their logs, teeth flashing, bellies shaking, hands clapping. The sound was loud, merry and unmistakable. Aleuts, one, Anglos, zip.

A slow grin spread across Johnny's face, and Jack mopped a heated brow. "Sheesh," he said, "you broads sure are hard on a couple of simple guys just trying to follow the hallowed Western tradition of raping the environment."

"Well, aunties," Kate said, draining her mug, "thanks for the tea. I'd better head on down the creek."

Jack shot up next to her. "Why? They aren't fishing, so they won't be delivering."

"You never know," Kate said. "Maybe they won't be able to stand Meany catching all that fish in their faces."

"Meany?" Auntie Joy said sharply. Auntie Vi looked at her.

Kate couldn't read either face, and her brows came together in a slight frown. "Yeah. The processors have dropped the price of reds to fifty cents a pound. The fleet's on strike. All except for Meany," she added, watching Auntie Joy. "Both his drifter and his setnet site have their nets in the water. The fish are hitting big-time, too. Even at fifty cents a pound, he'll make money."

Auntie Vi started to say something and Auntie Joy cut her off. "That one always make money." She snorted. "All he good for."

Kate looked at Auntie Vi, who was studying her toes with complete absorption. "Okay then," she said, rising to her feet and dusting unnecessarily at her jeans. "I'm off."

Next to her, Jack looked over at the four aunties, clearly uneasy at being left to their mercy. Kate saw the look and dropped her voice. "Don't worry, Jack, they're nice, kind, cuddly old ladies. They won't hurt you."

Jack's expression told her what he thought of that estimate of his hostesses, and she was hard put to keep her face straight.

"You come back tomorrow, Katya," Auntie Joy said firmly. "We catch lots, we need help with the cleaning and the hanging. You come back and help."

"Okay, auntie. Just as long as I don't get stuck with fire detail."

"Fire detail?" Jack said apprehensively. "What's fire detail?"

Kate refrained from telling him that fire detail was tending the fire in the smokehouse. It had to be maintained around the clock. It couldn't be too big and it couldn't be too small, and it could never, ever be allowed to go out. If the fire went out, the smoke went with it, and if the smoke went with it, the salmon would be ruined, and if the salmon were ruined, there went this year's smoke fish. It was an important job, maybe the most important job, and definitely the most tedious.

It was also the job most beginners got stuck with their first summer. Kate sternly repressed a grin.

He followed her down the creek bank. "Are we going to be able to get any real fishing in if we stay here?"

"Depends on what you call real fishing," she said. "I think Auntie Vi's definition is a little different than yours."

"You're telling me," he muttered.

She relented. "Of course you'll get some fishing in. Maybe not only the kind of fishing you came for, but you will fish." She laughed at his expression, and turned him to face upstream. "About half a mile up the left bank, there's a great hole for reds."

He brightened. "Really?"

"Really. Although you might be sharing it."

"You mean with other sport fishermen?"

She nodded. "George Perry will probably be landing a few on sandbars while you're here. There's even an airstrip about a mile inland."

"Why?"

"Why the fishermen?"

"Why the airstrip?" He waved a hand. "Why build one out here? Was there a herring cannery or a gold mine out here one time, or what?"

"No." Kate's smile faded. "RPetCo built it a couple years back. When they were sinking exploratory wells hereabouts."

"Oh." A touchy subject, and Jack knew enough not to pursue it. "So we're in Iqaluk."

"Pretty much everything you can see from here is Iqaluk," Kate agreed. She didn't want to talk about it, either.

Iqaluk was a fifty-thousand-acre parcel of land that included the eastern shore of the Kanuyaq River and part of the Prince William Sound coast. It was home to some of the richest salmon spawning grounds in the Gulf of Alaska, hence the name *iqaluk,* the Aleut word for salmon. It was also one of the last old-growth forests in the Pacific Northwest. Title to it had been clouded by competing claims, from the Niniltna Native Association, the Raven Corporation, the state of Alaska and the federal government. The federal government did not present a united front, either; the Forest Service and the Department of the Interior had been squabbling over Iqaluk since before statehood in 1959.

Everybody had a different idea about what should be done with Iqaluk. The Niniltna Native Association wanted the land deeded to them as part of the tribal entity's compensation under the Alaska Native Claims Settlement Act. Raven, the parent corporation for Niniltna's region, wanted the land so they could lease it out for logging and subsurface mineral explorations and development. Either idea was enough to send the state into orbit, because if the land was handed over to Raven or Niniltna the state wouldn't see a dime in taxes. The timber companies wanted the federal government in the form of the Forest Service to gain title, because the Forest Service had the charitable habit of building roads into old-growth forests at public expense for private profit. They went faint at the thought of the Department of the Interior gaining jurisdiction, because Interior would turn it over to the National Park Service, who would incorporate it into the national park system, which excluded exploitation of any kind, unless directed to do otherwise by Act of Congress. Which brought everything full circle, because if Iqaluk was turned into a park, limits would be imposed on hunting and fishing, and Auntie Joy and Auntie Vi would be in the front row of the rebellion.

Hell, they already were. "Civil disobedience," Kate said out loud.

"Huh?"

"Thoreau would be proud of my aunties. The federal government told them they couldn't fish subsistence here, and yet here they are, about to hook up their fish wheel."

A small plane approached, flying low and slow over the surface of the creek. It was George Perry's Super Cub, on tundra tires, following the course of the stream a hundred feet off the deck. They waved, and George banked a sharp left, folding down the window as he circled. "Hey," he yelled, "get a move on, you deadbeats, there's fish in that thar water." He straightened her out and took off again up the creek, rocking his wings in farewell.

Jack shook his head. "He does like to give his tourists their money's worth, don't he?"

"Probably stream surveying," Kate said.

"Oh yeah? Lamar?"

Kate shook her head. "He's got a new sidekick. Little gal, name of Becky something."

"She taking kindly to low and slow?"

Kate chuckled. "Not hardly. From what I saw of her uniform yesterday, she has yet to learn that she's supposed to stick to fish counting and leave the flying to George. That wasn't her, though, in the back seat."

"Oh yeah?" He squinted after the Cub. "Who was it?"

"I don't know, some guy." The profile of the man seated behind George had seemed vaguely familiar, but she couldn't quite place him. "Probably a fly fisherman going up the creek for a day. Mutt! Come on, girl, time to go!"

Mutt's head appeared at the top of the bank, her great yellow eyes peering soulfully over the tips of the rye grass. Kate read her expression without difficulty. "You want to stay?"

Mutt gave a joyous bark.

"Okay, stay."

Mutt leapt down to the beach with one graceful, arcing stride and loped over to the skiff. She hopped up to put her front paws on the side of the skiff and gave Kate a lavish lick of gratitude.

"Yeah, yeah, yeah," Kate said, shoving her away. "Just remember this the next time old Graybeard shows up and you want to get laid."

Mutt barked again, and took the bank in a single bound to disappear into the tall grass.

Kate stood in the bow, Jack on the sand. He looked down at her critically. "Well, I'm not going to lick you." He smiled, a long, slow smile. "At least not right now." He kissed her instead. It was a long, leisurely kiss, and it took Kate three tries to get Old Sam's older kicker started, because she kept tangling the cord. It didn't help that Jack stood grinning at her from the creek bank until she was out of sight.

When Kate's skiff emerged from the mouth of the creek, Meany's setnet site was still the only site fishing, and his drifter was still the only boat with a net out. He'd drifted a little too close to shore for his sixty-mesh, or thirty-foot, net, and so was pulling it, presumably prior to moving the boat farther off shore and resetting the net there, or perhaps prior to delivery, since he was riding very low in the water.

Only he had a problem, because half a dozen other drifters had crowded round him, their engines idling, making no effort to move out of the way.

Kate caught the barest glimpse of all this on her way back to the *Freya*, as she was preoccupied with dodging hatch-cover water-skiers and fireworks. Dewey Dineen tossed another cherry bomb that came a little too close for comfort, dousing Kate with water. She altered course to come alongside the *Priscilla* and share her feelings on the subject. He was half in the bag, so she let it go with a few pithy remarks that were received with a wide, unfocused grin and the offer of a beer.

Old Sam was standing in the bow of the *Freya*, and came down on deck to catch her line. She came up on deck and said, "What's going on?"

Old Sam grinned the grin that made him look like a cross between Lucifer and Linda Lovelace. "It's better than a Hollywood movie, Kate. Come watch."

She followed him up to the bow, from where they had an excellent view of the altercation shaping up off the port bow. On board the no-name drifter, Meany's son was pulling in the last of the gear, where it sat in a green pile of mesh on deck forward of the reel. Meany himself was at the controls on the flying bridge, trying to make way without much success, because he was being matched move for move by the half-dozen drifters surrounding him.

With immense enjoyment, Old Sam said, "He just took delivery from his beach site, and the rest of 'em won't give him sea room."

Kate eyed him, one eyebrow raised. Old Sam was maybe five feet, two and a half inches when he stood on tiptoe and weighed maybe 125 pounds after a nine-course meal—maybe. With the passage of time—he wouldn't say how much—the flesh of his face had wrinkled like a mass of contour lines on a well-worn map, but his step was firm, his eye sharp and his grin just nasty enough to make the people he turned it on feel for their wallets. "What are you grinning about, old man? If the fleet's on strike, so are we. This situation isn't putting any butter on our bread, either."

"Yeah, well, was I fishing instead of tendering, I don't

know's how I'd be risking a new drift net for fifty cents a pound myself."

"I guess Meany doesn't think so."

Old Sam spat over the side, an eloquent assessment of his opinion of the fisherman in question.

Kate looked over at the drifter, still surrounded. "He trying for us, or for town?" Beneath the green mesh of the net, the deck of the drifter was awash in a slippery pile of salmon, while her trim line was riding dangerously close to water level. If a squall blew up, the drifter could founder in an instant. It had happened before, when a skipper's greed overshadowed considerations of safety of ship and crew. It would happen again.

But not today. "Them boys ain't gonna let him do neither," Old Sam predicted.

He was only half right. There was the sudden roar of an engine and Meany's drifter, sluggish but determined, plowed straight for the midships of the *Esther*. Tim Sarakovikoff let out a yell of outrage, and Kate had a split second to wonder if he knew about Myra's extramarital activities. There was an answering roar of engines and a froth of water from the stern of the other boats, and the drifter slid through the sudden opening made between the *Esther* and the *Deliah* like waxed thread through the eye of a needle.

"Slicker'n snot," Old Sam said with reluctant admiration.

There was a furious roar from a dozen throats. Meany was called a lot of names, most of which would have offended his mother deeply, but he made it to deep water and out of the bay.

Old Sam spat over the side again. "Guess he's doing his own delivering today. Good."

Kate thought so, too. Fishermen had long memories, and

Old Sam and the *Freya* could ill afford to be seen as helping to break a strike, not if they wanted fishermen delivering to them in the future. On the other hand, Kamaishi signed their paycheck. It was a thin enough line to tread, sometimes too thin. "We heading for the barn? Not much point in sticking around here, if nobody's fishing."

What with Jack and Johnny marooned with the aunties up Amartuq Creek, she didn't really want to go anywhere, and was glad when Old Sam grinned his demon grin. "Here's where the action seems to be, girl. We might as well stay and watch the show. Hell, we got front-row seats." She opened her mouth to request permission to spend the night on shore, caught his choleric eye and thought better of it. Besides, Jack and Johnny needed a day or so to acclimate, anyway. Not to mention, if she stayed on board she could read instead of fillet fish.

Pete Petersen brought the *Monica* alongside and the two old men retired to the galley and drank beer and reminisced about the good old days, when the Fish and Game and the fish buyers and *wimmen* knew their places and kept them. Kate had heard it all before, and retreated to the wheelhouse. Settling herself comfortably in the captain's chair, feet propped on the console, she opened *The Heaven Tree Trilogy* and lost herself in medieval Wales, which at that point seemed a lot more civilized than modern-day Prince William Sound on the Fourth of July.

With Meany gone, the scene shifted from confrontation to celebration. The parade in Cordova started at two that afternoon and since the fleet was on strike the fishermen could have upped anchor and sailed for Cordova in time to catch it, but they didn't trust each other enough to stay on strike, so they all stayed out on the fishing grounds until the period was over, just to keep each other honest.

It was immediately obvious that most of them had prepared well in advance to celebrate Independence Day, strike or no. At two o'clock, precisely in conjunction with the parade they were all missing, the fireworks came out in force, a fountain of pyrotechnics generated from every deck. With the injudicious placement of a large Roman candle, Jimmy Velasco went so far as to set the roof of the cabin of the *Marie Josephine* on fire. His nearest neighbors downed punk and raised buckets and helped him get it out before it did too much damage.

Les Nordensen broke his left arm when the hatch cover he was water-skiing on caught the stern of the *Terra Jean.* Pete Petersen set it with a roll of *Playboy* magazines and duct tape, and Les went back to the party.

Also under the influence, Kell Van Brocklin fell hopelessly in love with Ellen Steen, and pulled the hook to follow his pheromones across Alaganik Bay. They were pretty effective; after nearly running down Lamar Rousch's Zodiac, which raised a doubt in certain suspicious minds as to just how drunk he actually was, he sniffed the *Dawn* out from a group of drifters rafted together at the south end of the bay and nosed up alongside. From the *Freya*'s wheelhouse it looked like the *Joanna C.* was trying to mate with the *Dawn,* but Ellen managed to repel boarders and steam off to a safe distance. Rejected, Kell lost interest, passed out at the wheel and ran the *Joanna C.* up on a sandbar, which effectively put him out of commission until the next high tide.

Joe Anahonak challenged Craig Pirtle to a joust, and a group of drifters made a lane between two unsteady lines of boats. The *Darlene* and the *Rose* charged at each other at full throttle, boat hooks at the ready. Full throttle on a Grayling bowpicker was only about eight knots; still, it was enough to bring the aluminum bows together with one hell of a clang, causing Kate to peer over the top of her book just in time to see Joe take a perfect, airborne tuck-and-roll over his own bow and Craig's as well, ending up in the water with a magnificent splash, big enough to cause a mini tidal wave that rocked nearby boats and caused two other fishermen to nose-dive for sea bottom. Craig was not so lucky, his boat hook somehow entangling itself in Joe's anchor chain. Either too dumb or too drunk to let go, or possibly distracted by a low-flying Super Cub, a grinning George Perry on the yoke, Craig pole-vaulted Joe's deck with a form worthy of an Olympic score of ten, to pancake on the roof of Joe's cabin, where, fortunately for him, Joe's spare set of gear was piled.

George waggled his wings in applause and headed off toward Cordova. Kate reached for the binoculars. The person in the rear seat sprang into focus. It wasn't the man she'd seen going up the creek; this time it was Auntie Joy. What was Auntie Joy doing going into town? Usually once she got out to fish camp she was there for the duration, like the rest of the aunties. The aunties didn't usually fly between fish camp and town, either; it was too expensive for all of them and supplies, too. If there were anything to worry about, Auntie Vi would have brought the whole bunch out to the *Freya*. Kate trained the glasses on the mouth of Amartuq Creek. It remained empty of anything but water and sand and occasional jumping salmon. She put down the glasses and tried not to worry.

Meanwhile, back on the jousting grounds, Yuri Andreev fished Joe out of the drink. Yuri was one of the teetotaling Old Believers from Anchor Point, fishing his first year on the

Sound, and he was torn between disbelief and disgust at the behavior of his fellow fishermen. Joe, unheeding, thanked Yuri profusely for the rescue and collapsed into Craig's arms to swear lifelong devotion to liberty, equality and especially fraternity.

The party went on. It was still going on when Kate finished the first part of the *Trilogy,* mopped up her tears with a shirtsleeve and turned in.

Possibly because of the unusual activity carrying on all night around the *Freya,* her dreams were disturbing. In one, Auntie Joy was tending her fish wheel, with Aunties Vi and Edna and Balasha cleaning and filleting the catch on the bank behind her. Lamar and Becky appeared, attired in clean uniforms with knife-edged creases on their shirtsleeves and pantlegs, and hats squared away at precisely the correct angle. Somehow Auntie Vi had a gun, and it went off. It was a shotgun, Kate noticed, because Kate was in the dream, too, but only as an invisible observer, and the shotgun kicked hard, knocking Auntie Vi over backwards. Lamar and Becky were miraculously unharmed, no speck of blood marring their crisp uniforms, but Auntie Vi's chest had been crushed by the recoil and she lay dead, staring open-eyed at the blue, blue sky.

Kate couldn't remember dreaming in color before, and she admired the effect, before the scene shifted to the deck of Meany's no-namer. He was beating his kid again, *thump, thump, thump,* his fist connecting with the boy's body in the one-two punch of a professional boxer, the meaty sound like someone smacking his lips together over and over again.

Or no, it was the sound of a heartbeat, *lub-dub, lub-dub, lub-dub,* slow, steady, inexorable. The halibut heart was back, and Kate stirred and moaned in her sleep. The dusky, humping lump of grainy flesh pumped against her hands, once, twice, three times, and she came awake in a rush, perspiration beading her forehead, her blood beating rapidly against her eardrums.

It was early yet, by the slant of the sun's rays no more than six. A light breeze caused the water to lap at the hull of the *Freya*. All else was calm, no sounds of jousting or other celebrations of fraternal love. There wasn't any halibut heart sharing her bunk, or crawling down the slant of the chart table, or lumping its way over the sill of the door between chart room and wheelhouse. She shook her head once, sharply, clearing the lingering trace of the dream from her mind, and took a deep breath and blew it out explosively.

Kate was not given to introspection, a nasty, addictive habit she believed led to self-absorption and a lifelong preoccupation with one's navel. Dreams weird enough to leave a shudder along the flesh were the best dreams to walk away from, as fast and as far as possible. Once upon a time, her dreams had been of former victims from her years as a sex crimes investigator in the Anchorage DA's office, children mostly, children and women too beaten down for too long to fight back. She shook off those memories, too, something it was getting easier to do with every passing year, although the scar on her throat would never let her completely forget.

She never would forget them, the children especially, their staring eyes, broken bodies and wounded hearts, but they no longer held her hostage to their memory, and she no longer felt guilty at having abandoned their successors to their fate. Five years was all she'd had to give, and she had given them, with every scrap of ability and dedication and passion she had to offer. When it was over, she came home, to recover her health, her equilibrium and her sanity, and to live out her life in a place that was as nourishing of spirit as it was calming of soul.

Understanding this in so many words for the first time, she felt her heart lift a little, and it was then she heard it, a faint, thudding sound, coming from below. She had to listen hard, but it was there, and seemed to be coming from the starboard side of the hull. "Sam?" she called.

There was no answer. Old Sam and Pete hadn't turned in until long after she had, and with no delivery to make to the cannery Old Sam was probably still sacked out. She scrambled into her clothes and hopped out to the catwalk running around the bridge, pulling her tennis shoes on as she went. A bit of breeze formed a small, regular chop, and it lapped against the hull with a regular beat. For a moment she thought that was all it was, and then, as she leaned out over the railing, she caught sight of what looked like a bundle of sodden clothes pressed up against the black hull of the *Freya*. In that instant, a wave caught the bundle and it rolled face upward, resolving into the body of a man, the skin of his face leached white in the morning sun.

Even at this distance, even with the water darkening the color of his hair, she could identify him. The broad forehead, the heavy jaw, the thick torso.

It was Cal Meany.

And his eyes, staring blindly up at the dawn of a new day, left her in no doubt, even if she hadn't seen the swollen tongue protruding from between his half-open lips.

He was most definitely dead.

Nine hours later Kate watched as an Alaska Airlines
737 rolled to a halt in front of the Mudhole Smith
International Airport, there to disgorge a full load
of passengers and two igloos of freight. Five of
the passengers on flight 66 were locals, had little
or no luggage and were whisked away by family
members driving rusted-out Subarus and four-
wheel-drive pickups; the rest were tourists, kayakers, sport fishermen, hikers and campers. One
couple was met by a Bluebird bus converted into
a recreational vehicle bearing Montana plates. An
Isuzu pickup with Idaho plates picked up a pair
of kayakers, with kayaks, and a tall, eager woman
with flying blond hair screeched up in a puke-
green Ford Econoline van with rapidly failing
brakes and no plates at all and leapt out to embrace a man half as tall and twice as thick as she
was, who returned her embrace with enthusiasm,
to the point that Kate delicately averted her eyes.

A baggage tractor lumbered up to the luggage window and began off-loading duffel bags, cardboard boxes fastened with hundred-mile-an-hour tape, frame packs, knapsacks, sleeping bags, fishing pole cases, tackle boxes and about fifty optimistically empty coolers. Passengers crowded around and the pile melted.

Fifteen minutes later the first of the small planes began taking off, a Cessna 206 so heavy with freight and passengers it used up most of the runway before becoming airborne. If they caught any fish at all, it was going to take them at least two trips to get everything back to Cordova.

The next small plane took off the second the Cessna was clear of the ground, this time a Super Cub on wheel floats with rifles tied to the struts and gear lashed to the floats. It, too, took an inordinate amount of pavement to get into the air. The third small plane was a TriPacer, sprightly on its tricycle gear and with its light load of one pilot, one passenger, one pole, one pack, one rifle and one cooler. A fisherman who believed in traveling light and in solitude. Kate approved.

At that point a Cessna 185 with the blue and gold seal of the Alaska state troopers embossed on the tail landed in a three-point runway paint job, and Master Sergeant James M. Chopin pulled up on the apron with a flourish. It was a new plane, and gleamed bravely even in the cloudy drizzle that was standard for Mudhole Smith. Jim emerged gleaming no less bravely, a tall, broad-shouldered, long-legged man clad in an immaculate uniform, shiny blue jacket zipped to just beneath the perfectly tied Windsor knot of his tie, hat freshly brushed and its brim pulled down just far enough to provide Jim's bright blue eyes with just the correct amount of shade. Jim was well aware of the cachet the Alaska state trooper's uniform lent the wearer, and he took care never to appear less than sartorially splendid, whether he was testifying in court in Anchorage, disarming a wife killer in Chitina or responding to the scene of a murder in Cordova.

"Kate," he said, giving her a formal nod, immediately spoiling the effect with a grin than reminded her of nothing so much as the expression on the snout of a great white shark on its second pass. "Where's Mutt?"

"At fish camp. Where's your helicopter?"

"In the shop. Fish camp?"

"On Amartuq Creek, with Auntie Joy and Auntie Vi."

"Right. On Walden Pond with Thoreau, Gandhi and Dr. King, learning to practice civil disobedience. Mutt ought to be good at that." It unsettled Kate when she and Jim shared the same opinion on any subject, and it was doubly unnerving when the opinion concerned her elders' perfectly legitimate actions in defense of their cultural history.

He sensed her uneasiness. His grin widened and he adjusted his hat a millimeter to the south. "Hear you found yourself another body."

"I don't exactly go around drumming up business," Kate said, irritated.

His dimples deepened. Master Sergeant James M. Chopin was a die-hard flirt who made his home as state trooper in residence at Tok, a small community to the north of the Park that didn't quite qualify as Bush because there was a road through it. Rated on both fixed wing and helicopter, he kept the peace of the Park's twenty million acres from the air, the only way to get around Bush Alaska, and had been doing so for the last fifteen years. He'd been seducing Kate's female relatives for at least that long, earning himself the nickname Father of the Park, used with affection by some (usually female) and with opprobrium by others (usually male).

His legendary charm left Kate cold, or so she told herself; she had fended off his advances in the beginning because she disliked the idea of standing in line, and now kept it up more out of habit than anything else. Habit and Jack, she reminded herself. She blinked in the face of that steady blue gaze and with an effort did not step back from it.

Flirtation aside, Jim was the consummate professional law enforcement officer, and she respected his instincts, his ability and his sangfroid in the face of the call of the weird. She remembered only too well the scene in Bernie's Roadhouse nearly three years ago, when the drunk pipeliner had pulled a gun and placed the muzzle at Jim's forehead. Without batting an eye, Jim had said, "What seems to be the problem here?" The drunk pipeliner, made aware of who he was up against, surrendered.

The feeling of respect was mutual, and he said, as he climbed into the cab of the rump-sprung pickup she'd borrowed from Gull, "What have we got, Kate?" knowing that her observational skills were acute, her judgment was sound and she would lay out events in concise, chronological manner, without histrionics and without coloring the facts with personal prejudice.

Although there had been a moment there, last spring, when he thought she'd shown signs of becoming less an adjunct to law enforcement and more a champion of tribal sovereignty. It was a moment, in fact, when by some mysterious alchemy she had taken on the authority of her grandmother. He still wasn't entirely sure she hadn't lied to him about that domestic disturbance he'd responded to in Niniltna, to find her already in place and the situation resolved. Just by the quality of silence that surrounded the incident he knew he'd missed something, but long experience with the parochialism of Bush villages kept him from pressing the issue. A few discreet questions had revealed that the parents had enrolled in the Native Sobriety Movement and that the kids were turning in B's and C's in school. He was all for local solutions to local problems, and so long as the situation remained stable and the kids were doing all right, he was willing to walk away.

Besides, if he accused Kate Shugak of obstruction of justice he'd never get into her pants.

Kate started talking when they turned from the airport parking lot onto Highway 10. It was thirteen miles from Mudhole Smith International Airport to town, and Eyak Lake had just appeared on their right as she came to that morning's discovery of the body.

"Where is the body?" Jim said.

"Wrapped in a tarp in Knight Island Packers' cooler."

He slanted a grin her way. "Meany deliver to Knight Island?"

Kate nodded. "When the price was right."

"Professional courtesy," he suggested.

She didn't smile.

He was sitting erect in the passenger seat, the round crown of his hat just brushing the ceiling of the truck's cab. His long legs were cramped because Kate had the bench drawn up far enough for her feet to reach the pedals, but he was the only person Kate had ever seen who could look dignified with his knees up around his ears, so it didn't matter. They came to the end of Eyak Lake and Le Fevre's street sign flashed by on the right. "Well, Kate," he said, ruminatively, "you going to tell me how he died?"

She took a deep breath, held it and released it slowly. "This one you should see for yourself, Jim, without any preconceptions."

"But it was murder? You're sure about that?"

She laughed, a short, sharp, unamused bark.

"Um." The sound was noncommittal. "What's your best guess?"

She snorted, slowing as they passed Eyak Packing Company and putting the blinker on to turn left on Railroad. "Motive we got, suspects we got more. He beat up on his son, who's big enough to have taken him out, by surprise anyway. He was screwing at least one wife, as personally witnessed by me, and Gull is only too happy to assure me that there were just dozens more, so there's all their husbands, plus Meany's own wife."

"She in town?"

"No, she's working the setnet site."

His eyes narrowed. First motive, and then opportunity, how nice. In law enforcement it was axiomatic that in murder cases the spouse was always the number one suspect, since ninety percent of the time the spouse did the killing. "You talk to her yet?"

She shook her head. "Waiting on you. Meany's setnet site and his drifter were the only nets in the water yesterday, when all the other fishermen were protesting the price drop, and I am here to tell you, the fleet don't like it when that happens." With which masterly understatement she braked to turn left on Nicholoff, passed Baja Tacos, the AC Value Center and Save-U-Lots stores and the harbormaster's office, to pull up in front of a rambling building with different levels of flat, corrugated-tin roofs, some one-story, some three-story, all walled with gray plastic siding. The parking lot was nearly empty, and Kate stopped in front of a door marked "Office" in big black letters, put the truck into second and turned off the ignition. She sat for a moment, staring straight ahead, hands gripping the steering wheel, as if making up her mind. He waited.

With a muttered curse she turned to face him, and when she did, the sight of his impassive expression caused a reluctant smile to cross her own face. "I don't want it to be the kid."

He nodded.

"It used to be a lot easier. You know?"

"I know."

When she'd worked for the Anchorage DA, her duty was clear. Identify the perp, build a case on means, motive and opportunity that would hold up in court, arrest him and assist the DA in prosecution, followed by, if everyone did their jobs properly, an extended sojourn at Hiland or Spring Creek or Palmer hosted by the ever accommodating state of Alaska.

She'd been a private citizen too long. She said abruptly, "Monday was the opener. July second. Flat calm, no wind, sunny, fish hitting everywhere you looked, fishermen filling up and delivering and filling up again and delivering again. Meany delivered that day. He had a load on, the drifter's trim line was damn near under water."

Still noncommittal, Jim said, "Lucky for him it was a no-weather day."

She nodded. "He had the son on board, kid maybe fifteen, sixteen years old. The kid did something stupid, something no worse than any other teenager with his hormones in an uproar hasn't done a billion times before anywhere in the world. Meany beat on him. He beat on him something fierce. He knocked him into the water, not once but twice. And then he kicked him."

He waited.

Her eyes met his. "The kid looked like it wasn't anything didn't happen once every day and twice on Sundays. He was used to it." She added, "I *really* don't want it to be the kid."

He thought. "Okay. So here we've got a fishermen, dead not by his own hand"—he cocked an eye at Kate and she shook her head—"who was beating on his kid, probably a repeat offender." He waited for Kate's confirming nod. "A fisherman who was viewed as a scab by a hundred striking fishermen. A fisherman who was screwing around with another fisherman's wife, and rumor has it, with others as well. That about cover it?"

"It does from what we know so far."

His gaze sharpened. "You have reason to believe there might be somebody else wanted this guy wasted?"

One shoulder raised, lowered. "Look at the pattern so far. This guy lived to piss off everyone around him." Kate remembered Tim's flushed, excited face late Monday afternoon, so proud of being high boat. *I know this guy,* Tim had said. And Tim had not mentioned his wife that day, only his mother. Unusual for a newlywed. Was the omission deliberate? Had he known Myra was screwing around? Had he known with whom?

She would have to ask him, she realized reluctantly, or Jim would, and it would be less threatening coming from her. She didn't look forward to it, though.

A memory of Auntie Joy's expression as she looked at

Meany from the deck of the *Freya* flashed through her mind. She gave a mental shrug. That at least was something she didn't have to worry about. Auntie Joy had been at fish camp surrounded by five witnesses, one of whom was the chief investigator for the Anchorage district attorney.

"Okay. We're lousy with motive and suspects. How about means?"

Kate got out of the truck. "The last time I saw him alive he was making for Cordova with a full load. Yesterday afternoon about one o'clock. He had to run a gauntlet of fishing boats to do it, with a lot of half-drunk pissed-off fishermen skippering them, but he made it."

"His son on board?"

She nodded. "On deck, picking fish out of the last of the gear and pitching them into the hold. But hell, that don't necessarily mean anything. We don't even know where Meany was killed."

"What do you mean? You found him at Alaganik?"

"Yeah, but who's to say he didn't get himself killed right here in the harbor, after he delivered?"

"He did deliver, then?"

She nodded again. "Mark Hanley, head of the beach gang, he says he pulled up to the Knight Island dock two hours after I saw him leave Alaganik."

"He remembers exactly?"

She gave a half-smile. "He was ticked at being called out. Nobody else was fishing, the beach gang was celebrating the Fourth with a barbecue and, as I understand it, Meany showed up just about the time the wet T-shirt contest started."

Jim grinned. "Not a happy camper."

"No."

"So you think the killer might have killed him here, driven his boat back out to the grounds and rolled him into the water?"

"Maybe."

"Why? To confuse anybody who comes looking for him?"

"Definitely to confuse someone. Wait till you see the body, Jim," she said, with emphasis. "This, you should pardon the expression, is overkill."

He grinned again. She didn't grin back. He sobered, and reached for the door. "Okay, then. Lead me to it."

It was a walk-in cooler, shelves on all four walls crammed with steaks and roasts and chops of beef and pork wrapped in white butcher paper, boxes of whole chickens wrapped in plastic, twelve-packs of corn on the cob, plastic gallon sacks full of peas and broccoli, and a case of frozen bread dough in two-loaf packages—a summer's worth of supplies for a perpetually hungry cannery crew. The harsh light of a single, hundred-watt lightbulb inside a wire cage illuminated everything clearly. The cannery superintendent, a thickset, dark-haired man who looked barely old enough to vote, hovered in the open doorway, clearly reluctant to step any closer to the tarpaulin-wrapped horror resting on the table that took up the center of the room. The surface of the table was streaked with old blood and scarred with knife cuts.

"We brought the table in from the slime

line," the superintendent said. "Didn't seem right to just sling him onto the floor."

Kate hated walk-in freezers. When she was a little girl, there had been a community freezer in back of the old city hall in Niniltna, a large room filled with shelves where everyone in town brought their moose and caribou. It had been her special task when she visited her grandmother in the village to go and get the evening's meat from the locker. She would get as far as the door, where she would stand, shivering, a sweat of fear down her spine, filled with an irrational knowledge that if she left the door to fetch the meat, the door would swing shut behind her, locking her in forever, leaving her there to die a cold and lonely death, just another package of frozen meat. It sometimes took her ten minutes to work up the courage to leap, snatch at the first package on her grandmother's designated shelf that came to her frantic grasp and leap back to stop the door from closing. Sometimes she lucked out and someone else would be at the locker at the same time. Mostly not.

Years later her fears came full circle when a murderer tried to kill her in just that fashion. She had outwitted him, barely, and the memory gave her the courage to walk into the cold-storage locker today without hesitation.

She stood on one side of the table, Jim on the other, minirecorder in hand. He gave the date and the time and continued, "Master Sergeant James M. Chopin reporting, standing in the walk-in cooler of Knight Island Packers in Cordova. Present are Kate Shugak, tenderman, who found the body, and Darrell Peabody, Knight Island Packers' superintendent, who has graciously offered the body house room."

Kate wondered how much editing was done on Chopper Jim's tapes back at his Tok office.

"The body has been identified as Calvin Meany, drift net fisherman, Anchorage resident, PWS permit." Jim read Meany's permit number, driver's-license number and Social Security number into the recorder, from cards extracted from the wallet Kate produced. "Body was discovered floating in Alaganik Bay at six-thirty a.m., this morning." He clicked off the recorder. "Okay, let's take a look."

Kate helped pull the tarp back, and heard Peabody swallow loudly behind her. Even Jim, who in the course of his professional career had seen just about everything bad that one human being could do to another, was surprised into expression. "Jesus Christ." The words, forced out of him, were compounded of surprise, disgust and not a little awe.

As Kate had seen from the catwalk of the *Freya*'s bridge, Meany had been strangled. Whether it was before or after he had been stabbed in the heart with a sliming knife, the white plastic handle still protruding from his chest, was yet to be determined. Whether he had died by strangulation, or stabbing, or from concussion from many of the blows he had sustained to the head and upper body was also yet to be determined. His left arm had sustained a fracture of both ulna and radius, ripping the skin of his forearm so that the bones gleamed against the shriveled shreds of skin around the edge of the wound. He had defensive marks from wrist to elbow on his right arm. Silently, Kate pointed to both sets of his knuckles. They were ripped and swollen. There were dark bruises on his shoulders and torso. Something sharp had torn at the skin on the left side of his head, tearing a gash from temple to jaw. He was bloated from his immersion in seawater.

There was a long silence. Their breath formed little clouds in the room's chill air. At last Jim stirred. Over the body, his eyes met Kate's. "My kingdom for a forensic pathologist," he said, and clicked the recorder back on.

Jim slammed the gate shut on the bed of the truck, removed his hat and tipped his head back to draw in a long, sweet gulp of fresh air. Across the road was the eight-hundred-slip boat harbor. The new harbor was accessible by three ramps leading down to the first, third and fifth of the five floats, each anywhere from nine hundred to twelve hundred feet long. The twenty-four-foot slips began on the left, and the slip size increased to the right, ending with sixty-foot-slips on the last float. The old harbor descended into the basin from the opposite side of the artificial basin, and consisted of four floats half the size of the new ones, with a quarter the slip capacity. The city had sorely needed the new harbor; looking at it now, all floats, old and new, filled to capacity, Kate thought they should have moved and extended the breakwater for a harbor twice its present size. Especially since Cordova was a typical Alaskan town in that it was perpetually broke, and the harbor generated 20¢ a daily foot, $4.55 a monthly foot, and $13 a yearly foot. Cal Meany's drifter had been thirty feet long; if he'd maintained a slip in this harbor it would have cost him damn near $400 just to park while he went for groceries. No wonder he kept sneaking into transient parking.

A door slammed and Kate looked down the road to see

Gull emerge from the harbormaster's office, step to the middle of the road and bend down to pick up something, which resolved itself into the limp body of a squirrel. His laugh carried clearly to where they stood, a hearty, heartless, even triumphant laugh, before Gull tossed the corpse into a nearby Dumpster and went back into his office.

Jim looked back at Kate. "What was all that about?"

Kate sighed. "It's a long story."

"I'm in the mood. Humor me."

Which Kate interpreted as a plea for a little light relief from the grim task so fresh in both their memories. "You know Gull."

"Big Chief Friend of E.T. Who doesn't?"

"The squirrels got into his insulation."

Jim raised an eyebrow. "Isn't that the diagnosis of record?"

A smile forced its way across Kate's face. "No, real squirrels this time. He said he could hear them, pitter-patting between the roof and the ceiling, night and day. Drove him nuts."

"Why didn't he set a trap?"

"He did. They took the bait and sprung it."

"Poison?"

"Said he couldn't take the chance his namesakes might get into it."

They both looked at the harbormaster's office, the ridgepole lined with seagulls keeping a collective beady eye out for anyone cleaning a fish down on the floats. Every now and then one would nip at another with a sharp yellow beak, and as they watched, a new gull came in for a two-point landing, missed his footing, backwinged, fell off the edge and was ridiculed by a raucous chorus as he came around for a second try. The roof was white with guano. "God forbid," Jim said.

"So," Kate said, "he planted a nut tree."

"A what tree?"

"A nut tree."

Jim digested this in silence for a few moments. "What kind of nut?"

"I have no idea. It's that little scraggly tree to the left of the office."

Jim looked at the little scraggly tree. "Uh-huh. What, he figures to grow nuts to give the squirrels something else to eat besides his insulation?" Kate shook her head. "What, then?"

"The squirrels live over there." She pointed at a stand of alder, birch, diamond willow and spruce trees covering the hill rising up toward town. "They have to cross the road to get to the nut tree. Gull figures with all the traffic, eventually they'll be flattened going to and fro."

"I see." Jim regarded the tree, which seemed to be missing some branches, not to mention some leaves. "Think it'll survive the winter?"

"I have no doubt whatsoever," Kate said. "Gull has invested heavily in fertilizer and tree wrap. The minute the temperature drops below thirty-five, he's out there swaddling up that tree like it's his firstborn child."

"Uh-huh." Jim's eyes wandered down to the empty transient parking slip. "You know, I hear the Cetaceans have developed a mini–force field that acts as a personal shield. They're test-marketing it on Rigel Five. Supposed to adjust its insulating factor to the current conditions. Fits in your pocket, not too expensive."

"Really?" Kate said politely. "If there were any Cetaceans in Cordova, I'd recommend it to Gull. As it is . . ."

"You're probably right."

Their eyes met and they smiled.

Jim resettled his hat, flat brim not a bubble off level, and straightened his already straight shoulders. He nodded at the corpse in the back of the pickup. "Give me a ride to the airport?"

"You going to fly him in?"

"Quicker than waiting for tomorrow's jet, and the sooner we get the body back to Anchorage and the techies in the lab, the better."

She nodded, and they climbed in.

Jim was silent until they were well out of town. He sighed, and said, "Beaten, strangled and stabbed. I wouldn't be surprised if Frank finds a bullet in him."

"Kind of emphasizes the killer's sincerity, doesn't it?"

"Kind of."

They passed the Powder House, a southcentral Alaskan institution on a par with Bernie's Roadhouse in Niniltna. From the stories Old Sam told, and hints she'd had from other old-timers and elders, Stephan had hoisted more than a few at the Powder House when he got this far south.

He hadn't hoisted any at home. He had left that to her mother. Kate shook the memory off before it took hold.

They were almost to the airport before Jim said, "Unless, of course, we've got more than one killer."

Kate slumped a little in her seat, sorry he'd put her fear into words. "I hate the weird ones. I *hate* the weird ones."

"Yeah."

Jim could afford to sound laconic. "I suppose you expect me to go on out to the setnet site and interview the family."

The shark's grin was back, wide and predatory, with entirely too many teeth showing.

"I'm tendering," she said. "Some of us actually have to work for a living, you know—we're not subsidized to live in luxury by a grateful state."

He let out a great shout of laughter that rang off the metal insides of the cab.

"Shit," Kate said, with feeling.

"Thanks, Kate," he said, still laughing. "I appreciate the offer. And the laugh."

"Up yours," she said.

With true nobility, he refrained from giving the obvious reply, but only because he needed help in muscling Meany's stiff and awkward body out of the truck bed and into the back of the plane. They slammed the door on the macabre object, ignoring the wide-eyed looks of a cluster of airport workers standing near the terminal. "I'll be back, this evening if I can, tomorrow if I can't."

"Hurry," she said, with emphasis. "If this strike continues, most of your best suspects are going to head south for the winter."

"I'll hurry."

"Meantime, I'll dig up what I can, but if they start fishing again, I start tendering."

He eyed her, considering. "You want me to put you on temporary staff? There's a per diem."

"God, no!" she said, genuinely horrified.

He spread his hands. "I offered."

"And I turned you down flat. Just get your sweet ass back here as soon as you can."

The grin flashed again. "Why, thank you, Kate. I didn't think you'd noticed."

Back in town, Kate narrowly avoided a squirrel darting across the road and pulled the truck up in front of the harbormaster's office. Through the window, she could see Gull sitting at his desk. He looked up and waved her inside.

"Thanks for the use of the truck, Gull," she said, handing over the keys.

He looked at them, thought about it for a moment and then, as if inspiration had struck, stuffed them into a pocket. Not a man who maintained a strict guard over the material things in his life, but then the truck was the property of the city, and there weren't many places to drive a stolen vehicle in Cordova.

"So, Chopper Jim get off with the stiff all right?" he said, sitting back and putting his feet on the desk.

She mimicked his actions, linking her hands and stretching so that her bones popped. "Yeah."

Gull scratched the back of his head. "Hell of a thing." It was an offhand observation; he didn't look shocked or horrified or disgusted, but then he could quote chapter and verse of a century's worth of atrocities committed against the noble red man by the base white man from the Mexican to the Canadian border. He wasn't one to get overly excited at a single murder, no matter how redundant in method. "What do you think happened?"

"I don't have a clue," Kate said. "Or rather, I've got too many of them. Did you see Meany when he came in yesterday afternoon?"

Gull snorted, and folded his gigantic paws over his chest. "Hell, I saw him yesterday evening. I had to run him out of transient parking. Son of a bitch. You know, Kate, it's not the fact that guys like him try to steal from the city that upsets me so much, it's the discourtesy."

"Discourtesy?"

"Discourtesy," he said firmly. "I mean, the Fomalhauters weren't having enough problems with the repairs to their exhaust duct—their *Star Grazer*'d taken a hit from a rogue microplanetoid—then this earthbound yo-yo tries to put a goddam drift netter up their tailpipe."

Kate wondered if Gull knew anything more about astronomy and the potential for extraterrestrial life than he did about the Native American. Probably not, but who was she to spoil his fun?

Then it hit her. "What time was that?"

"What, when the Fomalhauters landed?"

"No," Kate said gravely, "when Meany tried to drive up their tailpipe."

He scratched again. It seemed to help him think. "I don't know, about ten maybe? He always does that, or did it, coming in later in the evening, thinking I won't nail his ass."

"And did you? Nail his ass?"

"To the floor. I was practicing 'The Ojibway Square Dance' on my flute—it sounds better when you sit next to an open window—and I looked up and there he was, the prick, sneaking up on the float, without running lights, can you imagine? He's lucky I wasn't the Coast Guard. So I marched right down there and ran him off."

"Was he alone?"

"I didn't see anybody else," Gull said. He added, "Of course, Meany was on the flying bridge, and like I said, he was running dark. There could have been somebody in the cabin, I suppose. Like ten or twelve women," he added, "all married to somebody else. I'm telling you, Kate, the guy went for quantity."

"Did you have words?"

"I yelled at him," Gull said with satisfaction. "He didn't bother yelling back, he just slammed her into reverse so fast he rammed the slip and damn near stripped the gears. Some kind of boat jockey he is." He snorted, sounding like a disdainful bull.

Kate thought about that for a few moments, then for the time being abandoned it. Gull had no motive, other than the continuing battle over transient parking, a battle he carried with enthusiasm to every skipper of every boat, sport or commercial, seiner or drifter, who dared preempt a foot of the transient float. There ought to be signs, like the blue-and-white wheelchair they had for Handicapped Parking. Maybe a fluorescent decal every ten feet of float with a flying saucer on it. Alien Anchorage. Outlander Landing. Put it next to a red circle with the figure of a man in the center of it and a red slanted line crossing him off. Little Green Men and Bug-Eyed Monsters Only. Kate wondered what shape the Fomalhauters took, and decided not to ask. "So that was about ten o'clock."

Gull nodded, then brightened. "It must have been about twenty after when I came in, because I turned on the TV in time to watch Jackie Purcell lie about the weather."

So Meany was still alive at ten, and his son may or may not have been on board. She should head on out to Alaganik, start banging on hatches, talking to fishermen to find out if they'd seen anything at Alaganik the night before. But they'd chased him off hours before the period ended, none of them had given pursuit, none of them had been fishing except for Meany, and most of them had been drinking and partying besides, and Meany had been such a popular guy that none of them would be inclined to care one way or the other if the murderer was caught, anyway.

Except the murderer.

She ought to take a look at Meany's boat, too. They'd left it in Alaganik at anchor. Someone had given the son a ride to his family's setnet site, where his mother and uncle were supposed to be. Her next stop, she thought drearily.

They were startled out of their separate reveries by the crackle of the radio and Lamar Rousch's voice, rendered thin and reedy by the FM bandwidth, announcing the next fishing period. Gull leaned over to turn up the volume, and when Lamar signed off, turn it down again. "No period," he said. "Escapement must be down."

"For crying out loud," Kate said, "about a million reds must have gone up the Kanuyaq yesterday from Alaganik Bay alone, and nobody was hanging any nets in their way. Well, two, but hell."

Gull gave his head a sympathetic wag. "I wonder sometimes myself how accurate those fish counts can be. You know, there was a trader from Andromeda riding deadhead on the last SeaLandSpace freighter through here, he was telling me—"

A movement caught her eye and she looked up to see Old Sam heading down the ramp. "Oops. There's my boss. Gotta go. Thanks again for the truck."

Gull waved her off with a regal hand, very much master of all he surveyed. "Okay, Kate. See you."

She caught up with Old Sam as he was about to board the *Freya.* "Hey, Sam."

"Hey, girl." Nimble in the face of eighty winters, Sam hopped over the gunnel and landed lightly on the deck.

She followed him into the galley, and sat down as he began assembling the ingredients for dinner. With something of a shock, Kate realized that it wasn't even six o'clock. It had been a full day. "Listen, Sam?"

"What?" he said, pulling a package of mooseburger out of the sink where he'd left it to thaw at breakfast. He turned a burner on and got out a frying pan.

She sidled in next to him and made her own patty. She liked hers thicker than he did his. "Could we maybe head back for Alaganik after dinner?"

He paused. "Why? It's early yet. And we don't even know what hours the period's going to be, let alone is anybody fishing it."

"There isn't one," Kate said. "It was on the radio in the harbormaster's office."

"No period?"

Kate shook her head.

"Why the hell not?" Old Sam said indignantly. "Christ on a crutch, what about all the fish we saw heading north yesterday? And hardly anyone with a net in the water?" He slammed his patty into the frying pan with unnecessary force, and the resulting sizzle nearly took off his eyebrows. "It's those goddam sport fishermen, is what it is, and their idiot escape demands. That goddam Bill Nickle won't be satisfied until the only red taken from the Sound is taken with a silver spinner."

Kate set her patty down next to his. The subsequent tantalizing aroma made her mouth water. There was nothing better than mooseburger, especially in the middle of the summer, when it seemed you would never get the smell of fish out of your nostrils or the fish scales out of your hair. Frying mooseburger was the smell of fall, and dry land beneath your feet, and settlement time.

Kate waited until they'd eaten before broaching the matter of their departure a second time. Old Sam was much more approachable on a full stomach. For that matter, so was she.

"We might as well put 'er in dry dock," he said glumly, "all the fish we're likely to haul in this year. Hardly worth the price of copper paint."

Kate wasn't sure she'd ever seen Old Sam glum before. A mischievous, sometimes malicious, always impudent elf of a man, he enjoyed life and irritating the people in it too much to squander time brooding. As annoying as he usually was, she found she didn't like it when he wasn't. "Listen, Sam, I need to talk to some people on the Alaganik beach. Maybe even some of the drifters." She paused. "It'd be a lot easier to have the *Freya* as a base of operations."

He raised his head, examining her with sharp old eyes almost hidden in folds of wrinkles. "This got something to do with Meany?"

She nodded. "I promised Chopper Jim I'd nose around a little."

It was like she'd thrown a switch. He jumped to his feet and chucked plate, silver and mug into the sink on top of the unwashed frying pan. "Why didn't you say so, girl?" he said, grinning a grin that rivaled Chopper Jim's for sharkness. "Cast off, I'll wake her up."

As Kate went to the bow, she reflected that cops-and-robbers was the one game boys never really grew out of.

The beach that edged Alaganik Bay began in the west at the Kanuyaq River delta and ended in the east in the high cliffs that abruptly broke off the southward march of the Ragged Mountains. There were three creeks big enough to be named, Calhoun, Amartuq and Coal, and a dozen rivulets that only appeared at low tide.

It was a broad, steep expanse of fine, dark gray sand mixed with tumbled gravel. Heaped piles of seaweed and driftwood logs bleached white by the salt of the sea were scattered across the high-water mark. Tidal pools formed in the rocks exposed by low tide, sheltering stickle-backs and hermit crabs and sea urchins, and now and then a flounder or a bullhead, and oc-casionally a small salmon. Kate loved a tidal pool, and had ever since she was a toddler splashing after bidarkys.

No time for tidal pool exploration or a seafood harvest today. Kate stood on the bridge of the *Freya* and surveyed the beach through Old Sam's binoculars. Just above the high-tide mark the rain forest closed in, pine and cedar and alder and cottonwood and birch and spruce all jostling for place. The setnet sites had been hacked out of this jungle by main force, and the cabins built there constructed either of prefab kits freighted in by barge, or of the detritus of sea and land, their split log–tarpaper–plywood designs reminding Kate of Emaa's add-on, multilevel, anything-goes-for-siding-including-the-sawed-off-bottoms-of-beerbottles home in Niniltna.

The Meanys' nearest neighbor to the west was Mary Balashoff; to the east, the Flanagans. "Widow woman," Old Sam said briefly. "Got herself a couple of girl kids that are holy terrors. You can go talk to them all by yourself."

She wanted to talk to everyone all by herself, but Old Sam wasn't having any. He ignored gentle hint and loud protest alike and climbed down into the skiff like he owned it. He did, so she yielded the kicker and moved forward to sit on the thwart in the bow, feeling reduced to ballast. Mary Balashoff's site was on the west side of Amartuq Creek, Meany's on the east. It was far and away the richest creek that emptied into Alaganik Bay (Kate's ancestral elders had been no fools), and she wondered how Johnny-come-lately Meany had acquired title to the site. She asked Old Sam.

Old Sam took his time steering the skiff around a clump of seaweed. A sea otter kept a wary eye on them from the center of the clump, paws clutching a clam and a rock. "He didn't. He didn't need to."

"Why not?"

"Alaska beaches are public beaches up to the high-water mark. Setnet sites can't be personal property."

Kate knew this, but held her peace. Old Sam never passed up an opportunity to relieve her ignorance, whether or not she suffered any. He resembled Shitting Seagull in that respect. She turned her head to hide a smile.

"However," Old Sam said pontifically, "if somebody's family has been fishing the same site for a hundred years, it's their site for the next hundred, unless you want to try to move in at the point of a twelve-gauge."

Kate's gaze sharpened. "So you're telling me Meany brought a twelve-gauge?"

"Pretty much. Nate Moonin used to fish it, but he sold his cabin to the Ursins, a married couple from Anchorage." Kate remembered Lamar telling her that nearly a third of the setnetters on the Sound were neither traditional nor professional fishermen. "Teachers," Old Sam said. "Well hell, makes some kind of sense, I guess. Teachers get the summer off, so they buy a permit and move their families down for the duration." He grinned. " 'How I Spent My Summer Vacation.' "

"How'd Meany get in on the act?"

Old Sam shrugged. "Way I heard it, school got out and the Ursins came down and Meany was already on the site."

"That's all?"

Old Sam snorted. "Hell no, that's not all. I wasn't there, and Ursin didn't slow down enough to talk to on his way north, so I don't know what happened firsthand."

"But you can guess."

"I can guess," Sam said, nodding. "I figure Meany offered to buy the cabin, because Meany always was one to keep things nice and legal. Probably for ten cents on the dollar, but he sure as shit'd steal it legal." He paused, and added, almost reluctantly, "They had those three kids, ages ten and under."

It was a moment before Kate realized what he was saying. "You think he threatened them? You think Meany threatened to hurt the Ursin kids if the Ursins didn't sell to him?"

With flat conviction Old Sam said, "I think Meany did whatever was necessary to get the job done."

Kate thought again of the boy on the boat. Meany had been more than capable of beating on his own kid. Threats to someone else's would have come naturally to him.

The buzz of the outboard was loud against the silence of the day, the smell of salt water sharp and demanding. "That Mrs. Ursin, now, there was a nice gal," Sam said suddenly. "Womanly," he added with emphasis, nodding at Kate to make sure she got the idea that she herself might be somewhat lacking in that department. "Made one hell of a pineapple upside-down cake."

So do I, Kate thought, given enough Bisquick. But if she said so she'd be making two a week for the rest of the summer, so she kept quiet.

"They didn't know much about fishing, but they were learning. Didn't sell much, but then they canned half of what they caught. I was going to show them how to smoke fish this summer." He nodded toward the beach. "Jeff cleared a bunch of alder last fall, cut and stacked a cord of it next to the cabin. I see the Meanys been burning it, probably for fuel." He spat over the side, and shipped oars as the skiff's bow ran up on the beach.

Kate jumped ashore and pulled the skiff up, tying the bow line to a driftwood log above the high-water mark. She looked toward the cabin and saw a curl of smoke rising up out of the chimney. It was half past seven, and the sun was still struggling to fight its way inside the low overcast. The bay was like glass, and although most of the fleet had headed back for town on the morning tide, there were enough boats left with men occupying themselves with make-work jobs in their laps for Kate to realize she was under better surveillance than she could have hired through the Continental Op. She was not overjoyed to see that the Bush telegraph was doing its usual efficient job. Gossip tainted memories. She hoped potential eyewitnesses were keeping themselves to themselves, but it was a vain hope and she knew it.

She felt a nudge in the small of her back. "Well, come on, girl," Old Sam said impatiently, "what are you waiting for?" He set off up the steep slope at a brisk pace, and Kate followed. By the time she caught up with him, he was hammering on the door of the cabin.

It was a trim little building, one of the prefabricated ones, with a corrugated-tin roof and neat powder-blue plastic siding. It stood over the high-water mark on pilings, its back to the bank as the forest primeval leaned down and tried to snatch it up in great green arms. The deck was unvarnished cedar that had gone a beautiful silvery gray, and still smelled wonderful in the salt air. The door opened abruptly just as Old Sam was fixing to hammer on it a second time.

By her age and general air of wear and tear, the woman standing in front of them was the wife. "Mrs. Meany?" Kate said. "Mrs. Calvin Meany?"

"Yes." The single word was uninviting, either of further conversation or of entrance.

"My name is Kate Shugak. This is Sam Dementieff. We're the ones who found your husband's body this morning."

She didn't say anything, just stood in the doorway with her arms folded tightly against her. She had been pretty once, and with luck—widowhood, perhaps?—and a change of occupation might be pretty again. Dark auburn hair streaked with gray was matted against her skull, her skin was freckled and sunburned and her eyes were green and tired. Her figure was spectacular; from the neck down Mrs. Meany looked like Sophia Loren. Kate was impressed; anyone who could look statuesque in high-tops, filthy jeans and a faded brown plaid shirt was definitely out of the ordinary, and deserving of respect.

Mrs. Meany did not appear to be stricken with grief. On the other hand, neither did she appear to be overtly hostile, or nervous. "May we come in?" Kate said.

Mrs. Meany didn't move. A voice came from the cabin. "Better let them in, Marian."

A man appeared behind Mrs. Meany. He was short of stature and stocky in build, much like Calvin Meany, but the blunt, nearly simian features of Meany's face had been by some subtle transmutation thinned down, even refined here. The brow was broader, the nose high-bridged, even aristocratic, and when he met Kate's eyes there was no trace of the predator that had lurked at the drifter's shoulder. He was massaging a shoulder, and the knuckles of his hands were swollen and scraped and bruised. He looked as if a change of occupation might benefit him, too. "I'm Neil Meany," he said. "Calvin was my brother. This is Marian, his wife. Please come in."

A gentle touch on one shoulder and Marian stepped obediently to one side. She didn't close the door behind them, Kate noticed, but left it open, probably to encourage an early departure.

It was a one-room cabin, lined with pink insulation between the two-by-four studs. Two sets of bunk beds stood against the far wall, a table and six chairs in one corner and a stove, a sink and cupboards in another. There was one window in each wall, the panes stained with smoke. The room was dim except for the muted light of the cloudy evening through the open door. No one had bothered to light a lamp, and the stove, a converted fifty-five-gallon drum, was cold to Kate's casual touch.

The handle on the fuel door across the stove's belly was fashioned from an old metal doorknob, with latch. Kate had stumbled over a box of doorknobs just like it in the *Freya*'s focsle three days before. She looked over at Old Sam, who was glowering at her from beneath lowered brows, daring her to comment. She didn't.

"Please," the brother said, gesturing. "Sit down. Would you like some tea? Dani, why don't you put the kettle on."

The girl in one of the top bunks turned the page of her comic book. "Like, put it on yourself, okay?"

"I'll do it." Marian Meany moved swiftly to the stove, detouring around Kate and Old Sam and Neil, pouring water out of a white plastic jerry can into a large kettle and lighting the camp stove on the counter. She remained there, staring out the window that faced on the bay.

Marian Meany moved like a woman one step ahead of a clenched fist. Old habits were hard to break. Kate looked from the widow to the two men at the table.

The brother was on his feet, the younger man sitting down. The younger man had high, wide, slightly slanted brown eyes and a way of peering out from beneath tufted brows that gave him a distinctly vulpine look. His mouth was wide and full-lipped. He smiled at Kate, his face lighting with practiced charm.

She didn't smile back.

"I'm sorry," Neil Meany said, "what was your name again?"

"Kate Shugak, Mr. Meany," Kate said, "and this is Sam Dementieff, my uncle." Maybe not technically, but close enough for government work. "Sam owns the *Freya*, the tender anchored out in the bay there. Your brother delivered to us last period." Neil Meany glanced out the window and nodded. The light caught his face half in and half out of shadow; he looked tense and strained, natural enough in the circumstances. "Who is everyone else here, please?"

"Oh, I'm sorry," he said. "This is Frank and Dani Meany, my niece and nephew. And Evan McCafferty, our summer hand."

"How do you do," she said. The summer hand smiled again. She ignored it. "We took your brother's body back to town this morning." She paused, but nobody asked. "The state trooper flew in and took the body to Anchorage."

Meany frowned. "Anchorage? Why Anchorage?"

"Because there has to be an autopsy, Mr. Meany."

He went very still, eyes fixed on her face. "Autopsy?"

"Yes. To determine how he was killed."

"You mean he didn't just drown?"

"No." At the sink Marian Meany turned around. Her face was backlit by the window and Kate couldn't make out her expression. This was awkward but necessary. Kate said levelly, "It looks like your husband was murdered, Mrs. Meany."

"Oh."

She didn't seem much interested in how, Kate noted. Or perhaps she already knew?

The brother said it for her. "How was he killed, Ms. Shugak?"

"We don't know." She added, just to see the expression on their faces when she did, "It could have been one of several ways."

Neil Meany stared at her. "I beg your pardon?"

Kate hesitated, more over how to phrase it than over fear of hurting anyone's delicate sensibilities. "Well, you could say whoever did it wanted to be very sure your brother was dead."

An expression of revulsion crossed the mannered face, and Neil Meany put up a hand palm out. "Never mind. I don't want to hear it."

Marian Meany remained silent. Kate looked at the boy sitting on the bottom bunk. "Your name is Frank, isn't it? Frank Meany? Is there anything you can tell me about your father's death, Frank?"

"You're not the cops," the boy said, his heavy features, so like his father's, cast in the same sullen mold as the last time she'd seen him. "We don't have to talk to you."

"No, you don't," Kate agreed. "But you're going to have to talk to somebody, sooner or later."

The boy ducked his head down, refusing to look at her, but she could see the misery—and perhaps fear—on his face.

"Frank," Neil Meany said sharply. "This kind of behavior doesn't help us."

The girl in the top bunk turned her head to look at him. "Fuck off, Neil. Like, you know, you have anything to say about anything we do. Don't talk to her if you don't want to, Frank."

The silence in the little cabin gathered and grew. Kate kept her voice as nonthreatening as possible, and said, "Your sister's right, Frank, you don't have to talk to me. But you don't really have anything to hide, do you? Did you have another fight with your father? That's certainly understandable, after the one I saw on Monday. Is that what happened?"

A loud snort came from the top bunk. "Like, we never had a fight with our loving father, our loving father beat on us. There's a difference, okay?"

Kate kept her eyes on the boy. "I saw you on the deck of your dad's drifter yesterday, when he went to town to deliver."

The boy still wouldn't look up. "So?"

"So, we need to know when was the last time you saw him."

Making them all jump, the girl slammed her comic book shut and bounced down from her bunk. She stood between Kate and the boy, her green eyes narrowed with hostility. She had a figure like her mother's, better displayed in leggings and a halter top that bared her navel. All she needed was a veil and some bangles and she'd fit right into a harem. "Like, he went into town with our loving father, okay?" she said. "And our loving father as usual came up with some asshole excuse to start beating on him, okay? Like, you know, our loving father didn't need an excuse? So Frank ran away, okay?"

It was patently futile to look for grief from either of Calvin Meany's children. Kate couldn't blame them, and she would love to clear them of any complicity, but they weren't helping her much. "What time did you leave the drifter, Frank?" she said.

"Right after they pulled up to the cannery dock," Dani said hotly. "You can ask the beach gang, they all saw our loving father beat the crap out of Frank. He knocked him into the friggin' hold, for crissake, okay?"

It wasn't okay, but Kate didn't say so. "Where did you go, Frank?"

Again, Dani answered for Frank. "We do have some friends, okay? People who actually like us, okay? He went to stay with them."

Again, Kate addressed the boy. "Who did you stay with, Frank?" He kept his head down. "Frank." Her voice compelled him to look up, finally. "You can make me leave you alone by telling me their names."

He held her gaze for a moment, and then his head drooped again. When he spoke his voice was an inarticulate mumble.

"Who?" Kate said, the memory of Monday's scene keeping her patient with him as she would have been with no one else.

He raised his head again. "The Wieses. Paul and Georgina. I'm friends with their son, Joe."

"Thank you." She paused. "When you left the dock, was that the last time you saw your father?"

"Yes, it was, okay?" Dani said.

Kate looked up at the girl, and caught a flicker in Dani's angry eyes. She was holding something back, but the set of her jaw didn't look promising. "How did you get back to the site, Frank?"

"He hitched a ride, okay?"

"Who with?"

Dani tossed her head. She looked older than her brother but not by much, and not for lack of trying to look that way. Kids never looked like kids anymore, they all looked like adults by the time they were ten. Or were working at it as hard as they could. "I don't know," she said with an elaborate shrug. "Some fisherman type, they all look alike, all covered with slime and scales."

Frank actually spoke, his head still down, his voice muffled. "Wendell Kritchen. I saw him down at the harbor this morning. He told me Dad was dead, and gave me a ride out on the *Tiana*."

"I know you," Marian Meany said suddenly, staring at Old Sam. "You're Sam Dementieff. The one they call Old Sam."

"Yes, ma'am." The old man doffed his hat and bowed his head. Sam's company manners were faultless; he just didn't believe in wasting them on friends and family.

She pointed out the window. "You own the tender out there."

"Yes, ma'am."

Marian crossed the room and sat down, her hands on wide-spread knees, staring hard at Old Sam, looking more aware than she had when they arrived. "They say you're older than God, and that what you don't know about fish and fishing and fishermen isn't worth knowing."

"That would be about right, ma'am." There was nothing of false modesty about Old Sam, either. And, Kate reflected, what they said was right.

"Do you know anyone who would want to buy our permit and this cabin?"

Her brother-in-law stirred in his chair, his eyes fixed on Marian's face in a steady gaze, but like Kate he said nothing.

Old Sam looked Marian over with an assessing eye not entirely devoid of male appreciation. "You might want to try the Ursins," he said bluntly. "The people your husband forced out before you got here."

She didn't so much as blink. "Do you think they'd want to come back?"

"Depends on how much you want for the permit and cabin."

"Whatever my husband paid for it."

"Marian—"

"Hush up, Neil," she said. "You couldn't stand up to him alive any more than I could. Well, he's dead, and we're not going to pretend any of us ever wanted this kind of life. He bullied us to Alaska, and then he bullied us down here after he bullied the Ursins out. We were never any of us anything more than free labor for his little empire."

"I didn't—"

"We're selling out," Marian Meany said flatly. "The second after someone writes us a check."

Frank had raised his head and was looking at his mother with something approaching dumb adoration in his eyes.

She gave him a brief, wan smile. "It's going to be all right, kids. We're going home. We're selling the setnet site and the drifter and the house in Anchorage and we're going back to Cincinnati."

"Oh, goody," Dani, back in her bunk, said, and turned the page of her comic book.

"Knock it off, Dani," her mother said, the lack of hope she felt of being obeyed evident in the tired repetitiveness of the words.

"Like you have anything to say about what I do or don't do."

In the same mechanical tone, Marian said, "Of course I do, you're my daughter."

Dani turned her head and looked Marian straight in the eye. Her voice was low, almost gentle. "It's a little late for you to start playing mother, isn't it?"

Marian turned away from the fury in her daughter's face. It might not be too late for Marian, but Kate wondered if the same could be said for Dani.

The widow looked at her brother-in-law, the other adult, the one person in the room she might rouse to some enthusiasm at their changed circumstances. "You can go back to school, Neil. After we sell the boat and the permit, there'll be enough left for that, too. You can get your doctorate, teach Keats."

"Yeats," he said.

"Whatever." Marian turned back to Sam. "So, Mr. Dementieff? Do you know how to get in touch with the Ursins?" He nodded. "Will you?"

"I'll call them when I get back to town."

She smiled at him, a meaningless stretch of her lips. "Thank you."

Old Sam grunted and crammed his hat back on his head. "Ain't done nothing yet."

"Thank you just the same." Her company manners were good, too.

"Listen, folks," Kate said, feeling it was more than time to get back to the point, "I need to know where you all were last night. It's just routine," she added, seeing the protests form on the faces in front of her. "Trooper Chopin asked me to get some of the preliminary questions out of the way, so he'll have a head start when he gets back."

Dani sat up, comic book forgotten. "Chopper Jim's coming here?"

"Yes, later tonight, or maybe tomorrow, and he—"

The comic book went flying as Dani leapt from the bunk and ran over to a curtain made by hanging a length of unhemmed chintz from a wire stretched across one corner of the cabin. When she yanked the material to one side, the glow of colors behind it was momentarily blinding. Cherry red and lime green figured prominently.

"So where were you, Dani?" Kate said, patiently for her. She'd seen this reaction before in women expecting a close encounter of the trooper kind. Unbeknownst to Dani, Jim Chopin chose his victims carefully. They were all, without exception, over the age of consent, and they all, without exception, had vocabularies consisting of more than the Valley Girlisms "Like, you know?" and "Oh-KAY?" Kate was able to restrain any impulse she might have had to leap to the defense of the teenager's virtue.

"Where was I?" Dani said. She pulled out an almost transparent little black dress with a nonexistent skirt and no bodice to speak of and paired it with flowered leggings trimmed with lace, a new high in setnet site chic. She regarded the resultant ensemble with a critical frown, decided it didn't reveal enough skin and dove back into the closet for more. "What do you mean, where was I?"

Although from the look of things, Kate just might have to leap to the defense of Chopper Jim's virtue.

The summer hire rose to his feet, and went to stand in front of the window, looking out. The set of his shoulders was stiff. Kate gave his back a long, thoughtful look, and said to the girl, "Where were you last night, Dani?" Kate didn't have an official time of death, so she guessed. "Say, from yesterday afternoon until this morning at about six-thirty?" There was silence, and she said, "You can talk to me now, or you can talk to Chopper Jim later"—precisely the wrong thing to say.

Dani emerged from her makeshift closet with lip curled

and attitude intact. "Then I'll talk to Chopper Jim later." The girl tossed her head; her hair, a hundred miles from an electrical outlet, bounced around her face in perfect strands, looking as if it had been blow-dried by Vidal Sassoon himself five minutes before. There was so much in the gesture, all of it only too easy for Kate to sort and identify: rebellion, bravado, braggadocio and a current of sexual awareness that was as angry as it was intense. She'd seen it before, the unmistakable signs of a child brought to womanhood too fast and too soon.

"We were both here," Marian Meany said. "Right here in the cabin. The period ended at six o'clock. We came in here and crashed."

"That go for you, too?" Kate said to Neil Meany.

He hesitated. "Yes. I mean no. I mean, I cleaned up here first, and then I went up the beach for a while."

"Where up the beach?"

Before he could reply Dani said mockingly, "Like, you know, Uncle Neil's got himself a girlfriend."

The curse of fair skin is the inability to hide a blush, although Neil Meany's voice was steady enough. "I'm friends with the next setnetter up the beach. Anne Flanagan. She's got two daughters." His shoulders shifted uncomfortably beneath Kate's steady gaze, with what could have been manly embarrassment at having his manly affections discovered. "I found a glass ball in the gear. One of those Japanese floats. It was only a little one, but I thought the girls might like it."

"You got there when?"

He looked at his watch, a battered Seiko on a plastic band. "Well, I washed up first, and changed my clothes. Took maybe twenty minutes, maybe half an hour. I took the skiff to her site"—her site, Kate noticed, not their site—"maybe ten minutes all told. So I probably got to her place a little before seven. A quarter till?"

"And when did you leave?"

"She invited me to dinner, and we talked for hours. Oh yes, and played Monopoly with the girls afterwards. I didn't get back here until, oh, I don't know, one-thirty? Two o'clock?" He smiled briefly. "It's hard to keep track of time during an Alaskan summer. Too much light."

Kate looked at Marian, who shrugged. "I was asleep."

"Dani?"

"Hm? Oh, I was sacked out, too. I didn't hear him come home." There was something in the airy dismissal that made both her mother and Kate look at her sharply, but Dani was holding a cherry-red T-shirt beneath her chin and twisting into a pretzel to regard the effect in the very inadequate mirror hanging from a nail over the sink.

"And Marian and Dani were in bed when you came home?" Kate asked Neil.

"Yes." Again, he hesitated. "I guess so. When it isn't raining I sleep in a hammock out back."

Great, Kate thought. "And Frank we've already heard from." The boy looked up from contemplation of folded hands. He had green eyes like his sister, like his mother, with the same wary look in them. Inwardly Kate cursed that wariness. None of them were telling her all that they could, and some of them were lying in their teeth, but then she was getting the distinct impression that life with Meany had not rewarded telling the truth. Like anything else, telling the truth was a habit: The more you did it, the better at it you became. The reverse was equally true.

Besides, there was nothing like murder to start off someone on a career of prevarication that Baron Munchausen would envy. What she needed now was more information, the better with which to poke holes in their stories.

She looked at the silent, fox-faced young man who was leaning against the counter, arms folded. "And where were you last night, Mr. McCafferty?"

"Mac, please."

"Where were you last night, Mr. McCafferty?"

"On board the *Priscilla*. Dewey Dineen invited me to go water-skiing."

"And you returned here when?"

His narrow shoulders moved in a shrug. "I'm not sure." He tried the smile again, with as much success as before, and it faded again. "What with all the celebrating, I wasn't any too steady on my feet, you know? Check with Dewey, he might remember. It was late, I'm pretty sure of that."

"Anybody hear him come in?" Kate asked the question with all the hope it deserved, none, and was not disappointed. Neil had been sacked out in back in the hammock, Frank was in town, Dani and Marian were asleep. Or so they said. "You have any problems with Meany as an employer?"

Again the narrow-shouldered shrug. "His checks cleared the bank."

Her own view of life in the fishing industry, and clearly McCafferty's last word on the subject. None of them had any more to add, at least for the moment, and Kate decided it was time to collect more information from outside sources before she put what the people here had said to the test. She rose to her feet. "I think that's all for now. Due to the nature of the crime, I'm sure Chopper Jim would want me to tell you that he would prefer you remain here at present, at least until the matter is resolved to everyone's satisfaction."

With which fine words she decamped, Old Sam at her heels. Halfway down the beach, he said, "Nobody's got an alibi, do they? Except maybe the boy?"

"Nope," Kate said glumly.

He gave her a shrewd look. "You were pretty tough on him."

"I don't want it to be him," she said wearily.

He gave a satisfied nod, as if she'd confirmed something he already knew. "What about the girl? The way these things work out, you know she come in for her share." He added, his voice gruff, "And then some, probably, being how she's a girl and all."

"I know," Kate said. "I know." She paused, one hand on the bow line, and looked over at him. "You built that stove, didn't you?" She jerked her head. "The one in the cabin. I recognized the doorknob. You've got a boxful just like it in the *Freya*'s focsle."

He tugged unnecessarily at the bill of his cap. "They were good people. I might have helped them out a bit."

Not for a moment did Kate imagine that Old Sam was referring to the Meanys.

As they were about to shove off, Marian Meany came flying out of the cabin, stumbling through the gravel, sending rocks skittering down the beach. She fetched up against the boat, hands gripping the bow, panting, her face flushed. "Did you see him?" she said urgently.

"See who?" Kate said.

"My husband. Did you see the body?"

"Well, yes," Kate said, brows puckering. "I found him."

The older woman caught Kate's wrist. "Are you sure? Are you sure he's dead?"

Kate kept her arm very still beneath the influence of that desperate, almost painful grip. "I'm sure."

Marian Meany's eyes stared hard into Kate's, and the struggle over what to believe was plain to see.

"I saw him, too, Marian," Old Sam said from the stern, one hand on the kicker. "He was dead." He caught her eyes and repeated firmly, "He was dead before we ever hauled him on board the *Freya*."

"You're sure? You're absolutely sure?"

"We're sure," Old Sam said, more gently this time.

"Thank you," Marian Meany said in a faint voice. "I'm sorry, I was afraid . . ." Her voice trailed off, and she retreated a few steps up the beach, before turning to face them again. "Thank you," she said fervently. "Thank you very much."

Her face before she turned to head up the beach again shone with a light that was almost beatific, and she walked as if she had shed twenty pounds, her stride long and graceful.

Old Sam hauled at the starter with unnecessary violence. "Dumb bastard's better off dead, he ain't capable of appreciating the kind of luck that lets him climb into bed next to that every night."

Old Sam was right about somebody being lucky, but it wasn't Calvin Meany. It looked as if everyone in his family had just received a gift from God, in the form of his own death.

Except that in this case God had had a lot of help.

In spite of Old Sam's vow to leave Kate to the Flanagan children's tender mercies, he was ahead of her going up the beach to their cabin. It was one of the flotsam-and-jetsam cabins, built of anything that came to hand—driftwood, Blazo boxes, plywood that had obviously been left behind by the tide. The roof had a shallow peak and was layered with canvas. The canvas was weighted down with a dozen lengths of very old, one-inch manila line, also obviously scavenged. The lines had then been tossed over the ridgepole and weighed down at each end by large rocks, dangling beneath the eaves like participles, indicating a thought—and a roof—left unfinished.

As they approached the cabin the sound of raised voices could be heard.

"No. No I said, and no I meant. What word in that did you not understand?"

They rounded the corner of the house and

beheld a yard. The bank sloped more gently on this stretch of beach, and the cabin sat in the middle of half an acre of cleared ground. There was a single drying rack, half full of split, boned king salmon. There was a net rack with green netting folded over it. There were various toys, including balls and dolls and a set of children's playground swings that had been painted in bright, primary colors, now faded and rusting, but still working, if the little girl squeaking back and forth in one of them was any indication.

Her identical twin sister had planted herself in front of her mother, feet apart, hands at her waist. She had fair hair cut Prince Valiant style and from beneath the row of bangs brown eyes stared accusingly. "Always with you it cannot be done."

The mother didn't miss a beat. "Hear you nothing that I say? On you shame! Temper, disobedience—a Jedi knight behaves not this way!"

The daughter tested the determination in her mother's voice and found it firm. Bloody but unbowed, she stamped off to join her sister, indignation written in flame down the line of her spine, and the two of them vanished like wood elves into the undergrowth at the edge of the yard. The mother turned back. "Sorry about that," she said, and added, when she saw their expressions, "*Star Wars*. When they're not speaking to me, they're always speaking in the best Yoda. The only way to get through is to retaliate in kind."

Old Sam let out a crack of laughter, and she smiled at him. "Aren't you Sam Dementieff?"

"Yes, I am," he said, and doffed his hat. "I'm proud you remember me, Reverend Flanagan."

"Oh please, out here just call me Anne."

"Reverend?" Kate said.

"Sure," Old Sam said, his crooked, callused hand enveloping Anne's smaller, no less callused one. "Anne here's the minister of the Presbyterian church in Cordova. I thought you knew that, girl."

Kate looked across at the other woman, who was regarding her with a friendly smile and an outstretched hand. "No," she said slowly, reaching out to take the minister's hand in a very brief clasp. "No, I didn't."

"What did they want to do?" Old Sam said. "Your kids? They are twins, aren't they?"

"Yes, they are twins, may God have more mercy on me in my next life." Anne Flanagan smiled and set out a plate of chocolate-striped shortbread, Old Sam's favorite cookie on the planet. Old Sam looked like he was in love.

"They wanted to go up to Mary Balashoff's. Mary is kippering salmon today and they want to know how."

"Well hell, let 'em. Mary's been teaching kids to fish and such for the last thirty years." Old Sam dunked his cookie in coffee and bit into it with a satisfied grunt.

"Usually I do, but her place is across the creek, and the tide's coming in, and—" She paused, and busied herself at the sink, washing out a mug with special care.

"And they'll have to cross the site between yours and Mary's, and Meany's is that site, and Meany's just been murdered and you don't want your kids anywhere near the place," Old Sam finished for her.

Anne Flanagan turned from the sink to give the old man a rueful smile. "Silly, isn't it?"

He snorted into his mug. "No way, lady. You keep them as far away from that bunch as you can. Those folks got problems, and I don't mean just with the killing of their man. They give the word 'dysfunction' a whole new definition."

"You could go with them," Kate said. "With the twins to Mary's."

Anne Flanagan's fine blue eyes rested on her face for a moment. "I could," she agreed, "and I probably will, later, but for now I've got bread rising and half a dozen other chores left to do." She smiled again at Old Sam. "You know how it is with kids. They want everything yesterday."

"You've heard about the murder, then," Kate said, before this turned into Old Home Week at the Y.

The minister poured out a cup of coffee and sat down across the table from her. "Yes."

"Who told you?" Old Sam frowned at her abrupt tone, but she ignored him.

"Wendell Kritchen."

Wendell had brought Frank back from town, and couldn't wait to spread the bad news. The DEW line of the Bush telegraph, that was Wendell. "He tell you Meany was murdered?"

Anne Flanagan's mouth pulled down a little at the corners, with distress or distaste, Kate couldn't decide. "Yes."

"State Trooper Jim Chopin asked me to do a little preliminary investigating while he takes the body to the coroner in Anchorage," Kate said. "We've just come from the Meany place."

Anne Flanagan's eyebrows raised in a polite question.

"Neil Meany told us he was here for dinner last night, Reverend Flanagan."

Kate would have sworn on oath that the slight emphasis on the other woman's title wasn't voluntary. Anne Flanagan's eyes narrowed a little. "Why, yes, he was."

No invitation to call her by her first name, but then Kate didn't seek the privilege, thanks anyway. "What time did he get here?"

"Right after the period was over," the minister said readily. "He brought one of those Japanese floats over for the girls. I invited him to stay for supper. Spaghetti and garlic bread, leftovers warmed up from the night before," she added, her first trace of sarcasm, and surprised a snort of laughter out of Old Sam.

"When did he leave?"

"He helped with the dishes, and we talked. The girls were outside playing until late—I let them go to bed when they want to, out here—and when they came in, they wanted to play Monopoly. They like Neil, too. I made coffee, and Neil had one cup, and we played one game, and he left."

"What time?"

"I don't know."

"I beg your pardon?"

"I don't know," Anne Flanagan repeated, and smiled at Old Sam. "We don't have a clock. The sun was down by the time he left, had been down for a while, so it was late."

"Past midnight? One o'clock?"

"I'd guess the girls came in about midnight. Maybe a little before, maybe a little after, I don't know. They're such night owls, the two of them. And then the game, which took a while. Monopoly always takes a while."

"But you don't know how long a while?"

"No. Like I said, no clocks. And then we had another cup

of coffee, and then he went home." Anne Flanagan paused, turning her mug between her hands. "That's the rule, no watches, no clocks. No sundials, no hourglasses, no ship's bells, no poles in the sand, no chronometers of any kind."

One corner of Old Sam's mouth curled up and, encouraged, Anne Flanagan added, "This beach has always seemed to me like a place out of time. Our nearest neighbors are at anchor or four miles down. There are no roads, and while what with fish spotting and stream surveys and sport fishermen you can't get away from the planes, the only time one lands on our section is to bring us here or take us home. Time—" She shrugged. "It doesn't exist. It does exist, I know that, but—"

"Here you wag it, instead of it wagging you," Old Sam suggested.

An answering smile spread across Anne Flanagan's face. "Yes. This time of year it's easy. The sun doesn't go down, it just goes around."

At this latitude that was an exaggeration, but not much of one. Kate was skeptical. "How do you know when you can put your net in the water?"

The smile faded. "We wait until everyone else has theirs in the water. Sometimes Lamar Rousch goes by in his boat and says it's time."

Kate barely repressed a snort. "You can miss a lot of fish that way."

"It's not about making money for us, Ms. Shugak," Anne Flanagan said levelly.

"No?"

"No. It's about getting away from town, and all the noise that comes with it. It's about getting the kids away from the nuts that Anchorage Job Service unloads on Cordova canneries every summer. It's about me taking a break, from my job, from my church and from my parishioners." She shrugged, and drank coffee. "Truth to tell, half of them are gone fishing themselves, so it's not like I'm abandoning my congregation. And it's good to get out here and away from the telephone and the television."

"Back to nature?" Kate suggested, something not quite a sneer on her face.

Anne Flanagan's voice remained level. "If you like."

"The better to commune with God, I suppose."

A muscle twitched in Anne Flanagan's cheek. "If you like," she repeated.

Old Sam put his mug down and frowned at Kate. She ignored him. Neil Meany had said that he'd gotten home at one-thirty or two o'clock. "Did you watch Neil Meany go back to his cabin?"

One eyebrow went up, and this time there was nothing of polite inquiry in it. "No. Neil Meany is a grown man. I was sure he was capable of making it home without my supervision."

"Did Neil Meany talk to you about his relationship with his brother?"

The other woman hesitated, and Kate said, "What, he tell you under the seal of the confessional?"

Anne Flanagan stiffened in her chair. "I don't hear confessions, Ms. Shugak," she said coldly. "I am not a Catholic priest."

"Then what's the problem?" Kate was aware of Old Sam sitting very still next to her. She could feel the weight of his gaze boring into her but, again, she ignored it.

"Merely, I was organizing my thoughts. I am aware that, by virtue of my firsthand experience of the Meany family, I may have valuable insight into the situation."

"Read a lot of mysteries, do you?" Kate said unkindly.

Anne Flanagan sat up straight in her chair and, fixing her gaze at a point above Kate's right shoulder, reeled off a staccato recitation of events that Chopper Jim would have admired for its brevity, clarity and wholly impersonal tone. "I first met Neil the first of June, when school let out and we moved out to the site. His family was already here." She paused. "I was not impressed with his brother. Calvin Meany seemed to me to be a businessman of dubious ethics as well as a domestic tyrant. Marian—" She shook her head, as if to say, There is no there there. Kate was inclined to agree, but she didn't say so. "His children—" She shook her head again.

"His brother I did like. Do like. He has visited me and the girls perhaps eight, ten times over the past five weeks. Sometimes he stays for dinner, sometimes he doesn't. We've shared meals, played board games, talked about books we've read. He's quite a scholar. I gather he was studying for a doctorate in English literature before his brother brought him to Alaska. He is planning to return to school after next year's season." She took a drink of coffee. "How does—did he feel about his brother? He didn't like him, but then that was a trait shared by the entire family. Frankly, I have yet to meet anyone who did like Calvin Meany, in the family or out of it."

So had Kate. "If he disliked his brother so much, why follow him all the way to Alaska from Ohio and go to work for him?"

The other woman frowned. "I don't know, exactly." She

hesitated, her eyes troubled. "He misses school. He really wants that Ph.D."

"Now there's a motive for murder," Kate said admiringly. "Academic frustration. I'll try that out on Chopper Jim when he gets back."

Anne Flanagan's fair skin flushed a deep red right up to the roots of her hair. She looked at Kate and opened her mouth, looked at Old Sam and closed it again. Her chair grated against the floor as she stood up. "I think I've told you all I can," she said. "If you'll excuse me, I have chores to do."

"Thanks for the coffee, Anne." Old Sam got up, jammed his hat on his head and left without a word. Kate followed.

Halfway down to where the skiff was beached, not far because the tide was coming in, their ears were assaulted by a high, thin voice rising into a piercing shriek, coming from the trees that lined the bank. "This is your last chance, Jabba! Surrender, or die!"

Two disheveled twins emerged from the bushes, one with a slingshot, the other with a bow and arrow. Both weapons were loaded, and the enemy looked hostile.

Where was Mutt when she needed her? Kate thought, staring down at the twins. The twins stared back, pugnacious and unafraid.

Old Sam shot his hands up in the air and quavered in a high, falsetto voice, "We surrender! Don't hurt us! Please! Take us to your leader!"

This was more like it, and the twins relaxed without taking their fingers off the triggers.

Unwisely, Kate said, "Watch where you're pointing those things, you might hurt somebody."

Their expressions hardened instantly. "You should have bargained, Jabba," the twin holding the bow and arrow said ominously. She raised her weapon and sighted and an arrow whizzed between Old Sam and Kate.

"Hey!" Kate retreated a step. Old Sam was already beating feet for the skiff. A rock zinged past six inches in front of her startled eyes, and the enemy was reloading.

It was with distinct relief that she heard Anne Flanagan's voice raised from the cabin. "Caitlin! Lauren! You knock that off, right now!"

With more haste and less dignity than she would have liked, Kate retreated to the skiff, pushed it off the beach and jumped into the bow. By the time they were afloat, the twins had vanished back into the undergrowth, their mother in hot pursuit.

"I've got to hand it to you, Kate," Old Sam said when they were safely offshore, "when you hold a grudge, you hold a grudge."

"I don't know what you're talking about," Kate lied, sitting very erect on the midship thwart.

"The hell you don't," he said, his voice hard and flat and, yes, angry. "You had a run-in with that born-again zealot in Chistona last summer, so now you figure every preacher is tarred with the same brush. You know better, Kate, or you should. It just ain't so that everybody called to God is a fanatic fixing to burn your books. You ain't never been in Anne Flanagan's church. You never heard her speak. You don't know that she's anything like that Seabolt asshole." She heard the sounds of the starter cord being ferociously yanked, to no effect. "And you oughta know by the way I acted around her that she ain't nothing like him at all. You ought to march your butt right back up that beach and apologize." He yanked on the starter again. The engine spluttered and didn't catch. Old Sam swore. "I ought to by God march it for you."

Kate, momentarily forgetting who she was speaking to, bristled and snapped, "Try it on, old man. Just you try it on."

She was sitting facing forward, arms folded, jaw tight, glowering at the bow of the skiff. The next thing she knew, there was a hand at her collar and another at the waistband of her jeans and a sudden sensation of weightlessness, followed by a tremendous splash.

She came up spluttering and coughing. They were still close in to shore and the water was shallow enough for her to find her feet. She sluiced off her face with one hand and glared up at the old man. "What the hell do you think you're doing!"

"Teaching you respect for your elders," he said calmly, wrapping the starter cord around the top of the kicker. It caught this time, and he throttled it back to a low roar.

"Hey!" Kate said, as the skiff began to move slowly away from her.

His voice floated back to her. "Walk it off, girl. I'll be waiting for you at Mary's."

And he left her there, waist-deep in the Gulf of Alaska, as he put-putted peacefully down the bay.

It was five miles from the Flanagan setnet site to the Balashoff setnet site, and the distance was not made any easier by the soft, wet gravel underfoot, the weight of her soaking clothes, the sight of Anne Flanagan emerging from the trees, twins in tow, in time to see her squelch off, the knowledge that only ten or twelve fishermen had to be watching from the boats anchored around the bay and, last but most definitely not least, the sting of her own conscience.

Ekaterina Ivana Shugak was thirty-three years old, and the last time she had had to be reprimanded for disrespect to her elders was twenty-five years before, when at a potlatch she had failed to yield her chair to a visiting tribal leader from Port Graham. Her grandmother had said nothing of her granddaughter's breach of manners, nothing at all, not during the potlatch, and not for seven days afterwards. The other Niniltna elders had followed her lead, even Abel, who had turned the emotional temperature way down at his homestead for the longest week of her life. She had never forgotten it.

She had never repeated her error, either.

Until today.

The recognition of her violation of etiquette, of her dereliction of duty was slow and labored in coming. It took a mile of beach just to burn off her temper. She churned up the gravel better than a four-wheeler, and it was only exhaustion that slowed her down in the end. She was a grown woman, a person with education and experience, loved by her family, valued by her colleagues and looked up to by her community, not to mention feared by her enemies; what call did Old Sam have to correct her manners? One lousy little remark, not shouted, barely spoken, whispered even, and suddenly it was time to bob for apples, full-body-immersion style. This was the goddam Gulf of Alaska, after all, where the temperature of the water never rose above forty-two degrees Fahrenheit, she could come down with hypothermia in two minutes, count 'em, two, and go into shock and die right there on the beach, if not lose consciousness while she was still in the water and drown, and wouldn't Old Sam be sorry then.

By the second mile she'd slowed down enough to become miserably aware of her physical state. Damp denim chafed her thighs and her bra strap cut into the flesh beneath her arms. A residue of seawater tickled her sinuses and made her sneeze. Her skin was sticky, her shirt stuck to her back, her hair was falling out of its braid and, worst of all, her shoes squished. Above any other physical discomfort, Kate hated getting her feet wet.

By the beginning of the third mile she could see the

Meanys' cabin, and spent the next twenty minutes preparing to ignore with dignity any comment that might come her way. Her worst fears were realized; the two kids, Dani and Frank, were sitting on the beach, heads together, talking earnestly. They broke off as she approached, their expressions at first hostile, then incredulous and finally delighted. They had the same eyes and the same chin; there wasn't a lot of difference in their broad grins, either.

"Been wading?" Dani inquired in a bland voice as Kate stumped grimly by.

"You're supposed to take your clothes off *before* you get in the water," Frank added helpfully.

Another time, Kate might have been relieved to see that Frank could smile and joke; now, all she could feel was the red creeping up the back of her neck. She marched on.

It was another mile to Amartuq Creek. By then Kate was wet, tired and humiliated, and her defenses were down for the count.

She had been rude to Old Sam. She had been even ruder to Anne Flanagan—rude hell, actively offensive, deliberately so. Further, Old Sam was correct when he said that Kate's experiences at Chistona had colored her perception of Anne Flanagan from the moment she had been made aware that the woman shared a profession with the Right Reverend Simon Seabolt. Her grief for Daniel Seabolt had left scars, deeper ones than she had realized. Kate had never been one to agonize over past failures; nevertheless, under even the most superficial self-examination it was obvious that the events of the previous June had been nagging at her like an unhealed wound ever since.

And poor Anne Flanagan, her mere existence a prod at

the open sore, bore the brunt of an accumulated frustration Kate hadn't even known she was carrying around.

She had deserved the dunking for being rude to Sam, who had told her nothing less than the truth, and she had deserved the long walk in wet clothes for being rude to the Right Reverend Anne Flanagan, who had done nothing but offer Kate tea, cookies and her other cheek.

And here at long last was the creek, its sandy mouth stretching wide, the incoming tide hiding the sandbar bisecting its channel, salmon making V-shaped ripples as they struggled upstream against the current. She halted at the water's edge. And there was Old Sam's skiff, beached on the other side of the creek. With the tide coming in, the channel was full of water. There would be no skipping across the sandbar that guarded the channel, which meant her shoes would get soaked again, and they had yet to dry out from their first dunking as it was.

For a split second she was angry all over again, and then the humor of the situation struck her and she burst out laughing. It was slightly uncontrolled, maybe even a little hysterical, but laughter it was, warming and cheering. She felt a lot better afterwards. It didn't even bother her when, halfway across, she tripped over a red salmon, lost her balance and fell in, getting all-over wet for the second time that day. What the hell, at least it was mostly fresh water this time. She got up, wrung out her hair and squelched up the bank.

Mary Balashoff's cabin perched at the edge of the trees across the creek, a plywood shack with tarpaper shingles and the long bow line of a skiff tied off to a cleat attached to the deck. It had a small porch hanging off the front door, and on this porch sat two figures, one small, one large. The small one had his chair tilted back and his feet up on the porch railings. The large one was rocking slowly back and forth in her rocking chair.

Kate was dripping water like a rain forest when she came to a halt in front of the cabin. Standing with her head bowed, she said, "I'm sorry, uncle. I was rude. Please forgive me."

He grunted. Taking his time, he put down his mug, removed his gimme cap to scratch tenderly at the back of his scalp, resettled the cap to his satisfaction and finally leaned over to reach down to a tray resting in front of the door. From a chipped china teapot he poured her a mug of steaming Russian tea, liberally sweetened with honey squeezed out of a plastic bear. She cradled the hot porcelain thankfully between cold, clammy hands. The tea scalded all the way down. Grateful, she took another long swallow, and Old Sam, teapot at the ready, topped off her mug again, adding another dollop of honey.

Implicit in his pouring of the tea was forgiveness. Implicit in her acceptance of it was their mutual understanding that at the first opportunity she would also apologize to Anne Flanagan. The proper balance of aged authority and penitent youth restored, the subject was dismissed.

Mary Balashoff looked from one to the other. Kate was serene. Old Sam was imperturbable. She shook her head. "Jesus, you Shugaks. I never will understand you."

Kate looked at Old Sam, whose mother had in fact been a Shugak, and smiled. He grinned back, his usual face-splitting, people-eating grin. "Well hell, Mary," he said, "can't let you pluck out the heart of our mystery, now can we?" He cocked a hopeful eyebrow at Kate, who valiantly swallowed any astonishment she might have felt at Old Sam Dementieff quoting Shakespeare on the shores of Alaganik Bay. Thwarted by her lack of response, he reached over and pinched Mary on the behind.

Again he was disappointed. Mary shook her head. "Shugaks," she repeated, and heaved herself to her feet. An amiable giant of a woman, she stood six feet, one inch in her stocking feet and had startlingly blue eyes at odds with her brown face and black hair. Back when such things were not done, her father, a handsome Aleut from Tatitlek, had run off with the beautiful daughter of a Norwegian seiner. Speaking of Shakespeare, Kate thought. The seiner, a proud and bigoted man, had washed his hands of the affair and returned to his Ballard neighborhood of Seattle, also known as Little Norway, righteously to declare himself to be without issue from that day forward.

It had been a happy marriage, so far as Kate could remember the tale, made all the more so by the fact that the union had scandalized the Tatitlekers as badly as it had the Ballardians, which allowed the couple to live in happy obscurity on a homestead outside of Copper Center, unhampered by advice from either family. They'd had five children, four boys and one girl, all of whom had blue eyes like their mother and black hair like their father and all of whom grew to a minimum of six feet in height. The boys went off to school, moved Outside and never came back. Mary had stayed, and by default had inherited the family setnet site.

She had been fishing it for thirty years. The Amartuq fish camp had been abandoned by federal decree for almost the same amount of time, and until the aunties had gone back up the creek a generation of Park children, including Kate, had learned to pick fish from Mary's skiff, to mend nets at Mary's knee, to fillet salmon and to tend the fire that burned beneath the drying racks after they had been filleted. Park parents had come to regard the Balashoff setnet site as on-the-job training for those offspring unlucky enough not to be chosen as deckhands.

Mary had also had a longtime summer romance going with Old Sam. Kate remembered this interesting fact just in time for Mary to save her from further speculation by saying, "Come on, honey. Let's get you into some dry clothes before you catch cold."

Kate, shivering now in spite of the tea, followed her inside, and emerged a few minutes later dressed in a worn Aran sweater that hung to her knees and a pair of jeans rolled up twice at the ankles and cinched at the waist by a frayed length of half-inch polypro and a thick pair of wool socks. She sat on the porch with her back to the wall, and at that moment the sun broke through the clouds and bathed the bay in a warm, golden light. It was nine-thirty, and with the sun came a small breeze that rippled the surface of the bay, rocking the boats gently at anchor.

Mary refilled the teapot and they drank in comfortable silence. At last Mary stirred. "What's this I hear about someone getting killed yesterday?"

"Let me guess," Kate said. "Wendell Kritchen bring you the news?"

Mary grinned, showing off a set of perfect white teeth. "He stopped by this morning."

"He's better than a town crier," Kate said, and left it to Old Sam to explain. Mary rocked, and listened.

When he was done they sat in silence. Out on the bay, a bowpicker's engine turned over. Its skipper weighed anchor and headed west, Cordova probably. Maybe he wasn't coming back. Maybe, like Old Sam, he didn't think fifty cents a pound was worth tearing up his gear for. Kate sighed.

"Couldn't have happened to a nicer guy," Mary said.

Kate looked from the bowpicker to Mary and back again.

"No," Mary said. "Cal Meany. Now there's a name was well deserved. He was one mean son of a bitch."

"How did you know him?"

Mary refilled her mug from the pot. "He cut my nets." She saw their expressions and smiled without humor. "Oh yes. And not just once. Twice. The first time was during last month's king opener. Snuck down and cut my gear from the anchor."

Mary's anchor was a heap of sandbags on the beach, tied together and attached to the beach end of the gear. The sea end of the gear was weighted with a small Danforth and marked with a fluorescent-orange buoy. When the tide came in, the corks floated to the top of the water and the net hung below, weighted at bottom by the lead line. The salmon, swirling in schools along the coast on a course for the creek, encountered the net en route, or hopefully some of them did, and got their gills stuck in the mesh. The thrashing of the caught fish in the water below caused the corks above to bob, at which time Mary would climb in her skiff and move up and down the cork line, hauling up the gear and picking the fish and then letting the gear drop down again. When the period was over, she pulled her gear and delivered the fish to the *Freya*. Or she did when not on strike.

And when her gear was intact. The anchor end cut, Mary's gear would float free, causing a hazard to boat traffic, not to mention that a free end was illegal as hell and Mary could be fined big-time for it, maybe even jailed, maybe—Kate went a little pale at the thought—maybe even have her permit pulled. "Did you see him?" Kate demanded. "Did you see Meany cut your gear?"

"Honey, if I'd've seen him, he would have been dead before now," Mary said flatly. "No, I didn't see him, or at least not that night. But he dropped by after the period was over. Said he'd noticed I was having some trouble. Said he knew how tough things were on a woman fishing alone. Said it couldn't get anything but tougher. Said he'd be happy to make me an offer on the site, and for my permit, too."

Kate looked at her for a moment, and then said deliberately, "I don't know if I really care all that much who killed this son of a bitch."

Old Sam grinned his cackling grin. "Now, now, what would Chopper Jim have to say to that?"

"Who gives a shit?" She said to Mary, "You say he did it a second time?"

Mary nodded. "This Monday. I went down at five to start setting up. This time he'd cut the cork line in half a dozen places." She drained her mug. "I was thinking maybe I should get a dog." She smiled at Kate. "Now I don't have to."

Kate's heart sank. "Mary."

Mary took one look at Kate's apprehensive expression and burst out laughing. "Oh honey," she said, still laughing. "Oh honey, if you could see your face." She wiped away a tear. "No, I didn't kill him. I'd like to pin a medal on whoever did, but I didn't do it myself."

Kate examined the level of tea in her mug with all the scrutiny of a Socratic scholar trying for the perfect dialectic on surface tension. "Where were you last night, Mary?"

Mary raised an amused eyebrow. "Why, I was right here,

Kate, right where I always am every night of the summer, right where I've been since the end of May, right where I'll be until the middle of September. And no, before you ask, there wasn't anybody here with me to say I was." She reflected. "Unless," she added with an air of innocence that fooled no one, "well, unless you count Edna and Balasha." Her smile was benign, and it didn't fool anybody, either. "They came to dinner, and we played pinochle until, oh, midnight I guess."

"Mary!" Kate said, indignant. "Why didn't you say so up front?"

Mary laughed again. "Sorry, Kate, I couldn't resist. Probably my only chance to be suspected of murder."

Old Sam was laughing, too. "You always were a pisser, Mary. Shame on you."

Kate finished her tea and let them laugh. The overcast had dissipated completely by now and the sunlight was warm on her face. Her hair, braided back into its usual plait, was still wet and as thick as it probably would be for another eight hours, but the rest of her was dry and comfortable. Her stomach growled.

Mary heard it. "Should I feed you?"

"Not just a woman but a god," Kate said.

"How's leftover pirogue sound?"

"Yum."

By the time the late dinner—creamed salmon and canned mixed vegetables in a flaky crust, Mary's specialty—was ready, Kate's clothes, hung over the stove, were mostly dry and she changed into them. They ate in silence on the porch, and when they were done Kate cleaned up and put water on for coffee, which she served, again on the porch. The sun was low on the western horizon, outlining what Kate thought was the hint of an incoming front. She wasn't worried. For now at least, her feet were dry and her stomach was full. "Mary?"

Mary, stretched out in her chair with her feet propped on the railing, sounded almost as sleepy as Kate felt. "What?"

"Did you see anything last night?"

"Like what?"

"Like anything, like any goings-on over at the Meanys'. Do you know what Cal Meany's drifter looks like?"

"The no-namer?" Without hesitation Mary pointed to where it rode at anchor. "Sure. Saw it come back last night."

"You did?" Kate sat up straight. "What time?"

Mary squinted thoughtfully at the horizon. "Was about the time the girls left, midnight or thereabouts. Well, maybe closer to one."

"Did the aunts see him, too?"

"They might have. They were in their skiff by then, and I was waving from the porch. We didn't get a chance to comment."

Gull had seen Meany in Cordova a little before ten-twenty. If Mary saw him at one, there was just enough time for a drifter with that much horsepower to get from point to point. "Could you see Meany?"

Mary shrugged. "Sure. He was on the flying bridge."

"Did you see his boy?"

Mary shook her head. "There was a light on in the galley, though. He could have been inside." She frowned.

"What?"

"Come to think of it, Meany had to shinny down off the flying bridge to drop anchor. If the boy had been on board, he would have been in the bow, wouldn't he?"

Kate wished her sympathies were not quite so much with

the boy; when she got good news of this kind it made her heart lift, and it was much too early in the investigation for her heart to be doing anything of the kind.

"Clumsy," Mary added.

"Who?"

"Meany, last night. Stumbling around the boat like it was midnight January instead of midnight July. Course it was the Fourth, he could have been drunk," Mary added. "Most of them were. Idiots."

"Yeah," Kate said, but absently. Gull had said something like that, something about Meany nearly stripping the gears on the drifter. Clumsy, on deck as well as on the throttle? The stories Mary and Gull told didn't square with what Kate had seen. Meany had moved with a feral grace, quick, nimble, never putting a foot wrong, always reaching for the proper tool and wielding it with a casual competence that elicited, however reluctantly, admiration and even envy.

She sat up with a jerk.

"What?" Mary said.

"Huh? Oh. Nothing." Kate relaxed again, eyes narrowed in thought. If Meany hadn't been acting like Meany, either at the small boat harbor or in Alaganik, maybe it hadn't been Meany on the boat. Maybe it had been someone else. Maybe even the murderer, trying to extend the span of Meany's life while he, or she, set up an alibi.

Mary said, "Just what was all that business today with you and Old Sam and the wet clothes?"

"What? Oh." Kate drained her mug. "I behaved like a horse's ass, and he pitched me into the bay for it."

Mary grinned. "That's my boy."

Kate wondered when in the last hundred years anyone

had called Old Sam Dementieff a boy. Probably only Mary Balashoff could get away with it. She nudged Old Sam with her foot.

He'd been dozing, his head resting on the back of his chair, his mouth open and a gentle, inoffensive little snore rippling out at regular intervals. "Ggggsnort?" he said, his chair falling forward on its two front legs. "What?" He knuckled his eyes and yawned, his bones popping audibly. "Guess I must have dozed off there. Sorry."

"We're not," Mary said maliciously. "Gave us a chance to practice our girl talk."

Immediately suspicious, Old Sam demanded, "Girl talk? What? What did I miss?"

"We'll never tell," Kate said, and got to her feet. "Want to take a ride up the creek?"

"What, up to the fish camp?" Kate nodded and Old Sam said, "Been a while since I got a chance to visit with the old girls."

For "visit" read "aggravate," Kate thought, but was wise enough not to say so out loud. One dunking a day was enough.

Mary said nothing, and after a sideways look at her, Old Sam added, "But I think I'll stay put. You go ahead, take the skiff, pick me up in the morning."

By some trick of the slanting rays of the setting sun the water assumed the color and viscosity of molten gold, seeming to slow their forward motion while at the same time lending a touch of splendor to the journey. Kate dipped a finger over the side and watched tiny eddies appear, looking like the gilt tracings she'd seen in a book once, something elaborate and baroque and Italian—Bernini?

She shook her head, glad she didn't have to justify her smile to Old Sam. Impossible to explain that a trick of light on water made her think of a sculptor born on the other side of the world four hundred years before. Although if he was going to start quoting Shakespeare at her she might suspect him of taking telecourses from the University of Alaska.

She passed half a dozen bears fishing and eating and roughhousing on a sandbank, three eagles playing tag in the treetops and a couple of white-tail deer drinking out of the creek, which in her opinion paid for the gas before she even got to fish camp. To put the icing on the cake, Mutt was waiting for her when the skiff nudged ashore, and greeted Kate with a joyous bark and a generous swipe of the tongue. Kate wiped her face on the sleeve of her shirt and gave Mutt an affectionate cuff up alongside the head. "Where were you when I needed you?" she said.

"And what's that supposed to mean?"

She looked up and saw Jack at the top of the bank. "I was attacked by Jedi this afternoon."

"I beg your pardon?"

"Never mind. It's better you should not know." She gave Mutt a final pat. "But you're coming with me when I have to go back there." Mutt appeared willing.

"Kate!" Johnny's head appeared above the top of the grass. "You're back!" He catapulted down the bank and grabbed her hand. "Come on! Come see what I've been doing!"

What he'd been doing was helping the four old women pick fish out of the fish wheel, head them, gut them, fillet them so that they were split into two halves still attached at the tail and hang them to dry. The rack inside the smokehouse was full, and the little fire beneath was smoking nicely. Some of the strips were already turning a rich, dark red. Kate's mouth watered. When the process was complete, the resulting product, when eaten, would smell up the house for three days afterwards, and your jaws would ache for at least that long, but oh, the taste. There was nothing like Auntie Joy's smoke fish, nothing.

But the rule was you didn't get any if you hadn't helped the process along, and in the waning light Kate pitched in, splitting lengths of alder (like Old Sam, Auntie Joy swore by alder for smoke fish) and taking a turn feeding the fire. Fish smoking was a long process, involving days and, depending on the weather, sometimes a whole week, during which time the fire could not be allowed to go out.

By the time the sun went down they were sitting around a fireplace constructed out of smooth rocks excavated from the stream bed. It wasn't really cold enough for one, but when you have been in and out of an Alaskan creek a dozen times in one day, the warmth of an open flame is a welcome thing. There was something very social about a fire, too, Kate thought, looking at the faces seated around it. Balasha and Edna had their heads bent over a quilt, gnarled fingers deft with needle and thread. It was a forget-me-not pattern, and Kate wished she had the guts to ask for it when it was done. Forget-me-nots were her favorite flower, the first to bud in the spring, the last to lose its blossoms in the fall, a tiny, exquisite, blue-petaled work of natural art. Balasha and Edna had appliquéd a delicate forget-me-not in the center of every square; when finished, the quilt was going to be drop-dead gorgeous. "You just made a forget-me-not quilt," Kate said, remembering the quilting bee at Bernie's the previous spring. They hadn't given her that one, either.

Edna bit off a thread. "We cut out pieces for four, same time all. Then we make."

Kate tried to sound casual. "So, who is this one for?"

Edna cocked an eyebrow. "You marrying up soon, Katya?"

Kate had to shake her head, and Edna heaved a mournful sigh and shook her own in response. "Then I guess this one we make for Dinah."

"She got the last one," Kate protested. The wedding was coming up the first week of September, over the Labor Day weekend, after fishing season and before hunting season. It was going to be a fly-in affair since Bobby had friends from Metlakatla to Nome who had expressed a firm desire to witness the event. While everyone in the Park hoped that the ceremony would precede the birth of Dinah and Bobby's first child, Dinah was already the general size and shape of a Babylonian fertility goddess. Already on tap as best man and maid of honor, Kate figured she might as well add godmother to her list of wedding day duties.

But she stuck to the point. "Dinah already got a quilt," she said, trying not to pout and whining instead.

"Then we save to give to someone else." Edna pointed a needle at her. "You get married up, you get a quilt. That's the rule."

Kate grumbled something beneath her breath.

Auntie Joy chuckled. She had discovered a patch of early salmonberries, and was sitting over a pot full of them which she had flooded with water to float the trash away, picking out leaves and twigs and berry worms. Auntie Vi was sitting across from her, helping, and as they skimmed bits of twig and tiny worms from the surface they gossiped in soft Aleut gutturals. They paused once, looking Kate's way, and not for the first time did she regret her father's insistence that she learn English and only English as she was growing up. The most schooling he had gotten was the short boot camp required of Castner's Cutthroats, and he had always felt at a disadvantage in the English tongue, something he was determined would not be experienced by his daughter. And Abel, of course, had known of his wishes and had brought Kate up accordingly, not that he spoke anything but English all his life. Her grandmother might have rectified the situation, if she hadn't been so much like her granddaughter in character, strong-willed and stubborn, that they fought incessantly from the time Kate was a child. Kate had not been inclined to take instruction from Ekaterina. She smiled at the thought.

Johnny was practicing the fine art of net mending on a square of ragged gear. The green plastic needle swooped through the mesh, hesitated and came back up. Auntie Vi raised an eyebrow at the resultant tangle, took the needle and in a few deft moves had the section of mesh hanging evenly. Johnny sighed heavily, but he took the needle back and tried again. Not a quitter, Johnny Morgan.

Like his father. He was sitting across the fire, looking at Kate with love in his eyes. He jerked his head toward the creek. She gave a tiny nod and got to her feet. Mutt, sprawled next to her, raised her head. "Stay," she said in a low voice, and with a voluptuous sigh Mutt stretched out again.

Jack let maybe forty-five seconds pass before following her, pretending they weren't all perfectly well aware of where he was going.

They rendezvoused at the skiff. "Hi," Kate said.

"I feel like a teenager sneaking out of his parents' house," Jack said.

She laughed. "Fun, isn't it?"

"Fun, hell," Jack said, and tackled her, toppling them both into the sand.

"Oof," Kate said.

"You taste like salt water."

"Um."

"And you smell like woodsmoke."

"Um," she said, and that was pretty much all she was allowed to say for the next few breathless moments, except for "Ouch!" and "Never mind, do it again." Things were rapidly approaching the point of no return when they both became aware of the advancing sound of an engine. They looked up. There was still plenty of light on this Arctic summer night, and coming straight up the creek fifty feet off the deck was George Perry in 50 Papa, the grin on his face matching the grin on the face of the trooper sitting in back of him. The port window was folded down, and over the noise of the Super Cub's engine George yelled cheerfully, "I'll set her down on that RPetCo strip about a mile upstream! Take your time!" They roared past. Chopper Jim even tipped his hat.

The mood had definitely been broken. "Goddammit!" A furious Jack was on his feet, beating the sand out of his jeans and buttoning his fly with clumsy fingers. "We're out in the middle of the goddam Bush and I still can't find enough privacy to get laid! What's next, a goddam grizzly walks in on us?"

From the other side of the creek, a goddam grizzly huffed at them, a salmon hanging from his mouth, before ambling up the bank and out of sight, enormous hindquarters shifting back and forth like perambulating beanbag chairs.

Jack whipped around and looked at Kate, his expression fierce. In the next moment, they both burst out laughing.

Kate tucked in her shirt and smoothed her hair back with a shaky hand. "We'd better go see what Chopper Jim's got."

"A fat lip, is what he's about to get," Jack muttered.

"Somebody's been killed, Jack."

His hands stilled on his fly. "What?"

"Last night. Or early morning. We found his body in the water this morning."

"In the bay?" She nodded. "A fisherman?"

She nodded again, and told him. He listened in frowning silence, and when she came to the end, said, "Why didn't you tell me before?"

She thought of the boy, Frank, and of the girl, Dani, and said, "I just wanted to forget about it for a while."

He examined her face, saw what he needed to there and nodded once. "We'd better get up to that airstrip."

Kate led the way back to the fire. "Auntie Vi? We're going to head up to the strip."

"We heard, Katya. Go careful. There is bears here."

The warning reminded Kate irresistibly of the warnings written on the margins of ancient maps: "There be dragons here." Mutt trotted ahead of her, and Kate took comfort in her presence. Unlike most dogs, Mutt did not go berserk at the sight of a bear. She was too smart and had been too well trained for that. At 140 pounds, standing well over three feet tall at the shoulder, she had backed down more than one bear, and would do so again. And it was July, after all; the bears had been eating since the first kings came up the creek in late May. A full grizzly was a happy grizzly, and less inclined to bother with anything lacking fins.

Or so she told herself, and took care to step on every piece of deadfall she could as she moved through the brush. The cracking and popping of dry wood breaking was a whistle past the graveyard. Behind her, she heard Jack doing the same thing.

The trail was faintly marked and bore signs of having

been recently pruned, the white gashes of lopped limbs glowing white against the trunks of alder and spruce and cottonwood. It was also darker in the brush, and once Jack tripped over an exposed root and staggered against her. "Sorry."

She caught his hands, which were interested in more than merely catching his balance. "Sure you are. Knock it off, Jack." He muttered something, sounding injured, and she bit back something that might have been a giggle.

He sensed it and snatched her up in his arms. The most protest she gave was a halfhearted wriggle, until she felt a tree press against her back. "No, Jack, we've got to get going." He dropped to his knees. "Oh." She swallowed. When she spoke again, her voice was breathless. "Really. They're waiting for us."

His words were muffled. "George told us to take our time." He looked up at her and grinned. "I'm just following orders."

She pushed at his shoulders. "Get up. No, dammit, I mean it." She slipped free, fastening her jeans, and sprinted out of reach when he came up off his knees and lunged at her. They romped up the trail, alternately led and pursued by a barking Mutt, both of them aware of and keenly enjoying a sense of play that had been missing from their relationship for a long time. Life was too short to be that grim, Jack reflected, and copped a quick feel before Kate darted out of reach again, laughing and warding him off. They emerged on the little gravel strip ten minutes later, out of breath, disheveled and light of heart.

The strip was within sound of the rush of water over stone, the more or less flat surface cut down to sand that sank beneath their feet. Good thing George's Super Cub was on tundra tires, Kate thought, enormous, cartoon-balloon tires dwarfed only by the acre of wingspan that made the Cub the quintessential Bush plane. It was drawn up at one end of the runway. George and Chopper Jim were standing next to it, waiting. Mutt caught sight of Chopper Jim, gave an enthusiastic yip and tore across the strip, sand flying, to greet him bigtime Mutt style.

"Is there a female in the Park that doesn't go weak at the knees at the sight of that guy?" Jack said from behind her.

"Not a one," Kate said cheerfully, and walked down the strip.

Jack, who had been expecting her answer to be, "One. Me," followed, disconcerted. What he was feeling was written plainly on his face, and she took care to keep her head turned away from him so he couldn't read her expression, which would call for retaliation big-time Jack style.

"Where's the Cessna?" she asked Jim as they walked up to the plane.

He shrugged. "I wasn't familiar with this strip, and there wasn't a beach around here long or flat enough to take her. And you know how the state frowns on employees dinging its property. I met George dropping off fish at the airport, so—"

Alaska pilots never wrecked planes, Kate remembered. They dented them, they dinged them, she'd even heard one pilot say he had pranged one, but they never, ever wrecked them. It was the difference between pilot error and calculated risk, another had told her. And of course no one ever admitted to pilot error, either.

"Besides," he added, "it's after legal twilight."

Hadn't stopped George, but then the pilot could fly in and out of most Bush strips blindfolded. "How'd you know where we were?" She looked at George.

George Perry was a tall thin man with a long thin face in perpetual need of a shave, wearing his habitual oil-stained overalls. "You weren't on the *Freya*. We flew over and asked Mary. Old Sam was there, and he pointed up the creek, so we figured you were at fish camp."

"And there you were, and in all your splendor, too," Chopper Jim observed. He might have ideas about Kate himself, but he was never needy enough to be jealous of another man's good fortune.

Or at least that was the attitude he was trying to project. Jack read something else in the gaze regarding him steadily from beneath the brim of the trooper hat, something perhaps only another man interested in Kate Shugak would see. "Up yours, Chopin," he suggested amiably.

Jim eyed Jack's six feet four with a speculative glance that took in the other man's ruffled hair and misbuttoned shirt and traveled on to the T-shirt that bore signs of being hastily stuffed back into the waistband of Kate's jeans. He reminded himself he was in uniform, and sent Jack a bland smile.

"What have you got, Jim?" Kate said, impatient with pissing contests of any kind, whether she was first prize or not.

"Well, not you, for starters," he murmured, breaking eye contact with Jack to smile down at her. "Oh, you meant Meany? Kinda forgot there for a minute. Well, the pathologist is a tad upset over Meany, Kate. She can't quite figure out how he died. There's water in his lungs, but his trachea is crushed, and then there is that knife, and unfortunately, the wound did bleed, so he was stabbed before he died." He paused, apparently thinking he might have missed something. He decided not. "That's about all she could tell me. She'll have more tomorrow, and the final report by Saturday, if her boss okayed the overtime. State cuts, you know." His mouth thinned, leaving them in no doubt of his opinion of legislative cutbacks to law enforcement.

"So we still don't know exactly when he died?" He shook his head, and Kate swore. "Dammit, Jim. If we don't know when, we're never gonna find out who. It's July, for crissake, it's light pretty much round the clock." She waved a hand for emphasis at the twilight sky that passed for night during an Alaskan July. "Somebody killed that many different ways has to have been seen going down for the third time, dammit!"

"Which reminds me," he said. "What'd you find out on your end?"

She gave him a look to let him know she knew she was being sidetracked. "He was beating on his son again at the cannery dock last night, admitted to by the son and witnessed by the whole damn beach gang, his wife and daughter are abuse victims if I've ever seen them, he moved in on the Ursins' setnet site and ran them off by threat if not by force, he cut Mary Balashoff's nets not once but twice during the past week and Gull is ticked because he tried to park in a space reserved for visiting dignitaries from Alpha Centauri."

Jim raised one very bland eyebrow. "Anything else?"

Kate took a deep breath, held it and then blew it out explosively. "Well, I didn't like him very much, either."

The three men laughed.

Kate, regaining her poise, said, "Old Sam says the whole bunch of them came here two years ago from Cincinnati, and from what his wife says, Calvin Meany has been driving them all like slaves ever since. You might want to check with the Cincinnati PD."

Chopper Jim knew what she meant; if Calvin Meany had

been skating close to the edge of the law in Alaska, chances were he'd been doing the same in his previous neighborhood.

"You might want to talk to the Ursins, too. They live in Anchorage. And of course you'll want to talk to the family yourself. And you'll need to check the boy's alibi. He says he stayed overnight with the Wieses, Paul and Georgina, before Wendell Kritchen told him about his dad and gave him a ride back to the site." Suddenly Kate remembered the daughter. "You ought to interview the daughter yourself, Jim. Try to get her off by herself. I'm pretty sure she was holding something back."

George, standing behind Jim, hid a grin. He'd ferried groceries and supplies out to the Meanys' site a time or two, had had a close encounter of the third kind with Dani and had escaped virtue intact literally by a wing and prayer. But Jim was a big boy. He could take care of himself. George only hoped he got to be there to watch him do so. He'd like to be present when a little of that famous Chopin aplomb went south for the winter.

No fool, Jim examined Kate's smile with suspicion. "Really?"

"Really," Kate said, with perfect truth, just not with all the truth. She did not, for example, warn Jim that he ought to don a chastity belt before he went within a mile of the place. Really, it had nothing to do with the case, did it?

"I'm staying at The Reluctant Fisherman tonight," Jim said. "I'll be back out tomorrow morning. I've talked to most of the fishermen in town today—I figure on getting to the rest of them out here. From what I understand, it had better be sooner than later, before they all get on a plane for Anacortes." He touched the brim of his hat and walked back to the Cub.

George waited while the trooper climbed into the back seat. He climbed into the front seat, pausing in the act of folding up the door when a thought struck him. "Hey, Kate!"

"What?"

"Tell Joyce I loved the invisible-dog leash float in the parade." He grinned.

"What parade?" Kate said blankly.

" 'What parade?' What kind of American are you, anyway, Shugak? The Fourth of July parade in Cordova. I flew out and picked her up. Sarah Nicolo decided they couldn't do their thing without her and chartered me to bring her in."

Kate vaguely remembered seeing George's Super Cub buzzing the jousting tournament the day before. It seemed like a long time ago.

"Anyway, Joyce was the leader of the invisible-dog team. It was a scream," George told Jack, "about a dozen old women walking those dog leashes, you know the ones all stiff that look like they have an invisible dog in them? Joyce and a bunch of the other gals, Rosie Pirtle and Monica Peters and Crystal Van Brocklin and Deliah Nordensen and I don't know who else, being hauled down the road by these invisible dogs. With Joyce in front those dogs didn't want to follow the parade route real strict, either, they barged through the crowd and the downtown playground and through the Alaskan Bar and around the post office and just generally broke everyone up. None of the old broads cracked a smile the whole time, either. What a riot, you should have seen it. Hell, I almost forgot." He leaned back and said something to Chopper Jim, who turned to rummage behind his seat, producing a cheap trophy and handing it forward. George thrust it out the window. "Here. Rosie sent that out for Joyce."

Kate took it automatically. With a final wave, George folded up and latched the window. The engine roared to life, the prop rotated and a minute later they were airborne.

Kate looked down to find that the object she was holding was a small wooden trophy, a fake brass five-pointed star on top and a thin fake brass plate affixed to the front. She held it up in the dimming evening light to squint at the words.

FIRST PRIZE
for Best Entry in
the Open Invitational All Alaska
Independence Day Parade
Cordova, Alaska

The four old women and Johnny were still seated around the fire, which had been recently built up. Berries and gear mending had been abandoned for Monopoly, the board unfolded on a large round of sawed-off tree stump, and from the pile of money and property accumulating in front of Johnny, not to mention the smug look on his face, it seemed that he was winning. He rolled the dice, cruised on up to North Carolina, which he owned, and trained the forward guns of his battleship on the Short Line, which he didn't.

Edna hopped one-footed around Go, landed her shoe on Baltic, collected two hundred dollars and handed it over to Johnny with a sigh. He owned Baltic, too, and she was staying at his hotel. She sighed again and mortgaged Boardwalk to pay off the rest of the rent.

Auntie Vi looked up at Kate and Jack's entrance into the clearing and said instantly,

"*Ayapu,* you two, you better go back in the woods and finish what you started."

"That's nothing," Johnny told her, "you ought to see them in town." He rolled his eyes. "*Mush,*" he added in his best Grumpy imitation. "Yuck."

Jack put one hand to the side of his son's head and shoved. Johnny collapsed in a heap of sand, giggling. Mutt bounded forward and attacked and they roughhoused around the yard until they very nearly dumped the Monopoly board. When it tottered, Kate distinctly saw Edna reach out and with a slight nudge of one stubby forefinger give it a slight assist. The pieces went everywhere. Johnny leapt up with a cry of anguish and began scrambling after them.

Kate raised an eyebrow at Edna. Edna, all round-eyed innocence, blinked back.

"Tea, Katya?" Auntie Joy said, holding out a mug. Kate traded it for Auntie Joy's trophy, reading out the inscription in fine round tones, adding an embroidered version of George's description of the winning entry. Edna and Balasha laughed heartily.

"So that's why you flew into town on the Fourth," Kate said, and at Auntie Joy's puzzled look added, "I saw you in George's Cub. I wondered."

There was a brief pause, and then Auntie Joy exchanged a look with Auntie Vi that Kate couldn't read. "Yes, I go to be in parade," Auntie Joy said placidly, bending over the berry bucket once more. But she'd left it a little too long, and Auntie Vi looked a little too impassive, and Kate wondered what they were up to. They were grown women, they could get up to anything they wanted to, but still, she wondered.

She found space on a log and sat down. Jack stretched out next to her, picking up a stick to poke the fire. A clump of sparks flew upward to dissolve against the pale sky, the closest they would come to stars for another two months.

A comfortable silence fell. Kate closed her eyes, the better to enjoy the warmth of the fire, letting the various woes of the day leach out through her skin.

When she opened them again, Auntie Joy was looking at her. With a trace of sternness, she asked, "What this I see in your face, Katya? What happens?"

Next to her, Jack went still. Next to him, Johnny, one arm around Mutt's neck, leaned forward with an inquiring look.

She told them of her discovery—was it only that morning?—of Meany's body, that it was obvious he had been murdered, that the trooper had drafted her into some legwork.

When she came to the end of the story, the comfortable quality of the silence around the campfire had changed. Auntie Joy's mouth was closed in a stubborn line. "What, auntie?" Kate said. "What is it? Do you know something about Meany?" The older woman remained silent, and Kate said, "If there is something, you have to tell me. He was killed. We have to find out who."

"Why?" Auntie Vi said bluntly. "That—" From the back of her throat came a grating Aleut word that meant exactly what it sounded like. The Aleut language had a thing or two to teach English about onomatopoeia. "That one not worth killing, Katya, but if someone did, we thank him."

Johnny's face had paled. He looked over at his father. Jack's gaze held a clear warning. The boy gave a tiny nod, and some of the color came back into his face.

Kate didn't notice; all her attention was on Auntie Joy. "How do you know Calvin Meany wasn't worth killing, auntie? When did you meet him?"

Auntie Joy remained stubbornly silent. With a sideways look at her sister's face, Auntie Vi said, "That one come up creek last Sunday."

"Here?" Kate sat up. "Meany came here?"

Auntie Vi nodded, but before she could speak Auntie Joy burst out, "He come up creek like he own it. He say he want fish camp, we should sell to him. Pah!" She didn't spit but she came pretty close. "No one own land. Land belong everyone."

There were fierce nods from the other three old women seated around the fire.

Auntie Joy made a visible effort, and went on more calmly. "So then that one say if land belong everyone, then everybody can come fish here. He will bring them." She paused. "We laugh at him."

Kate stiffened. "What did he do?"

Auntie Joy exchanged a glance with Auntie Vi, who was sitting like a wooden statue, the shadows of the fire flickering over the lines of her face giving an illusion of expression. "He get mad. He say he file for permit for lodge with Parks Service. He say if we don't have title, he can build lodge here. That true?"

"I don't know," Kate said slowly.

Jack stirred. "Iqaluk's title is still under deliberation, Kate. He probably could have, a temporary one anyway, if he greased the right palms. With all the budget cuts in Washington, the Parks Service needs money bad."

The refrain of the nineties, Kate thought.

Jack reflected, and added, "And then once Meany got the

lodge up, he could claim grandfather rights to it. The way the Park rats did when the government created the Park around their homesteads."

Kate thought this over. "Greedy just doesn't even come close to describing this son of a bitch," she said finally. "He jumped the Ursins' setnet site, he cut Mary's nets, not once but twice, and then had the gall to offer to buy her out. The setnet sites on both sides of the mouth, and the fish camp, too—he wanted all he could get of Amartuq Creek. Did he come here again, Auntie Joy?"

"No." But the old woman had hesitated, just a fraction of a second, before answering.

"Auntie?" Kate said. "Is there something else?"

Auntie Joy glared. "Nothing else," she said with finality. She got up and stamped off. Auntie Vi followed. Edna and Balasha exchanged glances, gave Kate apologetic looks and left, too.

They left behind a crackling fire, an uneasy niece and a father and son with secrets to share.

It was well after one when the skiff nosed out of the mouth of the creek. The northwestern horizon was lit with a golden glow where the sun had put his head down for a four-hour nap. On the right, the windows of Mary Balashoff's cabin were dark. On the left, the soft glow of one kerosene lamp turned low outlined the door of the Meany cabin. Kate fancied she could see Marian Meany sitting next to the open door, gazing out into the night, perhaps listening to the sound of her children breathing deeply, peacefully in sleep behind her. Neil Meany and Evan McCafferty would be sacked out in the hammocks out back. Offshore, the no-name drifter rode at anchor, one of the few boats left in the bay. Most of the fleet had headed for port.

Good, Kate thought. Chopper Jim could nail them one at a time as they hit the small boat harbor. She wondered if he'd stopped at the Meanys' on the way back to Cordova, to be exposed to the full glory of the Meanys' oldest daughter. The thought made her smile, and forget for the moment that she was alone.

This circumstance was brought about by Mutt's understandable inclination to remain on shore, where she could roughhouse with Johnny and terrorize the local wildlife with equal abandon, and also by Jack Morgan's inexplicable decision not to accompany her out to the *Freya*, where, she had made sure he was aware, they would have spent what remained of the night all by themselves. She had to return to spend the night on board because Old Sam was busy adding another chapter to the thick volume of carnal commerce with Mary Balashoff, and it was a standing order that the tender be manned every night it spent out of the harbor. It was Kate's turn on watch. Jack was regretful but firm. Kate pouted, and even that didn't work, but she couldn't do much more because Jack had Johnny on a short leash, trailing along behind him like a lamb on a tether. She came as close as she ever had to wishing Jack's marriage had been childless.

She putted across the bay alone, torn between feeling frustrated and feeling rejected. It was in this schizophrenic mood that she nosed up against the *Freya* and climbed on board, bow line in hand. Preoccupied, maybe even still pouting, she bent over to loop the line around a cleat, and totally missed the hiss of the boat hook through the air as it came down on the back of her head.

The night exploded in a sunburst of red, swallowed up by a great, engulfing wave of black into which she sank without a whimper.

It took a long time, it took what seemed like forever, before the black faded to gray, a drizzly kind of gray. A drizzle, in fact. She was wet clear through, and shivering, and she couldn't understand why. This was July; one did not shiver in July, not with the temperature consistently above fifty degrees, the big five-oh that signaled the beginning of summer each May. Hell, sometimes it got up to a scalding eighty degrees in Prince William Sound, a temperature hot enough to drain the enthusiasm out of the most competitive Alaska fisherman.

Wet again. After her adventures in dunking the previous day, by rights she shouldn't have to get wet all over again outside of the *Freya*'s head or the galvanized stainless-steel tub on her own homestead. What the hell was going on here? Her brow furrowed with temper, and she struggled to open her eyes. It wasn't easy, as they seemed stuck together, but eventually she pried them apart.

The first thing that met her gaze was a black-painted wooden surface that, after painful cogitation, she recognized as the deck of the *Freya*. Her cheek seemed to be pressed against it. Her whole body seemed to be pressed against it, in fact, although plastered might be a better word, because there was a steady drizzle coming down. The deck was wet, her clothes were wet, her hair was wet.

Beneath her wet hair, her head hurt, a deep throb that kept time with her heartbeat. She groaned, which only made it hurt worse. She stopped groaning.

There were two objects on the deck in front of her, two faded blue knobs sitting side by side that appeared to be connected to something. With an effort, she raised her eyes, and found Old Sam staring down at her, his wizened face bearing a disapproving frown. The knobs must be his knees, she thought hazily.

"What the hell's wrong with you, Shugak? You drunk or something?"

She didn't remember much about the next hour or so. Old Sam must have pried her up off the deck and helped her into the galley, where he stripped her and muffled her in the scratchy comfort of an army blanket and plied her with mug after mug of steaming coffee. When she'd regained consciousness enough to make herself understood, he examined the back of her head with uncharacteristically gentle fingers.

The probing hurt enough to cause silent tears to roll down her face. This terrified him, and he overcompensated by donning a bluff and hearty demeanor. "Not much harm done," he said in a tone determined to be cheerful. "You've got a lump the size of a baseball but the skin wasn't broken. You must have a skull like a rock. You'll be fine in a day or two." He rolled a towel and put it around her neck so she could relax without leaning her head against the wall. "Don't suppose you saw the asshole that did this?"

"No." She almost shook her head. "I was climbing up over the gunnel when— Wait." She paused. "No. I was already on deck, I think." Her eyes closed against the glare of the galley light, and she said, spent, "I don't know."

He grunted. "Well, whoever it was was looking for something."

She struggled to take an interest. "What do you mean?"

"I mean he thoroughly trashed my boat, is what I mean," Old Sam said grimly. "Look at 'er."

Painfully, Kate opened her eyes. It was true. Everything in the lockers was now out on the floor—dishes, pots and pans, canned goods, fish tickets, tender summaries, pens, pencils, tide books, a mending needle, a sliming knife. A bright orange swath that resolved itself into a survival suit sprawled awkwardly across the table. The color hurt her eyes. She closed them again. "How about above?"

Old Sam's voice hardened. "The same. He yanked the charts out of the shelves, he busted the goddam compass, your stuff's scattered from hell to breakfast." He paused, and added with menace, "I sure wish you'd caught him in the act, Shugak."

"I think I did," she murmured, slipping into a doze.

She woke up sprawled across Old Sam's bunk, and turned her head to find Chopper Jim standing there, staring down at her, hat for once in hand. "Hey," she said.

"Hey backatcha," he replied.

She ran her tongue around the inside of a mouth that felt as if it were stuffed with cotton wool. "Water."

He left and returned with a full glass, putting an arm around her shoulders and holding it to her lips. She gulped gratefully. "Thanks," she said, stretching back out.

The tiny stateroom boasted a single chair. The trooper tipped it forward to let the dirty clothes heaped on it slide to the deck and seated himself next to the bunk, unzipping his jacket and adjusting his holster. "Tell me about it."

"Nothing to tell," she said, wincing when an unwary movement made her head throb. "I came back to the boat after one. Somebody coldcocked me coming on board. I never saw him."

"Amateur," he said.

A reluctant smile widened her mouth. "Prick."

They sat in peaceful silence. After a bit she felt well enough to scoot up against the bulkhead. Jim shoved a pillow behind the small of her back. "Thanks." She closed her eyes again. "What did you find out in Cordova?"

He produced a notebook and thumbed through it. "First off, the boy's alibi holds up. The beach gang saw him leave the dock with his father alive and well on the deck of his drifter, and the Wieses say he showed up at their house right after and stayed the night."

Unconsciously, Kate's breast lifted in a long, relieved sigh. "Good. How about the autopsy?"

He flipped a few pages. "Time of death, roughly midnight."

"Roughly?"

He shrugged. "The Gulf of Alaska's mean temperature is forty-two degrees. The body was floating around in it for at least six hours. It tends to foul up all the techies' fancy-dandy tests. And Kate? He drowned."

"What?"

He held up a hand, palm out. "He had help. His trachea was crushed, and there was water in his lungs."

"What kind of water?"

"Salt."

"So. Could have been either the harbor in Cordova or Alaganik Bay. Any way we can find out which?"

He shrugged. "Lab's running more tests. It won't help," he added with the jaded wisdom of long experience. "They'll find trace amounts of oil and gas in the water, but with as many boats as have been fishing Alaganik there's probably not much difference in composition between this bay and the harbor."

"There's a lot more glacial silt in Alaganik Bay, washed down from the Kanuyaq. They ought to be able to identify the water from that alone."

"Maybe." He didn't sound convinced. In his years as an Alaska state trooper, Chopper Jim had not had much cause to put a whole lot of faith behind forensic evidence, which in his experience led, in court, to a face-off between opposing so-called expert witnesses, each of whom contradicted everything the other said, leaving the jury more confused than enlightened and, consequently, resentful enough to take it out on the prosecution. Like most in law enforcement, he leaned toward catching the perp at the scene, weapon in hand, preferably in the presence of three eyewitnesses, one of whom was a priest.

"So the knife went in after the fact?" Kate said.

"Yup."

"After he was strangled and drowned, somebody stabbed him."

"Uh-huh."

"I hate the weird ones." Kate tried to figure out a scenario to fit the evidence, but the effort made her dizzy and her head started to hurt again. "What else? What about the cuts and bruises on his face and torso?" Something in the quality of the ensuing silence made her eyes snap open. "What, Jim?"

He made a pretense of consulting his notes. "After Meany delivered, he went over to the fuel dock and topped off his tanks. Shortly after which he had a visitor."

Kate made a face. "Female, no doubt."

"You're such a prude, Shugak," he complained. "Anyway, they both left the boat about six-thirty, according to Otis Swopes, the Standard Oil guy. Otis identified the lady as one Myra Sarakovikoff. And, of course, Otis lost no time in telling the tale to the first guy to wander by, in this case one Wendell Kritchen, also known as the Mouth of the Sound."

Kate closed her eyes again. "Shit."

"Yeah. You can almost guess what happened next."

"Tim Sarakovikoff came home."

"You win first prize. Not only home, but he tied up to the fuel dock right next to Meany's drifter, and took on the story from Otis and Wendell while he was taking on fuel." Chopper Jim smoothed his already immaculate hair. "Tim took off uptown. According to approximately twenty eyewitnesses, he caught up with them at the Cordova House. Whereupon he proceeded to beat the living shit out of Meany. Dick Bynum's words, not mine," he added. "Dick seemed kind of admiring. One might even say jubilant. He got a good-looking wife?"

"Yes."

"Thought so," Jim said, satisfied, and making a mental note to check out Dick Bynum's good-looking wife at his earliest opportunity.

"What happened next?"

"Near as I can figure, everybody went into the bar and

celebrated, leaving Meany bleeding on the sidewalk. This was the Fourth of July, Kate, and the celebrating started early on."

"No one's memories are all that clear," Kate suggested, and he nodded. "Shit," she said again.

"I heard that," he agreed.

"Myra?"

"Myra was on the first plane out of Mudhole Smith this morning, on her way to Anchorage."

"Did you talk to her first?"

"No," he said regretfully. "But I phoned APD, talked to Sayles. He said he'd track her down, get her statement."

She had to ask, even if she wasn't sure she wanted to know the answer. "What does Tim say?"

"I haven't talked to him yet. He wasn't home, he wasn't at his mother's house, and his boat's gone from the harbor."

She sat where she was for a few moments, and then swung her legs over the side of the bunk.

"Whoa there," he said, stretching out a hand.

"Help me up." She grabbed his arm and pulled herself upright. With this sudden ascent to the vertical her head felt as if there were no more than three jackhammers working on it at the same time. "Come on."

"Sure, Shugak," he said, the drawl back. "You might want to put on some pants first, though."

She looked down and saw that Old Sam had stripped her to T-shirt and panties. She swore halfheartedly and went to lean up against the wall. "In the chart room."

She waited. There was an eruption of male voices, followed by the angry thud of feet. The door crashed back on its hinges. Old Sam glowered at her. "Get your ass back in bed, Shugak."

She managed a grin. "Not even if you crawl in there with me, Old Sam."

He swore and snorted and in the end stamped off, outrage evident in the set of his shoulders. Chopper Jim returned with a pair of Kate's jeans in one hand and socks and Nikes in the other. He held the jeans for her to step into, and waited until she was working on the second leg before observing, "I've always dreamed of doing this. It's just that in my dreams I'm helping you out of your pants, not into them." She had no comeback and he was mildly alarmed.

Leaning heavily on his arm, Kate shuffled out on deck and up into the bow, trying not to throw up along the way. What with the strike, most of the boats were back in the harbor. There couldn't have been more than ten left, and it was easy to pick out the neat lines of the *Esther*. She pointed it out.

"Think Old Sam'll loan me his skiff?" Jim said.

"If I go along," she said, lying in her teeth.

He turned his head and looked at her. The cost of remaining upright was reflected clearly in the pale, taut lines of her face. "You know, Shugak, you give the word 'stubborn' a whole new meaning."

Tim saw them aboard with an impassive expression belied by the shiner he was sporting, and returned to his work. He was mending a hole in his net, and the green plastic needle with the Gothic arch to its tip looked tiny and fragile as he wove it deftly back and forth. His knuckles were swollen and bruised, which could have been from launching and hauling a hundred feet of gear every six hours, with or without salmon in it. Picking fish was as hard on the hands as it was on the back.

He didn't seem surprised when Jim told him why they were there. He even admitted to the fight.

Of course even the weather knew better than to rain on Chopper Jim, and the overcast had turned into a high, broken layer of cumulus clouds with enough blue sky between to allow shafts of golden sunlight to ripple across the water, illuminate the peaks of the Ragged Mountains and the erect figure of the trooper, dwarfing the deck of the bowpicker. The Alaska state trooper uniform was very distinctive, and even if it hadn't been, there was no mistaking that hat. Every boat left in the bay had its whole crew on deck, and Kate wondered how far their voices were carrying.

As if she'd spoken aloud, Tim's voice was low. "I wanted to kill him."

"But you didn't," Chopper Jim said, "is that what you're telling us?"

Tim's smile was lopsided and rueful. Not much was left of the joyous high boat of the season opener. "Didn't get the chance."

"Why not?" Kate said.

"Auntie Joy made us quit," he said.

Kate's heart skipped a beat. "What?"

"That would be Joyce Shugak?" Jim said.

Tim nodded, contemplating his hands, the bruises already fading to yellow, the scrapes drying to black crusts.

"Tell us about it," the trooper said. "All of it."

It was a short story. Tim Sarakovikoff had left Alaganik Bay at one minute past six p.m. precisely on Wednesday afternoon, when it was evident that the Independence Day celebration had reached a point where no one was going to be doing any fishing. By eight, maybe a little past, he was tied up at the fuel dock and, as they already knew, had been met by Otis and Wendell, eager harbingers of humiliation.

Tim's face, so open, so honest, so completely without guile, darkened like a thundercloud. "They'd seen him, they said, and her, going at it right on the deck of his boat. Right in the harbor!" His voice went up an octave, and all at once Kate was reminded of how young he was.

Jim gave one of those all-purpose trooper grunts that indicated comprehension, sympathy and the determination to slog away at the facts until the whole truth and nothing but was arrived at, if they both had to sit there till the last trump.

Tim must have recognized it for what it was because it didn't require any further prompting for him to continue. "I caught up with them on First. Looked like they were headed for our house. Probably wanted to try out our bed." Tim's broad shoulders moved in a shrug. "I didn't let them get that far."

"You confronted him?"

Tim gave a short, unamused laugh. "Yeah, I guess you could call it that." He looked down and picked up a section of mesh that was lying on the deck between his feet. The green twine was tangled and torn, a piece he'd taken out of his gear and replaced. "Myra was scared. She ran. Meany didn't even try to deny it. He laughed at me, said Myra wouldn't have come prowling around him if I'd been taking good enough care of her at home. So I hit him." He raised his hands, backs up, displaying the wounds of honorable battle. "Guy had a jaw like the blade on a D-nine. I thought every bone in my hand was broken, but I didn't stop. I keep hitting him, and I guess I was so angry he couldn't get through, except the one time." He touched his shiner. He raised his head and looked at Jim.

"To tell you the truth, Jim, I don't know what would have happened if Auntie Joy hadn't stopped me. I just hit him, and hit him, and hit him. It felt good. It would have felt even better to have kept on hitting him."

"But Joyce Shugak broke it up."

Tim nodded, looking suddenly exhausted. "I think she came out of the Cordova House. There were a bunch of people in there. Anyway, she brought out a pitcher of ice water and threw it on me. It shocked me, and I stopped."

Jim made another note. "What kind of shape was Meany in?"

Tim shook his head. "On his hands and knees. He was okay enough to call me a bunch of names."

"And then?"

"And then Auntie Joy chewed on my ass for ten minutes, and then she picked Meany up and took him away."

Kate jerked erect in a movement that made her head throb and the low-level nausea surge threateningly to the back of her throat.

Jim noticed the sudden movement and eyed her curiously. She said nothing, and he turned back to Tim. "And then?"

Tim shrugged again. "And then I went up to the house and kicked Myra out."

Good for you, Kate thought, momentarily diverted. As young as Tim was, she had feared the romantic in him would be willing to forgive all for love.

"If there was one guy, there would have been others," Tim added. "I can't—I won't live with that."

Jim gave the grunt again, examining his notes with a critical air. "About what time was this, do you remember?"

"Oh hell." Tim let his head fall back on his shoulders and thought. "Had to have been eight-thirty, nine o'clock anyway. Maybe a little past. I don't know for sure. I pulled the plug on Alaganik at six."

"Where did you go after you left Myra?"

"Out to the Powder House. Got drunk as a skunk. I don't remember the rest of the night too well." Tim tied off a knot, cut the twine and set the needle aside. "I woke up the next morning on the *Esther*. I couldn't stand being around town, with everybody probably talking about it and all. So I came on back out. Been here since." He sighed. "Might never go back."

Jim made another note. Tim watched him. "Could have been worse, I guess," he said.

"How so?" Jim said.

Tim gave a wan smile. "She could have been screwing you."

As he was assisting Kate up over the side of the *Freya*, Jim said casually, "What's bothering you about Joyce, Kate?"

Damn him, he'd always been quick as a snake. Not that Kate had ever seen a snake, but she could well imagine one with Chopper Jim's sly expression on it, and with Jim's habit of striking out at precisely the one thing in a conversation you hoped he would miss.

"What?" Old Sam said, hauling up Kate from the other end. "What are you talking about, what's wrong with Joyce?"

"Nothing," Kate said, shaking off her tugs. She was feeling better; she could inhale without wanting to barf the air right back out. Upon investigation her belly felt hollow. "What's for breakfast?"

"Try lunch," Old Sam said. "How about pork chops and applesauce?"

Pork chops and applesauce was Kate's favorite meal in the whole world. As a child she'd gotten it only as a special treat because none of the Park rats raised pigs and, after you added on the air freight, pork in the Park was more expensive than filet mignon in New York City. Old Sam knew this perfectly well, and Kate realized that the offering of pork chops and applesauce was his way of showing his affection, alleviating his anxiety and ministering to her needs. Not that he would for a moment outwardly demonstrate anything of the kind; if challenged, he would have said the goddam chops were freezer-burnt and they might as well start using up some of the applesauce before the whole goddam case rusted out in the damp air of the focsle. "Sounds great," she said.

"Good," he said gruffly. "I'll serve it up."

When Old Sam cooked, he cooked comprehensively. There were, besides the aforementioned pork chops and apple-sauce, chicken adobo, sweet and sour spareribs (Old Sam had taken a course in Filipino cooking from his previous deck-hand, a man from Seldovia who left him to open a restaurant in Homer), mashed potatoes, creamed corn, green beans with bacon and onions, and fruit salad. Kate spooned some of the fruit salad on her plate and said, "Hey, great, no marshmal-lows. You remembered."

Old Sam frowned ferociously. "We're out."

"Oh." Kate prudently said no more on the subject and fell to without delay. Chopper Jim had laid hat and jacket aside and tucked a napkin into his collar; the view from her end of the galley table indicated that he only just managed to refrain from wallowing in his plate like a hog in a trough. Kate didn't blame him. Everything was delicious, and when she finished she sat back and reflected on how nearly impossible it was to despair on a full stomach.

That comfortable, almost complacent thought was challenged in the next thirty seconds, when Trooper Chopin pushed back his plate, complimented Old Sam extravagantly on his table d'hôte and announced his intention of visiting Joyce Shugak at the fish camp. Kate's head snapped up. Chopper Jim met her gaze with an unwavering stare. He was determined, and she knew he was not going to be sweet-talked, sidetracked, misled or otherwise diverted this time. "Okay if we take the skiff again?" she asked Old Sam.

Jim took this determination to accompany him without a blink, although he did say, when they had cast off, "You remind me of this German shepherd I used to know, the better half of a K-nine team. Ornery, overprotective of his handler and frankly a colossal pain in the ass." He smiled gently at her stiffening expression, and pointed out, "I did say he was the better half."

She did not dignify his observation with a reply.

The bay was a mirror in which the Ragged Mountains regarded themselves with approval, until the wake of the skiff opened a widening V in the still surface and their reflection broke into a collection of fragments that rolled and rippled ashore, cast up on a gleaming expanse of gravel that divulged no secrets.

From on and above the waterline, various sets of people watched their progress, but only Mary Balashoff, with either audacity or a clear conscience or both, waved.

The fish wheel was shut down. Judging from the wear and tear of gravel leading to it, it had definitely seen recent and vigorous action. So much for state-imposed fishing periods, Kate thought wryly, or federally imposed injunctions, for that matter.

The skiff nudged on the gravel. Mutt heard them first, and bounded down to greet Kate with enthusiasm and Jim with ecstasy. Jack's greeting to Kate was wary, which baffled her. He was also, when he saw Jim, alarmed and, if she read the flash of emotion that crossed his face, embarrassed.

The four aunties brought up the rear, not descending to the water's edge but lining up on the creek bank, looking more than ever like four birds sitting on a branch, cedar waxwings maybe, all fluffed out against the winter chill. Cedar waxwings, Kate remembered, had black masks like raccoons, which made them look like cartoon bandits, or punk rockers. The aunties looked like neither, but there was a palpable air of solidarity about them, especially in their united regard of the trooper, and her heart sank. "Where's Johnny?" she said, trying to keep her voice light.

Jack, with an obvious effort, managed to match her lightness. "Downstream slaughtering salmon."

"Decided to strike out on his own, did he? Funny, we didn't see him on the way."

"Maybe a grizzly ate him."

"Nah." Kate shook her head. "Too full of fish."

"And he's got the twelve-gauge," his father added, reassuring himself.

Jim, once he managed to fend off Mutt's advances, doffed his hat and spoke directly to Auntie Joy. "Joyce, I'm sorry to have to bother you, especially at fish camp"—thereby showing respect for both age *and* culture, Kate thought in grudging approval—"but I understand you were a witness to a fight between Calvin Meany and Tim Sarakovikoff in Cordova the night of the Fourth." He paused. Auntie Joy said nothing, and he added, "I'm sure you've heard by now that Meany was killed that night. I'm tracking his movements, trying to find out who saw him when."

Auntie Joy looked at him with a blank expression and no reply.

One of the most effective tools an Alaska state trooper had was the quality of expectant silence that followed a question. They were taught it in trooper school, along with the need to establish one's authority at the beginning of an interview. His height, clad in all that dazzling blue and gold, and what Kate had once referred to as his Dudley Doright demeanor generally proved effective for the latter; for the former, Jim was relying on tried and true interrogative tradition.

However, in the matter of expectant silence an Alaska state trooper is no match for a villager from the Alaskan Bush who has been trained from birth to listen to her elders, to the land, to the river, to the very wind itself, before she opens her mouth to pronounce upon any subject, if she ever feels the need to do anything of the kind. The aunties sat tight in their little round row and waited for what the trooper would say next.

So Jim, not inexperienced in dealing with tribal elders, played dirty. He hooked a thumb at Kate. "Whoever it was probably bashed your niece over the head last night and left her for dead on the deck of Old Sam's tender. In the rain," he added, piling it on.

Jack's eyebrows snapped together. Kate, who had left her bandage back on the *Freya* precisely to prevent unwanted and unnecessary solicitude from either the aunties or the big man with the increasingly pissed-off expression, resisted the natural impulse to put her Nike right up Jim's elegant navy-blue back-side. "I'm okay," she said. "Really," she said, warding off Jack with an upraised hand. "Auntie," she said, stepping forward and addressing Auntie Joy directly, "Tim says you broke up his fight with Meany. Is that true?"

Auntie Joy said nothing.

"Kate," Jack said, "we've got to talk."

She shook off his hand. "In a minute. Auntie, Tim says you helped Meany after the fight. Did you take him somewhere? To Uncle Nick's house, maybe?"

Auntie Joy said nothing.

Behind Kate Jim stirred. "I think you'd better come back into town with me, Joyce."

Kate whirled. "No!"

Jim said, not without sympathy, "Kate, I don't see that I've got any other choice. She's a material witness to the hours directly preceding Meany's murder. She's not cooperating. What the hell else do you expect me to do?" He paused. "I could arrest her for withholding evidence, what do you say?"

From behind the aunties a new voice spoke. "You'll have to wait your turn, Jim."

Everyone looked up to see Lamar Rousch standing be-hind Auntie Joy, along with a very tall man with an abundance of gray hair and a smug expression on his face.

The gray hair was natural, the smug expression acquired. Bill Nickle had come into the country fifty years before, ap-prenticed as a deckhand on a seiner, worked his way up to skipper and made a pile of money during the golden days of commercial salmon fishing in the seventies. Like Meany, he put his family to work for him, to such good effect that within eleven years his sons had taken over boat and business for their own.

Bill never forgave them, and came up with the perfect revenge, starting a professional sport-fish guiding operation and agitating in the legislature at every session for reductions in the commercial catch. Over the past ten years, and with the influx of tourists into the state, he had graduated from being a petty annoyance to the commercial and subsistence fishermen to a very real threat. It didn't help that he was smart, informed, articulate, and charming when he wanted to be.

He wasn't bothering today.

"What are you talking about?" the trooper said.

"I've got prior business here," Lamar replied, and turned to Auntie Joy. "Joyce, Bill's brought it to our attention that you've been violating the federal prohibition on fishing Amartuq Creek. I'm here to serve you with a cease-and-desist order."

"Now wait just a minute—" Jim said.

"You're a little late, aren't you, Lamar?" Kate said.

"I don't know what you're talking about, Kate," the fish hawk said, trying and failing to look like it.

"Then permit me to enlighten you. She's been fishing this creek for the last five years."

The tall, gray-haired man bristled. "The main reason the sport fishermen's quota gets cut every year!"

Jack snapped, "Right, Bill, like there aren't commercial fishermen scooping up entire schools of fish the other side of the marker every period the whole friggin' summer."

"That's a goddam lie," Lamar said, his pink skin flushing scarlet to the roots of his blond hair.

"Not to mention a couple hundred trawlers with mile-long nets sucking up every living thing off the bottom of the north Pacific Ocean. Somehow I doubt that one piddly little fish wheel on Amartuq Creek counts for much in the grand scheme of things."

"Especially when the Fish and Game cut the catch on the creek and don't bother cutting it in the bay," Kate said hotly. "Like hauling entire schools of fish out of Alaganik doesn't have anything to do with the decline of reds up Amartuq Creek."

"Dammit, Kate!" Lamar said, his baby cheeks going pinker. "We don't have any numerical proof of that!"

"Now look," Jim said, trying to reestablish his authority with a deep, carrying voice, "Joyce is my witness, and I—"

"You subsistence fishermen think the world revolves around you. It's time the sport fishermen got a crack at the take, and by God, I'm going to see to it we do!"

"You only think you will, you fly-fishing son of a bitch," Kate snapped.

"I know I will, you—" His gaze encountered Jack's and he derailed that train of thought just in time. "We've got interests in this area," he said tightly. "Vested interests, and financial backing. We can generate more money in licenses and guiding and food and lodging than a piddly little fish camp that ain't good for nothing but providing dog food for a bunch of old-timers that'd be better off in the Pioneer Home anyway!"

Auntie Vi said something in Aleut that sounded distinctly uncomplimentary.

The old fart reddened. "You've got your orders, Lamar, from the commissioner himself. Serve her."

"Over my dead body!"

"That can be arranged, Shugak!"

"Quiet!" Chopper Jim bellowed out the command with all the authority of twenty-five years of experience.

It didn't silence the Amartuq Creek Debating Society, but it woke up a peacefully slumbering grizzly male in a clump of diamond willow across the creek, who had been sleeping off the stupefying effect of a dozen early silvers gulped for brunch. Jim's bellow startled him to his feet, where he tripped over a branch, somersaulted down the bank and into the creek with a tremendous splash, followed by an even more tremendous bawl of outrage that flushed birds from every tree in sight, startled a yearling moose out of a thicket and caused a family of otters to vacate their fishing hole for less boisterous habitation downstream.

The party on the opposite shore stared, finally and mercifully dumbstruck, as the grizzly, grousing and whining and generally indicating his displeasure with rude awakenings in general and this one in particular, shook himself off and lumbered up the bank, crashing through the brush in high dudgeon.

The noise of entire trees being felled seemed to go on forever, until the watching group began to realize that something else was crashing through the brush on the opposite side of the stream, something coming toward them. Jim put his hand on the flap of his holster. It was the first time in their acquaintance that Kate had seem him reach for his weapon. Just as his hand closed over the pistol butt, Johnny burst from the enveloping alders about twenty feet down from where the grizzly had disappeared. He and the grizzly must have passed each other like semis on an interstate, Kate thought, watching as the boy seemed to race across the top of the water in their direction. He was yelling something inarticulate at the top of his voice. His face was red, his hair on end, and he looked frightened out of his wits.

Mutt barked once and launched herself into the water, which quickly became too deep for walking. She paddled, inches ahead of Jack, who had moved smartly into the water a second behind her. Father and son and dog met at midstream, dog grabbed at son's sleeve and held him steady until father arrived and plucked son out of the water, tucked him beneath his right arm and plowed to shore, dog bringing up the rear. They collapsed heavily on the sand, panting and soaked to the skin. Mutt waded ashore and shook herself vigorously, which got everybody else wet, too, and went to Johnny to poke at him with her nose, an anxious whine rising up out of her throat.

The boy rested his forehead on her neck for a moment. "I'm all right, girl." He looked up. "I'm all right, Dad. Really."

When Jack got his breath back he yelled, "Then what the hell was that Charge of the Light Brigade all about!"

Johnny winced at the volume. "I found a body," he said, and his face contorted. "It's her, Dad!"

"You what!"

"Shut up, Jack," Kate said rudely, and shoved him to one side, Jim breathing down her neck. "Johnny, take a couple of deep breaths. Auntie, bring a blanket, and something hot to drink. Come on," she said to the boy, "get up out of the sand, sit on this log." She knelt before him in the sand and started untying his boots. He uttered an inarticulate protest and she brushed aside his fumbling hands. "Let me. You need to warm up."

Jim paced around in the background while blankets and hot tea were fetched and Johnny was stripped and swathed and dosed. "Okay," he said finally, "enough. Johnny, tell us about this body."

The boy huddled inside the blanket, shaking hands clutching the mug. "It's her, Dad," he repeated.

"Who her?" Kate said sharply.

Johnny didn't hear her, his eyes fixed painfully on his father. "The girl you saw the other night?" his father said. "Are you sure?"

The boy nodded, teeth chattering as much from shock as from exposure, and then he shook his head. "It's her hair, Dad," he said, and his eyes filled with tears. "I could see her hair."

"Did you see her face?" Kate said sharply.

Johnny shook his head violently. "No. I couldn't—I touched her and she was all cold and stiff. I just couldn't."

Kate got to her feet. "Show us."

The reason Kate and the trooper hadn't seen the body on the way up was because it was lying in a bend of the creek where a small brook had cut a smaller backwater into the bank, leaving a crescent-shaped sliver of beach and a prime fishing hole. They must have passed Johnny on the way, the rush of the creek and the noise of the kicker drowning out his passage.

They grounded the skiff and climbed out. "I spotted the hole on our way up on Wednesday," Johnny said, in dry clothes, wet hair tousled from a hasty finger-combing. "There were fish jumping everywhere."

"Oh there were, were there?" his father said with a determined attempt at flippancy. "And didn't think to share 'em with your old man, I suppose?"

Johnny gave a ghost of a smile. "Guess I forgot."

His father snorted.

The repartee, if not easy, eased the tension among the four of them, and made it easier for Johnny to point to the dark shape lying half in, half out of the water. "I didn't see her at first, I—I must have walked right by her. See, you can get to the beach across that fallen tree." He swallowed hard. "Then the hook got caught, and I walked the pole around the beach trying to free it up, and—well, that's when I saw her."

"Did you touch anything?" Jack said.

"Of course not!" Johnny retained enough spirit to be indignant at the very suggestion of such a thing. "You always tell me you're not supposed to touch anything, that the crime scene is as important to the investigation as the corpse, and sometimes even more."

"So I do." By way of apology, Jack removed his Mariners cap (signed personally by Ken Griffey, Jr.) for the sole purpose of putting it on Johnny's head and tugging it down over his eyes. "Daa-ad." Johnny's protest was halfhearted. He resettled the cap so he could see, and then turned his back to stare determinedly creekward as the others went to look.

The bank had been cut away by the eroding force of rushing water, and the resulting strip of land was mostly gravel at this point. Sand would have been better for tracks. The gravel was churned up, but that could have been as much by spring runoff and fishing bears as by any human passage. Cottonwood and alder and some currant bushes grew right out to the edge of the overhanging bank, and one spruce tree had had the roots washed out from beneath it and had fallen over, bridging the brook.

Branches had been broken from the top-facing surface of the fallen tree and the bark had worn away, but that could as easily be from exposure to weather as from traffic. The traffic didn't necessarily have to be human, either, as witness the porcupine chewing peacefully on an alder branch, who rattled his quills at the trooper in his own demonstration of civil disobedience and trundled off unhurriedly.

The body was lying facedown, head toward the brook, feet toward the creek, limbs sprawled out, blond hair darkened by the water spread out around her head in a swirling halo. Jack pointed, and Kate and Jim nodded. They could all see the darker patch on the left side of the back of her head.

"Let's get her out," Jim said, his voice curt.

Rigor was well established and the body flopped over like a starfish. The skin of the face was dark with lividity. The eyes, mercifully, were closed.

The trooper hunkered down on his knees and with one hand investigated the back of her head. "One blow. Her skull feels like mush back here."

"Probably didn't know what hit her," Jack said.

"No," the trooper agreed, his even tone belied by the fury in his eyes.

Kate stared down at the youthful face, and said to Jack, "Was Auntie Joy at fish camp last night?"

He looked at her with a good deal of understanding, and something else, something she was too caught up in her own concerns to notice or to interpret. "Yes."

"All night? You're sure?"

"Yes." He jerked a thumb over his shoulder. "My son the venture capitalist was whupping our asses at Monopoly until midnight. We're sleeping outside. I would have woken up if anyone had left the cabin during the night."

"All right," she said, unable to repress the wave of relief that swept over her, and immediately ashamed of it. To Jim she said, "This is Dani Meany."

Jim jerked erect. "Cal Meany's daughter?"

She nodded. If Dani Meany's murder was connected to Cal Meany's, as seemed likely, if they had been killed by the same person, which seemed even more likely, and if Auntie Joy had an unshakable alibi for the previous night, which Jack had just provided her, then Auntie Joy was in the clear.

The trooper read her mind. "She's still got to tell me where she went with Meany the night of the Fourth, Kate."

Her eyes met his in complete understanding. "She will," she said firmly. If I have to pry it out of her with a crowbar, she thought.

The trooper rose to his feet and thumbed up the brim of his hat. He stood staring down at the body with a brooding look on his face, and said out loud what they were all thinking. "It's gotta be connected." He raised his head. "Let's look around for a weapon."

"Could be anything," Kate objected.

"Handy," Jack pointed out. "If the killer just used a rock or something he grabbed up, we can't prove premeditation."

"I could give a shit about degrees here, I want the prick that would bash a teenage girl over the head and leave her," Jim said, and started casting about for a blunt instrument.

In the end Kate found it, a smooth, three-foot length of driftwood caught in the snarl of dead root at the opposite end of the fallen spruce. Balancing on the spruce's trunk, she very carefully knelt, one knee at a time, clutched a branch whose needles had rusted, and leaned down. The wound to her head throbbed painfully with the sudden rush of blood, but it was worth it when her groping hand grabbed the length of wood. She brought it back up and looked at the dark patch on the thick end that caught her eye. Could just be mud from the bottom of the brook, but she didn't think so.

She rose just as carefully to her feet, and stepped quickly down the trunk to the expanse of gravel. Mutely, she held the makeshift club out to Jim. He held it in his fingertips and scrutinized it carefully. The same thing that had caught Kate's attention caught his as well, a smudge of something at the thick end. "Could just be mud," he said, echoing her thought for the second time that day.

"Could be. But look." She stood facing the downed spruce. "Suppose the victim is about to step on the trunk to cross the brook to the bank. Suppose the killer is right behind her, and snatches up the driftwood."

"Pow, he brings it down on the victim's head—" Jim said.

"Right-handed, then," Jack said. "And then, when the victim falls face forward into the creek—doesn't matter if she's unconscious or dead, because if she's unconscious she'll drown pretty shortly—then the killer climbs up on the trunk, crosses to the bank, tosses his club in the water, he thinks to float away or at least to be washed clean, and goes on his merry way." He took the club from Jim and examined it. "Just dumb luck it fell wrong side down for the killer and right side up for us."

"And cold water always delays rigor," Jim added, "so the time of death is confused."

"If he knew that," Kate said.

"If he cared," Jack said. He took a deep breath, and raised his voice. "Johnny?"

Johnny turned reluctantly. "Yeah, Dad?"

"Need you to take a look."

The color, only just returned to the boy's face, washed out again.

"Jack," Kate said.

The trooper, sensing something off, said nothing.

"Come on," Jack said, beckoning.

Johnny came with laggard steps, his eyes on the ground. He stopped just out of his father's reach.

"Come on, kid," Jack said, his voice gentling. "Just take a look. Is she the girl you saw the night of the Fourth?"

"What?" Kate said.

Unwilling, irresolute, Johnny looked anyway. He didn't gasp or stumble backwards, but Kate got the feeling it was only because of pride. His voice was thin and shaky. "How come her face is so dark?"

"She's been lying facedown for maybe twelve hours," his father told him. "Blood pools in the down side of the body after death. Is it her?"

The boy swallowed hard, and nodded. "It's her."

Kate stepped between the body and the boy. "What the hell's going on here, Morgan?"

Again, Jack took in a big breath. When he spoke there was a quality to his voice that Kate hadn't heard before, a mixture of embarrassment and pugnacity. "Johnny has something to tell you. Something he should have told you yesterday. Something I should have made him tell you." He squeezed Johnny's shoulder. "Go ahead."

Johnny looked up at Kate, and then away. When he spoke his voice was low, and she had to concentrate to hear his words.

The gist of the story seemed to be that the evening of the Fourth, the aunties had sprung Johnny from his fish camp duties (they had become duties his first day on shore) and he had gone for a hike down the creek, scouting likely locations for fishing with a rod and reel. He'd taken his father's .30-06 in case he met up with a bear with attitude, and, as Jack said, "The only way he can get backwoods experience is to go out into the backwoods."

Involuntarily Kate remembered her father and the deer hunt. Jack mistook the quality of her silence and said defensively, "He wanted to go alone. The bears are mostly after fish now, anyway, Kate. I didn't think he'd come to any harm." He added, "And he didn't."

"I didn't either," she said, "and I was six when my father turned me loose with a twenty-two. It's all right, Jack, I do understand. That part of it, anyway. Go ahead, Johnny. Tell us the rest."

Johnny cleared his throat and resumed his story. "It was getting late, and I'd run out of Jelly Bellys so I was thinking about turning around and heading back to fish camp for some dinner, when I heard somebody scream. It sounded like a girl, and it sounded close by, so I went to take a look." A slow flush climbed painfully up into his face. "I saw them across the creek. Right here, actually, on this beach. It was a girl, and she was with somebody. They, ah, they had all their clothes off, and they were, well, you know, they were doing it."

By now Johnny's face was as red as his shirt, but he struggled to get the story out nonetheless. "I was curious," he said, trying to meet Kate's eyes and not having much luck with it. "So I watched."

"They didn't see you, or hear you?"

If possible, his face became even redder. "No. They were—um—noisy. Especially her."

"This is her?" He nodded. "What happened next?"

He squirmed. "Well, they—they finished, is all. And after, they got dressed and left."

"How?"

He nodded over their heads. "They walked across that tree trunk and went into the woods."

"You ever see the guy before?" He shook his head. "What did he look like?"

"Uh—skinny, dark hair." He floundered. He hadn't been watching the guy.

Kate rescued him. "That's it?"

Her matter-of-fact tone seemed to hearten him. He squared his shoulders. "That's it. What do we do now?"

She was up on the trunk and halfway across before the trooper caught up with her. The trunk shook beneath his added weight, and then shook again when Jack and Johnny mounted it.

It wasn't simple erosion, others had walked that trunk before her, and not just Johnny. Once on the bank, she could see a faint but clearly discernible trail leading through the brush, a trail which appeared to parallel the direction of Amartuq Creek. Could be a game trail, she thought. Certainly could have started out as one, and been used by the occasional sport fisherman.

Not to mention the occasional murderer.

A hand grabbed her arm. "Hold it, Kate," Jim said. "We can't leave her for the critters to eat on."

"They left her alone overnight, didn't they?" she said impatiently.

"So we got lucky," he said. "Come on."

"You go, you bring her out in the skiff. I'll meet you on the beach, at the Meanys' setnet site."

"You take the body, I'll take the trail."

She snorted. "Yeah, right," she said, and was gone.

Before Jim could stop them, Jack and Johnny had shoved past and vanished in her wake. He swore once, and then, realizing he was alone with a body that would only ripen with the day, taking any forensic revelations it had with it, he turned back to the grim task of removing both it and himself from four-legged temptation.

The undergrowth was still wet from the rain, and they were soon soaked through to the skin. No one complained, not even Kate.

"I'm sorry," Jack said, crashing through the brush behind her. "Johnny should have told you what he saw."

"Why didn't he?"

"I told him not to."

"I see." The trail turned sharply and she passed beneath a low-lying branch without giving warning of its existence. She was pleased with the resulting crack of wood on bone, followed by a yelp of pain and a curse.

"You okay, Dad?"

"I'm all right," Jack muttered, and raised his voice. "I know it was stupid, Kate. I know it was interfering. Hell, it was probably obstruction of justice. I just—" They came to a dry creek bed with steep sides. The trail led down into it and up again, and without hesitation Kate bent her knees and slid down it and up the opposite side.

Breathless behind her, Jack continued, "From your descriptions of the Meany family, I figured it was the daughter and the summer hire. But I didn't think it had anything to do with Meany's murder." She glanced briefly over her shoulder. "Okay, okay, everything has to do with murder." He quick-stepped over the gnarled root of a very old Sitka spruce. "I just didn't want Johnny involved. Not in any of it, not even peripherally. I'm sorry," he repeated, like a mantra, or a magic charm powerful enough to exonerate himself. "I—"

"Don't be an idiot," was her comforting reply, and his head snapped up to see her stopped on the trail, smiling at him. "You're supposed to be overprotective, you're his father. It's in the job description."

He stared at her for a moment. Then in a movement so quick she didn't have time to dodge back out of the way, his hand whipped out and caught the back of her neck.

Johnny, who had fallen a little behind, came panting up from the rear. "Jeez, you guys!" He pushed through the bushes to get around them and was off up the trail like a hare in front of the hounds.

Confession, absolution and a Mariners cap and Johnny was ready once again to take on the world. Boys of thirteen believe they are strong and true and immortal and invincible, and drawing attention to the fact that they are only aspiring heroes with a long apprenticeship ahead of them is tactless in the extreme. Kate didn't try, merely fell in behind.

Jack, crashing along in their rear, said, "Who looks good to you for this one?"

"It has to be the same person who killed Meany."

He agreed, but played devil's advocate anyway, a routine they'd performed a thousand times before. "Why?"

"He made it back to Alaganik after all, and somebody finished him off there, not Cordova, like I thought."

"You thought he'd been killed in Cordova, and his body brought back to Alaganik?"

"Yes. Gull saw Meany trying to tie up his drifter at ten o'clock. Said Meany rammed the slip and stripped the gears."

"This would be Shitting Seagull of Intergalactic Space Dock fame?"

"He's a perfectly reliable source," Kate snapped.

There was a brief silence as they pushed through the brush, which Jack broke with a reluctant laugh. "Jesus. Kate, we've got to talk."

"And Mary Balashoff saw him drop anchor in Alaganik two hours later. She said he was clumsy, stumbling around the deck. That wasn't the man I saw when he delivered on the opener, so I thought it was somebody else. The boy, maybe, or the brother. Then we found out about the fight."

"I've met Tim Sarakovikoff," Jack observed. "If I'd had that young man teaching me my manners, I might not be walking any too steady my own self."

"True. So Meany did make it back to Alaganik, which means he was killed in Alaganik."

"And you think Dani Meany saw something she shouldn't have, and got dead for it."

"Yes."

"What was she like?"

She thought for another ten feet. "Lolita with heart," she said at last.

He digested this as the trail narrowed to snake around a knoll of mountain hemlock. "You liked her."

She remembered Dani's angry face during Kate's interrogation of her brother in the Meanys' cabin. "I admired her loyalty to her brother."

"Was she capable of blackmail?"

Kate's laugh was short and unamused.

"I see." He followed in silence for a moment. "So? Who looks good to you for Meany?"

"You mean besides the Anchorage family he screwed out of the setnet site, the setnetter whose gear he cut loose, the aunties whose fish camp he wanted to usurp, the husbands of the other wives he screwed and the fishermen whose strike he broke?"

"Besides those," Jack agreed.

She shrugged. "The family looks best, like always."

"Morgan's First Law," he agreed cheerfully.

"Now excluding Dani. And Frank's got an alibi."

"So. The wife or the brother."

She nodded. "They were here, anyway. The brother's got a weak-kneed alibi, but I haven't been able to figure out how he'd get from the beach to the drifter without anybody seeing him. I'm telling you, Jack, I'm still surprised there was only one death that night. It was totally nuts out."

"Nuts how?"

"Fourth of July nuts. They were jousting with boat hooks and water-skiing on hatch covers and playing chicken, for crissake!"

"Uh-huh." Jack nodded. "Maybe drinking a little, too?"

Kate snorted. "Yeah, maybe. Anyway, pretty much everybody was pretty much up all night. If the brother went out to the drifter, if he wasn't spotted, he would have been run over and sunk."

"Or just lost in the crowd," Jack pointed out.

Kate had thought of that, too. "True."

"And the wife?"

Kate remembered Marian's hurtle down the beach to their skiff. *You're sure he's dead?* she had asked them. *You're sure?* Kate gave a mental shrug. It wouldn't be the first time a suspect had acted the part of the grieving survivor. And now Dani was dead, Dani who had been the only witness to whether or not Marian had spent the night of the Fourth in the cabin. Kate could understand, even approve of the impulse to kill Cal Meany. But a teenage daughter as well? Still, "Meany was strangled. His trachea was crushed."

"By hand?"

"I don't know."

"Rope burns, like that?"

"Jim didn't mention any."

"Then there weren't any. How strong did she look to you?"

"Not that strong."

They shoved through wet salmonberry bushes. "She still could have done it, Kate. Remember the time it took us plus six cops to subdue that woman up on Hillside?"

"I remember."

He raised his voice. "Johnny! Slow down!"

After what seemed like an unnecessarily long time thrashing through the brush the three emerged together into a clearing. Beyond the clearing was the mouth of the Amartuq. Through the trees they could see beach, driftwood, drifters and *Freya* riding peacefully at anchor. The tide was almost all the way in, the ceiling had come back down and it was threatening rain again.

Kate turned east. A small plume of smoke spiraled up out of the chimney of the small cabin. The trail they were on led almost directly to it.

"That the Meanys' cabin?" Jack said.

She nodded.

"Convenient."

She nodded again. "Johnny?"

"What, Kate?" The boy's color was back to normal, the awful beginnings of shock checked by the excitement of the chase.

"How long does a game of Monopoly last?"

He was taken aback, convinced this was some elaborate grown-up joke with a punch line that was going to come at his expense.

"I mean it," she said. "How long?"

Johnny grinned. "Depends on how good one of the players is." He added, "And on how you play."

Kate frowned. "You mean there are different ways to play?"

"Uh-huh. You can deal out the deeds, that shortens the game a lot. And if you don't put any money in Free Parking, the game could last forever."

"What's the shortest game you ever played?" Jack said.

Cocky, Johnny said, "Twenty-three minutes."

"You win?"

With the flip of a hand Johnny dismissed the question as not worth answering.

"So," Jack said, "Neil Meany could have come home earlier than he told you, seen the drifter drop anchor on his way back to the cabin, taken a little detour and killed his brother, and been back on shore and in his bed before anyone was the wiser."

"Or Calvin Meany could have come ashore for a little TLC after his beating in Cordova and gotten a little more than he expected from his wife," Kate said.

"Let's go find out whodunit," Jack said. "Johnny, keep behind us. If there's action, run."

"Daa-aad!"

"Run," Jack repeated firmly, and in another of those odd flashbacks Kate remembered the bear charge and her father telling her to run. She hadn't. She saw the determination in Johnny's eyes, and knew he wouldn't, either.

She led the way to the cabin. Her knock on the door echoed hollowly, and for a moment she thought there was going to be no reply. Then the door swung inward.

A fire burned briskly in the barrel stove, and there were signs of packing, a suitcase open on one lower bunk with a strip of bright blue material hanging out of it, a box on the counter half full of toiletries.

No one was home. This fact registered at the same time they heard a shout. Kate turned to see Marian Meany coming down the beach at a fast clip, son in tow. "Where's my daughter? Have you seen my daughter?" She skidded to a halt, panting and disheveled. "My daughter is gone. She was gone when we got up." She grabbed Kate and shook her. "Where is she? Where is she?"

Over her shoulder Frank was frightened and belligerent about it. "Where is she? Have you seen her?"

It was to him she spoke. "Bring your mother inside."

Something in the quality of her reply must have warned them. Frank's face went white. Marian gave a low moan and sagged. Jack caught her before she fell, only to be shoved away by her son. "I'll take her." Frank put an arm around his mother's waist and assisted her inside. Kate and Jack followed them in. Johnny remained on the porch, staring in the open door with wide eyes.

"I knew something was wrong, I knew it." The words were wrenched out as if by force, and seemed to drain all the energy from Marian's body. She slumped into a chair. "She wouldn't talk to me, she just wouldn't, and I couldn't force her. Could I?" Marian raised her head. Her face was wet with tears. "Could I?"

Frank, looking far older than he should have, said quietly, "Where is my sister?"

Kate said, as gently as she could, knowing it wouldn't do any good, "She's dead, Frank. I'm sorry."

Marian stared at her through blurred eyes for a moment, and then she screamed. It was a loud, long, drawn-out scream that raised the hair on everyone's neck. It went on and on and on, and might never have stopped if Anne Flanagan had not stepped around Johnny, frozen in the doorway, and dealt Marian Meany a deliberate slap across the face. The sharp crack of skin on skin echoed around the cabin, and Marian's scream cut off abruptly. She stared at the minister dazedly for a split second before dissolving into sobs.

"It's all right," Anne Flanagan said. "It's all right, Marian." She shouldered Frank to one side and drew the other woman into her arms. "Shhh, now. Everything's going to be all right. Shhhh, now." She looked over the sobbing woman's shoulder. "Could somebody maybe make some tea? And if there's any liquor in the house, now would be the time to get it out."

"I heard that." A grim-faced Jack rifled the cupboards, lit the camp stove and put on the teakettle.

Kate motioned Frank outside. He followed, stumbling a little. "When did you first notice Dani was missing?"

His eyes were dull with grief and fatigue, his voice numb with grief. "This morning. We woke up and she was gone."

"So she must have gone out last night sometime. You didn't hear her leave?"

He shook his head. "What happened to her?" He swallowed. "Did she—was she—"

Kate, watching him intently, said, "Was she what? Murdered? Yes. Somebody hit her over the head with a chunk of wood. She either died at once or fell face forward into the water and drowned."

His white face turned green. He stumbled to the edge of the deck and vomited over the side. She waited, motioning Johnny back when he would have gone to help the other boy. They waited. He retched until he couldn't bring anything else up, and staggered over to the bench and sat down limply. "Frank," Kate said, "I know this is the worst possible time for you to have to answer questions, but I have to know everything you know, and I have to know it now. What was Dani doing up the creek last night?"

"She was meeting Mac," he said, his voice exhausted. "She'd been meeting him on that little beach all month, since after the first day Dad hired him."

Kate frowned. "You're sure it was Mac she was going to meet last night?"

"Who else could it have been?"

"Where is Mac?"

"I don't know." The boy looked around as if expecting to see the hired man spring out of the air.

"Was he here this morning when you got up?"

"No."

"So they met last night, and neither of them came back?"

"I guess so. I don't know, I didn't see him, either." His eyes filled with tears. "He sleeps out back in a hammock. Uncle Neil said he got up early and went hunting."

Hunting? Kate thought. In July? "Where is your uncle? Was he home this morning?"

He nodded. "Yes. We were all here. All except Dani." A tear slid down his cheek.

"Where is he now?" He didn't answer and Kate, remorseless, repeated, "Where is your uncle now, Frank?"

"Ms. Shugak." Kate looked up to find Anne Flanagan in the doorway. "I think that's enough. The boy's had a considerable shock, and it's not helping him to have you hammer away at him."

"I'm not enjoying it any more than he is, Ms. Flanagan," Kate said curtly, "but a young girl has been murdered, and every minute that goes by, every second, lets her killer get that much farther away. Where is your uncle, Frank?"

He blinked at her, as if she might be a little fuzzy around the edges to him. "I don't know. He didn't come with us to the Flanagans'. I don't know," he repeated in that same monotone. Frank Meany had had as much as he could take and no more.

A low buzz sounded from the mouth of the creek, and

Kate looked up to see Chopper Jim grounding Old Sam's skiff. "Johnny. Find a tarp and take it down to the skiff. Move!" she said when he hesitated.

"There's one under the porch," Frank said, his head leaning back against the railing, his voice exhausted.

Johnny looked at Jack, and Jack nodded. Johnny went.

"Ms. Shugak." Anne Flanagan's voice was calm but urgent. "Do you think Mac McCafferty killed Cal and Dani?"

"No. Mac McCafferty had nothing to gain from these murders. I don't think he killed either Cal or Dani." She paused.

"What?" Jack said.

She met his eyes. "I don't think he killed them, but I think he knows who did."

Jack examined her shrewdly. "And you do, too."

"Well, hell, Jack," she said with asperity, "who's left? Ms. Flanagan, what kind of Monopoly game did you play with Neil Meany the night of the Fourth?"

The other woman stared at her with gathering anger. "I don't see what that has to do with anything."

"Dammit, did you play the short way? Did you—" Kate had forgotten what Johnny called it.

Jack said, "Did you deal out the deeds?"

The minister's mouth tightened, but she answered. "Yes, we did."

"How long did the game last?"

"I don't know." Anne Flanagan made a visible effort to collect her thoughts. "Neil won. He's very good at it." She paused. "It was a short game," she said slowly. "He bankrupted the girls in nothing flat. I held on longer, but not much."

Kate told Jack, "Any Monopoly game I've ever played lasted three hours or more. I figured Neil Meany was at the Flanagan site long past the time his brother made it back to Alaganik, and Chopper Jim says the time of death was figured around midnight. Roughly."

From where he come to a halt on the beach below the deck, Chopper Jim said, "There's a lot of leeway in that figure because of the time he spent in the water."

"Yeah, but that's just about the time he got back to the bay, according to Mary Balashoff. And, if they were playing Monopoly the short way, Neil Meany headed for home right after, and probably saw the drifter from the skiff. An easy detour for him," she added, using Jack's words.

"Okay," Jack said, frowning, "but Neil Meany on the drifter with a what? Why such—" He searched for the right words. "Why did he have to be so damn thorough?"

"You save up enough mad for a long enough time . . ." Kate said, and left it at that.

"Motive," Jim said. "Does he inherit?"

Kate shook her head. "I think Cal Meany was playing real-life Monopoly, and I think it might have been going to interfere with his brother's plans." She walked into the cabin. "Frank, do you have a pair of binoculars?"

Frank had gone back inside to sit next to his mother, who had her head pillowed in her arms. He blinked at Kate, helpless in his own grief. "Binoculars," she repeated, and he raised an arm and pointed. They were sitting on the windowsill on top of a tide book. She took them out on the deck. The clouds had made good on their promise of rain and the resulting drizzle had soaked into her hair and the shoulders of her shirt.

She ignored it and concentrated on the scene revealed by the lenses.

There wasn't much to it. Meany's drifter rode placidly at anchor, a good distance from the few other drifters who had chosen to remain at Alaganik during the hiatus between openings. Probably they were avoiding contamination from close proximity to the scab boat. The hatch to the cabin was closed, no light shone through the galley windows and there was no other sign of any activity on board.

She lowered the binoculars and handed them to the trooper, still standing on the beach below, also impervious to the rain. He scanned the drifter. "Doesn't look like there's anyone to home."

"He's there," she said, and pointed. The buoy used to anchor the Meanys' skiff was empty. "And look." She pointed again. Barely still in sight through the increasing fog and rain, a skiff was drifting out of the bay on the ebbing tide. "Bet that's the Meany skiff."

Jim looked at the skiff, puzzled. "If he couldn't be bothered to tie up the skiff, why hasn't he pulled the hook and hightailed it for town?"

"Let's go out there and ask him." He remained skeptical. "Where's Evan McCafferty?" she said bluntly. "He sure as hell isn't hunting, Jim. Not in July, not in Alaska, and even if he was poaching, sure as hell not in a place with as much traffic in and out of it as this one."

His face changed. "Let's go."

They climbed into the skiff and Jack shoved them off, most displeased at not being allowed to accompany them, but, as Jim pointed out, he shouldn't even be bringing Kate with him, and he wouldn't be if he knew what Neil Meany and Evan McCafferty looked like.

And if he didn't need backup against a man who had already murdered twice. Jack stooped to slide his hands beneath the tarpaulin-shrouded body of Dani Meany, and carried it to the cabin.

By the time they closed in on the no-name drifter, the weather had socked in so low that they were bumping their heads on the clouds. The beach had long since vanished, they could barely make out the outline of the *Freya*'s hull off to starboard, and the other boats were next to invisible. A steady drizzle collected on the brim of Jim's trooper hat and dripped down the back of his jacket. Kate had no hat and her hair was soaked through, leaving her braid a wet rope lying down her spine. She was engulfed in Jack's windbreaker, which gaped at the neck and didn't provide a lot of protection. All they needed now was for the wind to start to blow, she thought sourly, and as if in response a breeze caught at the rigging of the drifter and produced a low hum that startled them both.

For the rest, the boat sat silent and dark. It looked deserted, and forlorn, as does any working boat without its gear in the water and a crew hustling go for broke on deck.

"Looks like you were wrong, Shugak," Jim said. "There's no one on board."

"Then why are we whispering?" Kate put her hand out to catch the rain-slick gunnel, and in that moment a dark figure rose up off the deck and brought a boat hook down on the trooper's head with a solid thwack that echoed off the fog and rain. Without a sound Jim fell face forward into the bottom of the skiff.

In falling Jim had cut the throttle. The kicker sputtered and died. The bow of the skiff bumped into the hull of the drifter, and Kate used what forward momentum that gave her and both hands to pull herself up over the gunnel into a tumbling somersault that should have carried her past Meany and his boat hook to the other side of the deck. It would have, if the hold hadn't been open and she hadn't somersaulted right into it.

She hit heavily, not on the bottom of the hold itself, but on something just as solid but softer.

It took her a minute to get her breath back. When she did, she raised her head and opened her eyes.

She was lying full length on the body of Evan "Mac" McCafferty, Cal Meany's summer hire, Dani's lover and the only witness to both of their murders. He was unconscious. She pulled herself to her knees to take a closer look. His pulse was rapid and thready, his skin clammy and his respiration labored. Blood clotted the hair at his temple, his left arm was twisted back to front. His ribs moved loosely beneath her hands as Kate got to her feet.

Neil Meany, standing at the edge of the open hold,

reached down with the boat hook. The sharp metal hook at the end of the wooden handle caught Kate on the twisted flesh of her scar. It stung, and she felt a warm trickle pool in the hollow at the base of her throat.

It was not so very long ago that Kate herself had used a similar boat hook in her own defense. They were very effective weapons, as the grave in Dutch Harbor could attest to. She stood very still, and met Neil Meany's eyes.

He was very calm, too calm. "I'm good with this," he said.

"So I see," Kate said, her voice level.

"My brother didn't think so. My brother didn't think I could do anything. I guess I showed him."

Kate knew a momentary desire to laugh out loud and fought it back.

"He wouldn't let me on the boat, did you know that? Did you?" he repeated, nudging her with the boat hook.

"No," she said. "No, I didn't know that."

"Come on up," he said, urging her with the hook, as if he were going to tug her on deck the way he would a gaffed halibut. "Come on."

She swallowed convulsively. "You'll—you might skewer me with that thing if you keep it on me while I do."

He glanced at the boat hook in some surprise. "Oh. Yes. Of course." And he removed it, as simple as that.

In the hold looking up, with no access to the controls or escape, she had no tactical advantage. On deck would be better. If he didn't gaff her over the side first. Besides, the smell of gas fumes that had collected belowdecks made her head swim, and she knew she had to get out of them if she was going to retain either sense or consciousness.

The hold wasn't that deep, but she was barely five feet

tall. She flexed her knees and swung her arms, once, twice, on the third swing jumping to catch the edge of the hold with her hands. An agile twist and she was on deck. She could still smell the gas fumes, but they weren't as strong on deck as they were in the hold, and her head began to clear.

Not five feet away Neil Meany faced her, holding the boat hook across his chest in both hands in the manner of an infantryman waiting on the order to charge. Fix bayonets, Kate thought giddily, and gave herself a shake. This would do no good, no good at all.

Gentle wavelets lapped at the hull. The rain had eased off into a heavy mist. The skiff was gone, and Jim with it. No cavalry. Fog swirled around the drifter, over the deck and around Kate and Neil Meany.

McCafferty's labored breathing echoed up out of the hold, and Neil Meany made a gesture of distaste. "Close up the hold," he said.

She thought of the gas fumes, looked at the boat hook Meany was still holding and closed up the hold. When she was done, he said, "Thank you."

Just as politely she replied, "You're welcome," and again had to repress a fit of hysterical laughter. "Neil," she said when she could, "put down the boat hook."

"No," he said. "I know how to use it. I told my brother I did. He didn't believe me, but I did. I showed him."

"You certainly did," she said, entirely without irony. "But now that you've showed him, you don't need it anymore. Put it down."

His eyes flashed and for a second he looked exactly like his brother. "Don't tell me what to do!"

"All right," she said. "I won't."

"Don't tell me what to do," he said more calmly. "My brother always told me what to do. I don't like it." As one recalled to his manners, he said, "I'm sorry, Ms. Shugak, I don't know where my head was at. There's a deck chair right behind you. Unfold it—slowly!"

She froze as the boat hook flashed out within inches of her face.

"Slowly," he said. "That's right. Please. Be seated."

She sat. "Thank you."

"You're welcome."

She sat and he stood for a few silent moments. She was wet clear through Jack's windbreaker and her jeans, but her feet were still dry. As long as her feet were dry, there was hope. She looked across the deck. Neil Meany seemed settled into position for the duration. She was careful to speak politely and formally. "Can you tell me about it, Mr. Meany?"

He looked at her blankly. She tried again. "What convinced you to come to Alaska with your brother?"

He actually laughed, an incongruously robust roar of merriment that seemed to ring off the enclosing mist. "He loaned me money to go back to school and get my master's degree. He loaned me the money to study for my Ph.D. It was all very formal, papers drawn up by a lawyer, notarized, the whole nine yards."

His mouth twisted into a mirthless grin. "He didn't talk me into coming up here, Ms. Shugak. He called the loans, and said I had to work them off, working up here for him. He said he wasn't asking for much, he said any summer we couldn't gross two hundred and fifty thousand was a summer that wasn't worth fishing, and that I'd get a deck share." He shifted. "When he put it like that it didn't seem so bad. But I didn't work out on the boat. I couldn't read charts, he said. I kept almost running her aground, he said. I had no feel for running the reel, he said. And"—his voice dropped, as if he were confessing a sin so terrible it was almost too much to speak it out loud—"I get seasick."

The mist swirled across the deck, engulfing him in a shroud of white for one brief moment, then wafted away.

"So he put Frank on the boat and me on shore."

It didn't take Kate more than a few seconds to grasp the importance of this. "And the crew share on a setnet site is a lot less than the crew share on a drifter, and it would have taken that much longer for you to pay off your brother's loan."

He looked pleased with her, as if he'd spent too much of his life reducing his thoughts to words of one syllable and welcomed the opportunity for a higher level of discourse. "He said," he repeated, as if the repetition alone were enough to convince anyone of the rightness of his actions, "he said if I crewed three summers for him, I could pay him off and have enough left over to finance the rest of my course work, and enough to support me while I wrote my dissertation."

He brightened. "I'm a Yeats scholar, did I tell you?" He straightened and declaimed to the fog, " 'The Land of Faery, where nobody gets old and godly and grave, where nobody gets old and crafty and wise, where nobody gets old and bitter of tongue.' "

The sound of the Irish poet's verses died away, and he slumped back against the console, face lapsing into sorrowful lines. "Bitter of tongue," he said again. "My brother was nothing but. Just like my father." He looked across at her. "What was your father like, Ms. Shugak?"

He didn't raise me to kill people, she thought, but fortunately Meany wasn't all that interested in her reply.

"Mine was just like my brother. He hit us. Whether we did what he said or not, he hit us. Damn him. Damn him!" He struck the deck viciously with the boat hook. "Damn him!"

Yeah, yeah, Kate thought, here we go, let's blame two, maybe three murders and two felony assaults on a repressed memory of child abuse. The smell of gas tickled her nostrils, seeping up insidiously from the crack between hatch cover and deck. She wondered if there was a leak somewhere. If there was, she wanted off this boat right now.

Deliberately, she checked the beginnings of Meany's rage with a question, maintaining the polite and formal manner of an envoy from the undersecretary. "What happened that night, Mr. Meany? What happened the night of the Fourth? Did you see your brother bring the drifter into the bay on your way home from Anne Flanagan's?"

"Yes," he said obediently, and then looked surprised at himself. "Yes. I was on my way back to the setnet site, and I saw him drop anchor."

"That would be at about midnight?" Kate deliberately fudged the time to see what he'd say.

He frowned. "More like one. Probably closer to one-thirty. I went out to talk to him." He looked at her and said earnestly, "You see, I'd just spent the evening with Anne and her children. You know Anne Flanagan?" Kate nodded. Meany's sigh was ecstatic. "A wonderful woman, Ms. Shugak. She reads poetry, did you know that? We talked of poetry that night. She could quote lines from 'The Second Coming.' His face contorted. "God, how I miss it, the conversation, the erudition, the simple awareness of the existence of literature. People call it an ivory tower, but they don't know. They don't know, Ms. Shugak. I would have given anything, anything to get back to it."

Kate remembered, from a long way off, sitting in Anne Flanagan's cabin and sneering at academic frustration as a motive for murder.

"And on the way home from Anne Flanagan's on the night of the Fourth," she said, nudging him back to the narrative, "you saw your brother's boat arrive."

"And on the way home I saw my brother's boat arrive," he said obligingly, "and I went out to talk to him."

Before she could stop herself, she said, "How on earth did you get out there without anyone seeing you?"

His smile was sly. He sang, "And the rockets' red glare, the bombs bursting in air, gave no proof through the night that my skiff was still there. They were partying so hearty on the bay that night that I could have stripped naked, painted myself purple and set fire to the skiff and no one would have noticed."

Lost in the crowd, Jack had said. "What did you say to your brother?"

"I told him I wanted to go back to school. I told him I'd overheard his conversation with Bill Nickle, that I knew what he was trying to do—"

"Conversation with Bill Nickle?" Kate said sharply. Neil Meany looked surprised, and she apologized at once. "I beg your pardon, Mr. Meany. Please continue."

"I told him I knew what they were up to," he said, like a child reciting his lesson for the day. He made a sweeping gesture with his hand. "A single-destination resort, that's what they called it. Can you imagine? 'Down the mountain walls from where Pan's cavern is'? He was going to bring in tourists to copulate in the foam with the nymphs and satyrs. Can you imagine?"

Kate couldn't.

"I may not want to live here," he said, "but I can certainly appreciate what is and what isn't appropriate to the region. My brother," he added disdainfully, "was planning some kind of northern Las Vegas. Really."

"He laughed at me," Neil Meany said, his face flushing. "That night? He laughed at me, just like he always laughed at me. I hit him with the boat hook, and he stopped laughing." He paused. "He was surprised, I think, that I was strong enough. But I was. Of course," he added, with the true scholar's meticulous regard for the truth, "somebody had been before me. He looked like he'd been in a fight. He was all bruised and bloody." His smile was blinding. "It was wonderful."

Especially wonderful that he wasn't moving as quickly as he usually did, Kate thought. "You didn't quite kill him."

He stared at her. "What?"

"There was water in his lungs. He was still breathing when you pitched him overboard."

"Really." His brow furrowed. "I strangled him with the boat hook. I pressed him back against the cabin, right here"— he pointed to a spot that Kate didn't bother to look at—"and pressed the handle against his throat, as hard as I could. He made the most awful gurgling sounds. I was certain he was dead before he went over the side." He thought it over in frowning silence, and then dismissed it with the wave of a hand, clearly deciding it didn't matter.

He hadn't denied pitching his brother overboard, so Kate decided that cause of death didn't matter, either. "Where did the knife come from?"

He shrugged. "He grabbed it off the deck. I took it away from him and stabbed him with it before I threw him over."

"Why? If you thought he was already dead?"

He smiled again. "I liked killing my brother, Ms. Shugak. I liked it so much I wanted to do it again." The smile widened into a wholehearted grin. "If I could have figured out a way to hang him from the yardarm, I would have done that, too."

"How about Dani, Meany?" she said, abandoning formality now that she had his confession. "Did you like killing Dani, too?"

The grin vanished, and the bastard actually got tears in his eyes. "No, Ms. Shugak. No, I didn't. But they saw me."

"Dani and Mac?"

He nodded. "They saw me come ashore that morning, on their way back from their little beach."

"You didn't know they had at first, did you?"

"No." He said it sadly. "They told me. They told me they wouldn't tell if I gave them money. Money to get away, they said." He looked at her, earnest, sincere, lethal. "But I couldn't give them money, could I? I needed it for tuition and fees." He smiled again and it was all Kate could do not to flinch away from what it did to his face. "So I said I would, and then last night I followed them upstream. Mac ran when I killed Dani. I had to run after him. He made me run after him. I had to chase him all the way down the trail to the beach. He was at the skiff when I caught up with him. This was in the skiff." He held out the boat hook, made a face and gave a little-boy shrug. "I was angry. He made me angry."

"You hit me, too, didn't you?" she said. "You were on board the *Freya* last night, looking for—what were you looking for, anyway?" The smell of gas fumes was growing stronger by the minute, she thought, vaguely alarmed. There had to be a leak somewhere.

"You frightened me with your questions," he said reproachfully. "I wish you hadn't, but you did. I had to know what you knew. And then you came back, and the only way off the *Freya* was through you." He raised a hand, palm up, as if to say, What else was there for me to do?

She didn't bother asking him if he'd meant to kill her. She'd been waiting, on alert, for an opportunity to jump him, but the toxic vapor from the leaking gas made her head swim. She fought off a wave of nausea, and asked a question at random. "How did you get to and from shore without my hearing or seeing your skiff?"

The sly expression was back. "I wasn't in the skiff. Or I was only in it as far as this old girl." He patted the bulkhead affectionately. "Then I put on a survival suit and swam over, holding on to a log. Nobody saw me, did they?"

Once Kate had donned a survival suit herself, only she had done so to find a killer, not become one. First the boat hook, and then the survival suit. Déjà vu all over again. Kate suddenly felt very tired. "No. No one saw you." No one had seen him go up the path after Dani and McCafferty, no one had seen him chase McCafferty back down to the skiff, no one had seen him haul McCafferty out of the skiff and drop him into the no-name drifter's hold, no one had seen him climb over the side of the drifter, clad in a survival suit, and swim over to the *Freya* and no one had seen him swim back. McCafferty had seen him kill Dani, but it didn't seem tactful to say so at the moment. "You certainly had an active night," she observed. Her head felt increasingly light on her shoulders. "But no. No one saw you."

He gave a satisfied nod. "I didn't think so. My brother told me I couldn't do anything. I guess I showed him, didn't I?"

"I guess you did," Kate agreed, and this time she didn't feel in the least little bit like laughing. Her tongue felt oddly thick in her mouth. She groped for words. "Meany. You have to know it's over. You might get away with clobbering me, you might even get away with murder, but you'll never get away with hitting an Alaska state trooper over the head with a boat hook. They'll hunt you down whatever hole you bolt into, with ferrets if they have to."

"Over?" he said indignantly. "Nothing's over." He patted the bulkhead. "I'm driving this baby to the nearest harbor and selling her for the most cash I can get, and after that I'm flying straight back home—first-class, mind you—and enrolling at the University of Chicago." He straightened and turned toward the control console. "I'll give you a ride into town, if you want." He looked over his shoulder. He was smiling again, a glitter in his eye she could see even through the gloom. " 'Things fall apart; the center cannot hold,' " he said, and stretched out a hand to press the starter button.

His last words registered, along with the now omnipresent smell of gas, and suddenly she knew what he meant to do. "No!" she screamed, and leapt from the deck chair, too late, too late.

The engine turned over and, finely tuned piece of machinery that it was, caught at once. A split second later the deck of the drifter disappeared in a roaring burst of flame. Kate felt herself raised up as if by a mighty hand, as if by Old

Sam's mighty hand, as if he were rendering a second and, this time, a final judgment.

Up, up, up she rose, ascending past the fog and the rain and the clouds unto the heavens, unto the stars themselves, and then down, down, down she came, down and down, and the cool, clean waters of Alaganik Bay closed over her head, and she knew no more.

Time passed, and she swam beneath the surface of the sea. It was dark there, and warm, and she let the currents take her where they would. Occasionally she sensed others nearby, their words drifting to her on lazy bubbles of dimly heard sound.

"—fumes built up beneath the deck, and he didn't know enough to run the blowers before he hit the starter."

Oh yes he did, she thought.

"We found McCafferty. What there was left of him."

"And Meany?"

"A bowpicker reeled him in this morning. He hardly looks touched."

"Like Kate."

She wasn't ready, and the current took her away again.

"She was mean to Mom."

"I know, but—"

"It'll only make her wet the bed, Lauren, don't be such a baby. You get her hand out from under the covers, I'll fill the pan with water."

"Lauren! Caitlin! I've told you before, do not be drawn to the dark side of the Force. A Jedi knight does not these things."

She drifted, lost on a sea with no shore, although every now and then she heard the surf, and within it, the sounds of different voices.

"Katya, you know we are here. We stay here and wait for you to come back. Young lady with sword, you stab me again, I sacrifice you to Raven for a good silver run."

"Wake up, lover. You and me, we got some unfinished business on the bank of that damn creek."

An anxious whine, a cold nose pressed to her cheek, and she was almost tempted to rise to the surface. Almost.

"Goddam you, girl, get your ass outta that goddam bed. The fish hawks give us a period and canneries come up with a semidecent price and the fish are humping each other up the goddam river. I'm supposed to take delivery of the whole friggin' fleet all by my goddam self?"

"Kate, um, they say I'm supposed to talk to you." A pause. "You look out cold to me, but here goes. We're taking you in shifts." Another pause. "You're shift work, Kate." A snicker. "I get the first shift, Auntie Joy gets the second, Dad gets the third, and like that until you wake up. Anyway, I'm first. Remember those Heinlein books you gave me last fall? I brought *Between Planets* with me, and I'm going to read it to you." He cleared his throat and began the tale of the planetless boy, and Kate listened, drowsy, drifting.

She did surface, eventually and in her own time, swimming up through deep green depths filled with silver schools of salmon that darted out of her way, tickling her cheeks with their fins as they passed. Her head broke the surface of the water and she heard voices.

"Never, never, never put money in Free Parking," said one. "All it does is keep it out of circulation. If somebody goes broke in real life, they go broke."

"But this is a game," another voice objected.

"You want to win or not?" the first voice demanded.

"We want to win," a third voice said firmly.

"Okay, then. First thing is, you buy everything you land on."

"Even railroads and utilities?"

"Absolutely. If you wind up with all four railroads, that's two hundred bucks every time another player lands on them. You can clean somebody out of their Go money every round, and that's four safe places for you to land, don't forget. Utilities, okay, they're cheap, but they pay for themselves, especially if you have both, and if you own them, that's two more safe places for you. The most important thing is, you buy everything, and I mean everything you land on. Because if you don't, the property goes up for auction before the other players."

"What?"

"I never heard of that!"

"It's in the rules," the first voice said firmly. "Second most important thing is, buy houses but don't buy hotels."

"Now this I do not understand," a fourth, older voice said. "You get more rent with hotel when someone land on it."

"That's true, Auntie Edna, but if you have three properties with four houses each on them, that's twelve houses the other players can't put on their property and charge you rent for. Get it?"

There was a brief pause. "*Alaqah, poijken,* no wonder you all the time bankrupt us. I don't play with you no more."

"But you're getting good at it, Auntie Edna."

"I am, too, aren't I?"

"No, Lauren, if I take the battleship, you take the cannon. If both are gone, take the racecar."

"What's wrong with the horse and rider?"

"Who cares? A token's a token, isn't it?"

"Hey," the first voice said sternly. "Attitude is everything."

"Jedi knights play Monopoly?" Kate said.

There was an instant of silence, followed by a rustle of movement. A warm hand felt Kate's forehead. "You're awake then," a new voice said.

Kate opened her eyes and blinked up into a face that resolved into Anne Flanagan's calm features. "I'm an asshole," she said. "I'm sorry."

Anne Flanagan's face broke into a wide and very unministerlike grin. "I'm sorry you're an asshole, too."

Kate smiled back, and slipped down again into the warm green depths.

The second time she surfaced, the subject had switched from commerce to faith.

"What I hate," said a voice, "is when you go to a wedding, and the minister tries to convert from the pulpit."

"What, are you kidding?"

"Nope. One of my co-worker's daughters got married last February, and the minister raced through the 'dearly beloved' stuff and settled into a nice long harangue about how marriage was the natural order of things, and how unnatural it was to be single. Where do they get off doing that during a wedding?

Everyone has friends of different faiths. Of all ceremonies, a wedding has to be the most cross-denominational religious event there is. Or it should be."

"Try a funeral," a third voice said. "Don't look at me like that, I swear it's the truth. One of my department head's kids got killed in a car wreck. We all turned out for the funeral, and the preacher said maybe two words about the kid and then ran what pretty much amounted to a revival meeting standing over his coffin. No lie, he actually said that if anyone wanted to be saved during the service, all they had to do was come forward to the altar."

"Jesus. That deserves a gold medal in bad taste, at least."

"There's a line from a poem by Yeats," the second voice said thoughtfully. " 'The best lack all conviction, while the worst are full of passionate intensity.' "

Another Yeats fancier, Kate thought dreamily. Who had been talking to her about Yeats? She couldn't quite remember, and she let it go before it began to worry at her.

"They get all the press, too, the born-agains."

"Not the born-agains, the born-again fanatics. The crazier they talk, the more likely they'll end up on film at eleven. The news media just eats up stuff like that. Look at Jim Jones."

"David Koresh."

"Ian Paisley."

"The Ayatollah."

"And the anti-abortionists. Pictures of a bomb blowing up an abortion clinic are a lot more productive of advertising revenue than a bunch of people working hard, raising kids and going to church every Sunday."

"You're such a cynic, Dad."

"Just a realist, son."

"It's got so anymore the fanatics are defining the parameters of the debate. You can't be pro-choice without being a murderer, and you can't be anti-abortion without being a zealot."

Like Simon Seabolt, Kate thought, and realized by the cessation of conversation and a scramble of feet that she had spoken the words out loud. She opened her eyes and found a ring of faces staring down at her.

"I'm hungry," she said.

Jack's laugh masked the wave of relief that washed over him.

Johnny grinned. "She's baa-aack!"

"Some tomato soup to start?" Anne Flanagan said.

Mutt reared up and began to wash Kate's face with a lavish tongue.

The twins looked as if they had not had cause to doubt Mutt's taste in humans, until now.

The next day Kate demanded up and got as far as the front porch. There were fluffy clouds scudding across a blue sky with bright sunshine winking between. There was a breeze brisk enough to ruffle her hair and keep the mosquitoes off, but not brisk enough to cause a chill. Or so Anne Flanagan said, anxiously tucking a blanket around Kate's shoulders. Kate parried offers of Red Zinger tea, Crystal Light lemonade and just plain water, and waited for Anne to stop fussing before asking, "What day is it?"

"Monday."

"I was out for two days?" Kate said, appalled.

"More like a day and a half."

"How did I get here, anyway?"

The minister sat down next to her and brought out yarn and knitting needles. "Jim Chopin picked you up out of the water."

"How did he find me in all that fog?"

"He said you practically landed on him when the drifter blew up. He hauled you in and headed for shore."

"Again, how'd he find it in all that fog?"

Anne smiled, twisting yarn over her right hand to cast onto the needle held in her left. "After that bang on the head, he wasn't thinking any too clearly himself. He thought he was headed for the *Freya*."

"We're lucky we didn't wind up aground on Middleton Island."

"Yes," Anne said somberly, "you are. It took Jim a while to regain planet Earth."

"I wish I could have seen that," Kate said wistfully.

"George brought Eunice—you know, the public health nurse from Cordova? George flew Eunice out to take a look at you, and she said that other than some scrapes and bruises, all you had was a slight concussion and to let you sleep until you were ready to wake up." She took up a loop of yarn and began a knit row. "Is it really true? Did Neil Meany kill his brother, and Dani?"

Kate stretched, testing the new skin growing over fresh wounds, and leaned back carefully so as not to aggravate the sore spot on her head. "Yes."

The bay was once more filled with boats, shore to shore, cork lines strung out behind them like beads on a string. To the west the *Freya* sat at anchor, the *Dawn* to port, the *Esther* to starboard. Kate hoped Tim had a hold full to overflowing. "Who did Old Sam get to replace me?"

"A young guy, I can't remember his name. Oh yes. Billy Mike. Or no, that's your tribal chief, isn't it. His son, that's it, Dandy Mike."

"What!" Kate sat up straight in her chair.

"Sit back and relax," Anne said, in a voice that brooked no refusal.

Kate sat back, grumbling. "Easy for you to say. Dandy's probably seducing Ellen Steen in the focsle even as we speak."

"That would be Old Sam's problem, not yours. And Mr. Steen's, if there is one."

There had been a smile in Anne Flanagan's voice when she replied, and Kate looked across the deck to find no distaste or censure in the minister's expression. Humor, yes, sympathy, understanding, kindness, tolerance, yes, all these things in abundance, but no rush to judgment, no disapproval, no condemnation. She didn't look much like an Old Testament prophet, either. "You're an odd sort of minister."

Anne raised an eyebrow. "How many have you known?"

"Touché." Kate faced forward again.

Anne dropped a stitch and reached for a crochet hook. "The problem most fundamentalists share is that they mistake metaphor for fact."

Kate's smile was sour. "What? You mean Joshua's trumpet didn't bring down the walls at Jericho?"

"Pastor Seabolt would say it did."

"And you? What would you say?"

"I'd say it's a great story, one that always gets the kids listening and, true or not, teaches a good lesson about the power of faith." Anne put down the crochet hook and picked up the knitting needle again. "Have you ever noticed how all the best biblical stories begin with *J*? Joshua at Jericho, Jonah and the whale, poor old Job."

"Jesus and the Crucifixion," Kate said.

Anne laughed. The sound didn't surprise Kate as much as it would have a week before.

The Flanagans' gear was riding the incoming tide, with two skiffs out picking it. One was filled to overflowing with three kids and one big man who even at this distance looked harassed. Kate's heart went out to him. The second skiff was filled with four old women, their hands a blur as they picked fish after gleaming fish, and with a shout of triumph topped off their load before the first skiff was even half full. Jack shook his fist at them, and their laughter as they headed for the *Freya* reached Kate in her chair on the deck.

"I liked him," Anne Flanagan said, her hands stilling. "Neil Meany. I liked him a lot." She closed her eyes briefly. "I must be the world's lousiest judge of character."

Kate started to shake her head and thought better of it. "No. I saw his brother in action. Believe me, Calvin Meany was enough to drive anyone mad."

A pause while Anne began her second row. Eyes intent on her work, she said, "Was he mad?"

No, Kate thought. Despite the histrionics on the deck of the drifter that evening, she believed that Neil Meany had known exactly what he was doing. "I think he'd been pushed to his red-shift limit. It happens, to all of us."

"But most of us manage to rein it in. Most of us don't wind up killing three people."

"No. Most of us don't."

"Thank God." Anne Flanagan said the two words in a soft voice, with absolute sincerity and unquestioning belief.

Kate wished she had the faith to believe that God had both the power and the inclination to curb the more homicidal urges of the human race. It would have been very comforting.

"Why did he stay?"

"What?" Kate said.

"He took the skiff and Evan McCafferty out to the drifter that morning. You and Jim didn't show up until late afternoon. Why didn't he just raise anchor and sail away?"

Kate had wondered about that, too, with no result. "I don't know."

Anne increased a stitch. "Maybe he wanted to get caught."

"Maybe." And maybe he had, maybe Neil Meany had waited for discovery, not knowing who would come, knowing only that someone would. Which might put an entirely different interpretation on whether he knew what he was doing when he pushed the starter. If he had, he'd not only have been committing suicide, he would have been committing his third and fourth murders. Maybe his brother had been right, maybe he was too dumb to drive a boat.

It was all academic at this point, anyway, Kate thought. Neil Meany had killed two people and had taken a third with him when he'd killed himself, accidentally or by design. Either way, he was bent on self-destruction, and Kate had no time to waste on the self-destructive, who all too frequently managed to be as destructive of the people around them as they were of themselves. She thought of her mother.

No. Life, as Old Sam might have said, was too goddam short.

There was a whoop from offshore, and they looked out

on the water to see Jack hold up a king salmon, balancing carefully in a skiff that was rocking exuberantly from side to side with the enthusiasm of its crew.

Anne's eyes narrowed. "Sixty pounds?"

Kate squinted. "Fifty, maybe fifty-five."

"We'll give it to Mary to smoke."

"Good idea."

Anne began the next row. "He was a Yeats scholar. Neil Meany. He could quote everything Yeats ever wrote."

"Um." Kate turned her face more into the sun and closed her eyes. "I never did like Yeats much myself."

"But he's terrific!" Anne was shocked. "He loved women."

Kate snorted without opening her eyes. "Yeah. 'The broken wall, the burning roof and tower and Agamemnon dead.' I remember the first time I read that, I thought, Yeah, and Iphigenia, too, Agamemnon's firstborn daughter, sacrificed by her father for a lousy fair wind to Troy."

There was a brief pause. "You didn't like Neil Meany much, did you, Kate?"

Kate opened her eyes and said flatly, "I don't like killers. Neil Meany killed his brother, killed his niece, killed Evan McCafferty and tried like hell to kill me, twice. Lucky I have a harder head than Dani, and that he assaulted me on the deck of the *Freya*, not in some little upstream backwater where he could have finished the job. No. I didn't like Neil Meany. And no, I'm not sorry he's dead."

Anne worked a few stitches. "You'll have to forgive him, you know. Forgive him, to get past it."

"No." Kate was definite without being overly emphatic. "No, I won't."

"What did you do with Cal Meany the night of the Fourth, auntie?"

"Not much, Katya," Auntie Joy said with elaborate nonchalance. "I just take him down to dock and shove him off."

"Auntie!"

The old woman heaved a deep sigh and added, "But tide is in. He just trip and fall on knees on his own deck."

The four aunties burst into gusts of merriment at the expression on Kate's face.

"Make big cuss words, too," Auntie Joy added, to the sounds of additional merriment.

Evidently there would be no potlatch held to honor Calvin Meany's memory, Kate thought. He would not be missed. She thought of his wife and son, now on their way back to Ohio. He would not be missed by anyone.

It was maybe eight o'clock by the slant of the sun, and all of the sailors were home from the sea, and one hunter home from the hill as well. Aunties Vi and Joy were still at the Flanagans' cabin, Aunties Edna and Balasha had gone back to fish camp. Jack and Johnny were scarfing up the last of Anne Flanagan's superb spaghetti. Anne was washing dishes, Kate drying.

Chopper Jim, none the worse for wear, looked Kate over with a critical and not wholly approving eye, nodded once and said, "I guess it takes more than blowing up a boat to kill a Shugak."

He had a lovestruck twin on either knee. Kate was relieved to see that the little monsters had some human instincts.

The trooper said to Auntie Joy, "Why didn't you just tell me that you'd taken Meany back to his boat, Joyce?"

Auntie Joy got up and left the deck. A moment later they heard the creak of the outhouse door.

"Because she's stubborn," Kate said, stacking plates in a cupboard. "Because it's an insult that you asked her to account for her time, like some village kid answerable to his parents for checking the fish wheel or the smokehouse fire. She's an elder. She's not answerable to you."

"Because I'm a trooper?"

Kate shook her head. "No. Or it's not first on the list."

"What is?"

Kate smiled. "You're thirty years younger than she is."

Mutt jumped up and barked once. A shout made everyone look from her to the beach. Auntie Balasha was at the edge of the outgoing tide in the fish camp dory and she was waving her hand urgently enough to ship water over the dory's sides. "Where's Joy? She must come! The fish hawk is back with his paper!"

"Son of a bitch," Kate said, and dropped the towel to head for the door.

When they got to the fish camp they found Auntie Balasha and Auntie Edna sitting on their stumps around the campfire, faces set in unrevealing lines. Auntie Vi and Auntie Joy went to sit next to them without a word.

Also next to the fire were Bill Nickle, who had seated himself, and Lamar Rousch, who had not, by which Kate deduced that neither had been invited to. "I don't have much choice in this, Kate," Lamar said the moment he saw her. "The governor ordered me out here this time."

Bill Nickle looked smugger than ever. "What's he here for?" Kate said, nodding at him.

Lamar was unhappy and he didn't care who knew it. "He's got a seat on the board of Fish and Game. He's a gubernatorial appointee. The boss said to let him come if he wanted."

"And I wanted," Bill Nickle said. "Give it to her."

Mutely, Lamar held out a document, folded in thirds. Kate took it and ripped it in half and handed the pieces back.

There was a murmur from the four old women. Auntie Vi permitted a wintry smile to cross her face. "The case is still in federal court, Lamar," Kate said. "The state can put their cease-and-desist orders where the sun don't shine."

Bill Nickle erupted to his feet. "Now wait just a goddam minute!"

"Watch your goddam language in front of my aunties," Kate snapped.

"Oh, why don't you just fuck off, Shugak! This is none of your goddam business, anyway!"

Jack, standing at the rear of the group, stepped back out of range and sent up a prayer of thanks that there hadn't been room in the skiff for Chopper Jim. In the telling, felony assault could always be reduced to a misdemeanor.

Kate moved forward swiftly, and Nickle raised himself hurriedly to his feet. He was eight inches taller than she was, but Kate didn't seem to find it a disadvantage. "It is my business, Bill. These are my aunties, and this is our family's fish camp. We come here every summer—"

"Yeah, right, where were you for thirty years, when the rest of us were working at building up a state!" It was nothing but empty bluster and they knew it, and after the words were out, so did he.

"—and we fish to eat," Kate continued without missing a beat. "We don't fish so we can stuff the skin and give it glass eyeballs and hang it on a wall somewhere and brag about the big one that got away. We take the fish and we dry it and we can it and we kipper it and we smoke it and we fill our pantries with it and then we by God eat it, and no one, especially not some jacked-up old fart from Anchorage that some other jacked-up old fart from Juneau misnamed to a state commission is going to tell us different." She stepped back. "Now get out. And don't come back."

She didn't add a warning to the last command. She didn't have to.

Nickle appealed to the fish hawk. "You have to stop them. The judge says so. The governor says so."

"The governor in on this little deal you and Meany cooked up?" Kate said.

"What deal?" Lamar said.

Nickle paled. "What deal? I don't know what you're talking about."

"What deal," Kate mimicked him. "Why, the big fly-in fishing and hunting lodge you and Meany had planned for Amartuq. What did Neil Meany say you called it? A single-destination resort?" As she spoke, she remembered the scene at Mudhole Smith International Airport, all the sport fishermen with their fly-fishing gear taking off for fishing holes unknown. There was one hell of a market there, even she could see that. How much more of a temptation would it have been to Meany, clearly a man with an eagle eye on the main chance? And then there was a perfectly serviceable airstrip less than a mile from fish camp. He would have thought he'd died and gone to heaven.

Instead, he'd just died. To Bill Nickle she said, "Meany acquired the Ursins' setnet site, by means that will not bear close examination. And then he tried for Mary Balashoff's site so you could nail down both sides of the creek, probably for a moorage, and you wanted the fish camp for a lodge because it's the only site on the creek suitable for one, never mind that it's also the only one suitable for the people who actually live here to have a fish camp."

Her lip twisted. "And what the hell, with virtually no overhead after the initial investment because you good-old-boy guides don't have to pay a lick in taxes, and since there's an old guide network in state government that goes back to territorial days, you figured you had it made. You almost did."

She laughed. "You know, you're nothing but a carpetbagger, Nickle. You don't give a damn about the land or the people, you just want to make a buck however you can." She looked around at the aunties, four round brown faces lined with patience and stoicism and a fortitude that had endured and survived a three-hundred-year threat of racial and cultural extinction.

That fortitude was not going to be put to the test today. Kate looked back at Bill Nickle. "Take your fishing flies and your bamboo pole and your two-pound test and get lost."

Faint but persevering, Nickle appealed once more to Lamar Rousch. "They can't do this. We've got the law on our side. We've got a goddam judge on our side!"

They stood there, at an impasse, the rushing sound of the creek loud in their ears. At last Lamar Rousch sighed and shoved his hat to the back of his head. "You know what, Bill? I'm just not ready to start World War Three, right here, right now. Okay?"

"No, it's not goddam okay! They're not supposed to be fishing here, you've got the papers, serve them!"

Lamar, well aware that he was putting his entire professional future on the line, smiled and said cheerfully, "No."

The aunties did not cheer as the two men disappeared into the grass, which was probably a good thing. At this point, they had Lamar on their side. Kate waited for the sound of the Zodiac's motor, and then waited longer until it had faded from earshot. When it had, she said, "Jack?"

"What?"

"Could you and Johnny take a walk, please? Like up the trail to the airstrip and back?"

He looked from her to the four aunties, perched in their solemn row, and said, "Want us to take our time?"

She smiled at him. "No. Normal speed is fine."

"Sure." He fetched his rifle from the cabin. "Johnny?"

"Daa-aad."

"Come on."

Johnny tugged off his Mariners cap with the Ken Griffey Jr. signature on it, beat it a couple of times against his leg, resettled it just so on his head, heaved a martyred sigh and followed his father into the brush.

Kate, now that the adrenaline rush that always accompanied flouting authority had faded, sat down on a tree stump, facing her aunties. She looked only at Joyce, however. "I know all about it, auntie."

Auntie Joy said nothing. Neither did any of the others, but Kate detected a group stiffening of spine, and was satisfied. "I had breakfast with Lamar Rousch in town last week, at the Coho Cafe. When we got the news about the price drop, a man at the counter offered a penny more a pound. Lamar said he was Joe Durrell, and that he was an independent fish buyer. Lamar said Durrell usually bought for the restaurant trade, in Anchorage and in cities down the West Coast, but I heard that sometimes, when it looked like he'd make a buck on the deal, he'd buy in bulk for Japan, too."

Auntie Joy maintained her owl-eyed stare.

"Guess where I saw him next? Mr. Joe Durrell?" They didn't answer her, but then she didn't expect them to, not now, not ever. "He was in George Perry's plane, on his way up Amartuq Creek." She paused. "Could I have a little of that tea? With honey, please. I've been so thirsty since I finally woke up." She threw in a wince and a hand to her sore ribs for good measure.

Woodenly, Auntie Balasha rose to her feet, poured out a cup of tea from the pot on the spider grill at the side of the fire, anointed it with honey and handed it over. Kate sipped at it gratefully. "Thanks, auntie. I needed that. Now, where was I? Oh, yes. Durrell on his way up Amartuq. Yes, well, I wouldn't have thought anything of it, in fact I didn't even recognize him at first, but then George came back without him." She sipped tea. "He had you in the back seat instead, Auntie Joy."

She cradled the hot mug between her palms and regarded her aunties. They stared steadily back, without expression, it seemed without blinking. "I couldn't figure it out, why you'd be going to town, and especially why you'd be flying to town. And then I got too busy to think about it, until I got laid up." She smiled at the four old women. They didn't smile back. "Nothing to do but think when you're laid up."

She drained the mug and set it down. "The way I figure it is this, aunties. You've been fishing subsistence, all right. But I took a look at that pile of bones behind the camp. That's an awful big pile. You've been catching yourself a bunch of fish."

"I've got a bunch of family," Auntie Joy said. Auntie Vi put a calming hand on her knee.

"Yes, you do," Kate said, nodding. "Yes, you do, auntie, but the amount of fish you've got smoking doesn't square with that pile of bones." She waited. She waited in vain, and sighed. "Okay. You're selling them to Durrell, aren't you? King salmon, filleted and boned and ready to slap on a grill. Nobody fillets a salmon the way you do, aunties. How did you hook up with Durrell, anyway?" They didn't enlighten her, and she waved a hand. "Never mind. It doesn't matter. What happened on the Fourth? Did he commit the cardinal sin of paying by check? So you had to go into town and cash it in the bar, while you held him hostage, along with his fillets?" She grinned. "Or did you just con him into a round-trip ticket to the Fourth of July parade?" She laughed, but she laughed alone. "Whatever. I have to admit, you guys got style."

Her laughter seemed to break the spell. The aunties shifted in their seats, exchanged covert glances. Auntie Balasha even got up to refill Kate's mug.

"Thanks, auntie." She sipped at the brew, strong and sweet and reviving. "You know, aunties," she said dreamily, gazing off into the distance, "if you sell the fish you catch on that fish wheel, you are not subsistence fishing, you are commercial fishing." She looked across the fire at the four old women one at a time, all trace of laughter gone. "And there are only two places in Alaska where you can legally commercial fish with a fish wheel. One of them is the Tanana River, and the other is the Yukon, and Amartuq Creek doesn't run into either one of them."

No one claimed ignorance of geography.

"Refusing to serve a questionable legal document, and a federal document at that, is one thing." She took a deep breath, and let it out. "But Lamar's a natural born fish hawk. He believes in what he's doing, and he's good at it. I got a sneaking suspicion he might already have an idea of what you're up to. And aunties, if Lamar catches you selling a subsistence catch to a commercial buyer?" The firelight flickered across her unsmiling face, and her voice held no trace of its former laughter. "He catches you at that, and he'll have you out of here in two seconds flat, tribal history, cultural imperative and all."

Footsteps sounded in the brush behind her, and she rose to her feet. "Thanks for the tea, aunties. Hey, guys. What, Jack, you couldn't find a bear to feed the kid to?"

———

Kate smiled at the eagle sailing thirty feet above the creek. The eagle, not overwhelmed by her charm, glared balefully back, and backwinged to land in a treetop to scan the creek for unwary salmon.

"What?" Jack said.

She raised her hand. "Taste."

He took her hand automatically. "What?"

"You said I tasted salty. The last night we were on the bank of this creek. Don't you want to make sure?"

His eyes lifted quickly to hers, and his slow smile told her exactly what he was thinking. Still, he hesitated. "How are your various aches and pains?"

"Variously achy and painy," she said, "but don't let that stop you."

"In that case." He accepted her hand and took his time pushing back her cuff. His lips were warm against her wrist, his tongue warmer. "Um," he said. "You do taste kind of salty."

"As salty as the other day?"

One eyebrow quirked up. "Let me check."

Checking took a while, and involved unbuttoning the cuff of her shirt and rolling the sleeve back to her elbow.

The sun had tangled in the tops of the trees, flushing the clouds with a rich pink-orange glow, and the fish camp had settled into its routine of gutting and splitting and hanging the day's catch, followed by dinner and, Kate was startled to see, the production of the Monopoly board. Edna caught up the dice and shook them like she was standing at the craps table in Vegas. She saw Kate looking and one of her eyelids lowered in a long, slow wink. Johnny, for a change, was asleep.

Jack had declined an invitation to play on the grounds

that he was taking Kate down to the creek to watch the stars. Four pairs of brown eyes looked up at the pale blue sky, and four old women diplomatically refrained from comment.

"Well?"

"Huh?" He raised his head and blinked at her.

"Do I? Taste as salty as the other night?"

"I'm still not sure. Let me—"

She stiff-armed him, and he fell back on the sand. She came up to lean over him. "Because I couldn't possibly."

His hands wandered. "Couldn't possibly what?"

"Um, yes, right there. I couldn't possibly taste as salty as I did Thursday."

"You sure talk a lot."

"But it's such a good story."

He sighed heavily. "All right. What? And hurry the hell up, would you?"

Kate let herself lean against him. This was the hardest part, but if she was ever going to talk about it to anyone, it would be to Jack. "That business last summer with Seabolt got to me, Jack. More than I knew. A lot more."

His arms tightened.

"Christianity—it's just too start-and-stop for me. Too . . . I don't know, too static, I guess. You're born, you live, you die, you go to heaven or hell." She paused. "Heaven's never been that much of a lure."

There was a smile in his voice. "Or hell that much of a threat?"

She smiled. "I guess not." She was silent for a moment. "I've never felt so helpless as I did last summer. Or so frustrated. Or so bewildered. I've never believed, so I didn't understand. I still don't." She took a deep breath. "It's been a long time since I've hated that much, or that strongly." Her laugh was shaky. "I forgot how much it takes out of you."

He made a comforting noise.

"The first time we went to talk to her, when Old Sam introduced Anne to me as a minister, I kind of lost it."

"You tarred Flanagan with Seabolt's brush, is that it?"

She nodded. "I pretty much ridiculed her every time she opened her mouth." She closed her eyes and shook her head. "Old Sam knows her, and likes her. I think he's even attended one of her services, and you know Old Sam is the biggest unreconstructed heathen around."

"Except for you."

"Except for me," she agreed. "So, afterwards, we got into the skiff to leave, and he told me what he thought of my behavior." Kate winced. "Of course he was right, so all I could do was tell him to stuff it."

"What did he do?"

She smiled against his chest, anticipating his reaction. "He took me by the scruff of the neck and the seat of the pants and tossed me over the side."

Jack pulled away to stare down at her incredulously.

"And then he took off with the skiff, and made me walk the whole five miles from the Flanagans' site to Mary's. Soaking wet."

Jack's jaw dropped and stayed that way.

"I had to cross the Amartuq on foot, on an incoming tide." She looked at him out of the corner of one eye. Jack's face was turning a slow purple. "Halfway over I tripped on a salmon and fell in and got wet all over again."

He laughed so hard he slid a foot down the sand. The tears rolled down his cheeks and he wrapped his arms against his belly and rocked back and forth, the laughter booming out of him and echoing across the surface of the water with such force that it startled the eagle into irritated flight, his great wings beating audibly at the air.

"Oh, Lord," Jack said, gasping for breath. His head fell back against the log. "Oh, Lord."

She waited patiently.

He sat up finally, wiping his eyes with the heels of his hands. "Why did you tell me? Old Sam never would have."

"He'll never tell anyone," Kate agreed. Old Sam wouldn't, either. If someone ever asked him about it, Old Sam would draw himself up to his inconsiderable height, stare down his beaky nose and invoke the sacred rite of Family Business. Old Sam didn't hold with no outsiders poking their noses into his goddam business. When Old Sam saw a problem, he took executive action, and that was the end of it.

"Why, then?" Jack persisted.

Kate smiled down at him, a wide, sweet smile that made his heart skip a beat and then start hammering high up in his throat. "You needed a laugh."

"Why?" he said, although he was pretty sure he knew.

"You're still mad at yourself that you didn't make Johnny tell me he saw Dani Meany and Evan McCafferty down by the creek."

He looked away.

"I like that about you," she said.

He was amazed. "What, that I'd withhold evidence?"

"That you would put your son first."

He reached for her but she pulled away and got to her feet. "No way, Morgan. Coitus interruptus once on this beach is about all I can stand." One eye closed in a bawdy wink and she turned.

He tackled her.

"Hey!"

He was laughing down at her when she wrestled her way around to face him. "What the hell," he said, grinning. "We haven't tried the skiff yet."

He slung her over his shoulder in a fireman's hoist and dumped her into the skiff. The next thing she knew, they were in midstream and Jack was heaving the ten-pound Danforth over the bow.

"You planned this," she said incredulously when he began to unfold an air mattress.

He didn't deny it. "You know what Whitekeys says."

"What?"

"Spawn, spawn, spawn till you die, baby." And he tackled her again.

On the bank four little round brown birds sat side by side, bright eyes observing with interest. Fish camp had a long and honorable history as a site for seduction, as the four of them, had they been of a mind to, could have personally testified.

"Hope they don't scare fish," Edna said to Joy in soft Aleut.

"Hope they do," Vi answered, a frankly salacious glint in her eye.

The four aunties collapsed into muffled giggles.

The couple in midstream didn't hear them over the rush of water down Amartuq Creek.

And if they did, they didn't care.